Publisher's Note:

Thank you for purchasing this book. It began as an idea, was shaped by the creativity of its talented author, and was subsequently molded into the book you have before you by a team of editors and designers.

Like all EDGE books, this book is the result of the creative talents of a dedicated team of individuals who all believe that books (whether in print or pixels) have the magical ability to take you on an adventure to new and wondrous places powered by the author's imagination.

As EDGE's publisher, I hope that you enjoy this book. It is a part of our ongoing quest to discover talented authors and to make their creative writing available to you.

We also hope that you will share your discovery and enjoyment of this novel on social media through Facebook, Twitter, Goodreads, Pinterest, etc., and by posting your opinions and/or reviews on Amazon and other review sites and blogs. By doing so, others will be able to share your discovery and passion for this book.

Brian Hades, publisher

THE HAUNTING OF WESTMINSTER ABBEY

A NOVEL BY
MARK PATTON

EDGE SCIENCE FICTION AND FANTASY PUBLISHING
An Imprint of HADES PUBLICATIONS, INC.
CALGARY

The Haunting of Westminster Abbey

Copyright © 2020 by Mark Patton

This is a work of fiction. Names, characters, places, and incidents are the products of the author's imagination or are used fictitiously and are not to be construed as real. Any resemblance to actual events, locales, organizations, or persons, living or dead, is entirely coincidental.

EDGE SCIENCE FICTION AND FANTASY PUBLISHING
An Imprint of HADES PUBLICATIONS, INC.
P.O. Box 1714, Calgary, Alberta, T2P 2L7, Canada

The EDGE Team:
Producer: Brian Hades
Editor: Ella Beaumont
Book Design: Mark Steele

ISBN: 978-1-77053-185-7

EDGE Science Fiction and Fantasy Publishing and Hades Publications, Inc. acknowledges the ongoing support of the Alberta Foundation for the Arts and the Canada Council for the Arts for our publishing programme.

Library and Archives Canada Cataloguing in Publication
CIP Data on file with the National Library of Canada
ISBN: 978-1-77053-185-7
(e-Book ISBN: 978-1-77053-097-3)

FIRST EDITION
(20200123)
Printed in USA
www.edgewebsite.com

Dedication

To Sophie and Tigger and my lovely wife Nikki.

Prologue

The Arrival

The fisherman grunted and pushed hard onto the riverbed
with his pole. His punt moved up and over the reed bed
that had blocked the opening to the tributary. Now he and
his passenger were in clearer water, not a chocked channel,
but a meander, snaking through a wetland wood of willow
and alder. A gibbous moon cast silhouettes of the old trees
across the river. Here and there moonlight broke through
the canopy, landing on clumps of yellow flag that lined the
bank. The flowers hinted color in an otherwise black and
grey, silver-lit landscape. The boatman had heard nothing
from his passenger since their trip began at the headwaters
of the Tyburn and he did not expect to. The hooded man
hunched into himself, draped in his garment at the stern of
the little skiff. Smells of rotting leaf litter and mold began to
give way to the pungent stink of pig. Odors from the manures
of various farm animals intensified as the limbs overhead
began to thin. The spaces between the trees widened and
then suddenly the trees were gone, replaced by pasture.
Here the river split, going both to the left and the right to
circumnavigate around a small island. The island was an
insignificant bend in terms of the route of the river, but not
at all insignificant to the people who inhabited the river's
shore.

Seeing the island the passenger rose up and nodded
to the fisherman, who then stuck his pole fast into the
deep thick river muck. Small fires on the island had gone

unattended and were winking out. The men who had made them had long ago fallen asleep. Some scaffolding was still about. It would be pulled down in the morning before the priests came to consecrate the site. There had been an old abbey built here long ago by King Edgar. By command of King Edward the Confessor it had been torn down and this new one built in its stead.

These two iterations of Christian piety were not the first ceremonial stages for spiritual observances upon this site. A thousand years before Thorney Island had become a monastic community it had provided space for a temple to Apollo. Apollo, the Roman god of music, poetry, prophesies, and plague was also known as Phoebus Apollo, god of the sun and light.

As the cloaked passenger had come to his feet he had felt no need to steady himself. He was comfortable with the rocking of the boat. Reaching down he lifted a closed lantern from the deck of the punt. It was lit and small seams of light escaped through ornate slits near the ring of the handle. Raising the lantern high with one hand, he unfastened the hasp to its little bronze door with the other. As he opened the lantern, a cold thick mist rose from the surface of the river. Tiny droplets of water hung in the air, fattening and shimmering in the moonlight. The mist began to spread; expanding across the riverbank till it blanketed the entire island in a thick fog. Strange blue humanlike shapes then appeared as the cloud like atmosphere pulsated with lurid incandescence. Ancient events, now not constrained by the rhythm of time, burst forth to replay scenes that once happened. Lightning flashed... but flashed silently. Armies clashed... but clashed silently.

A young red-haired queen was hoisted up in the soggy haze, stripped naked, and then hung by her hands. Roman legionaries appeared. They whipped this queen, Queen Boudicca, mercilessly and raped her daughters beneath her dangling feet. But there were no screams or cries of horror. The scene faded and gave way to Celtic tribes massing under the queen's standard. With her daughters by her side, Queen Boudicca rode out in a royal chariot seeking vengeance. Yet her rage was inaudible. Warriors and horses crashed through the mist, colliding with a Roman legion and shattering it. The city of Londinium burned in the fog. All of this happened within seconds and as silently as a leaf settling upon the surface of the Tyburn. Strangely, while everything was being hacked, fired, or pulled down, the Roman's temple of Apollo was left alone. The victorious Celts crept around it, and then moved on.

As the fog continued to pulsate, older things appeared. Events came into form that took place well before there had been a Christian abbey built upon the island or a Roman temple. What was now happening had happened long before the Romans had countered the Celtic revolt, long before Queen Boudicca took poison and died. Thorny Island was now just a grove of trees. But what trees! Ancient trees! Towering oaks and elms formed up within the mist. Druidic priests came into view as they suspended sacrificial victims in wicker baskets from the higher boughs. For the first time, as they set fire to the baskets, sounds could be heard. It was not the screaming of victims that could be heard but the chanting of the priests. It was barely audible, as though it was being muffled by the centuries still concealed within the mist.

"Belenus the Shining one," "Belenus the Bright One," "Belenus the God of the Sun."

The door to the cloaked man's lantern was now fully open. Light flashed out— more light than could have been contained within a single lantern or two or a thousand lanterns. Like a burst of sunlight but containing the light of many suns, it dissolved the mist and engulfed the newly built abbey. Then, the lantern door closed.

Chapter One

Wallace Butterfield

It wasn't a surprise. It was a total shock. Wallace Butterfield had never imagined that he would be asked to meet with the chairman of the Westminster Abbey Foundation. When the invitation came in the post, he thought it was a joke. His first reaction was to call up his few friends and let them know that he was onto them. "Ha-ha, very funny, you had my heart racing for a minute." That sort of thing. But no one 'fessed up. In fact, people became irritated with his questioning. When he did call the Abbey Foundation, he was directed to a Mr. John Bradshaw, personal secretary to the foundation's chairman Reverend Poda-Pirudi.

It was no joke. He had been asked to meet with the Reverend concerning some sort of architectural issue. Mr. Bradshaw could not be precise. He did not know what the issue was. He apologized that the Reverend's schedule was so pressing that he could only meet with him at night, but assured him that it would be worth his while to attend.

Wallace Butterfield had no idea what it was about, but if the Reverend wanted him to clean out the Abbey storm drains or dust off the books in the gift center, he was the man for the job. It would be a marvelous opportunity, something for his curriculum vitae. He could see it now, consultant to the Dean of Westminster Abbey— well, maybe not to the Dean but to this Reverend Poda-Pirudi. Butterfield wished that the Reverend might have had more of a British sounding name, not something Italian-sounding, but a nice double-barreled Anglo-Saxon name like Calvert-Beetlestone. That would have better suited his résumé. But whatever, Poda-Pirudi or Poda-Pirudi-Smythe, the Reverend's name was going to the top. Something had to go there. But, then again, Wallace knew that his own name would be on the same résumé.

Wallace Butterfield— what a horrible name. He'd thought of changing it. Butterfield that was so lame, so ridiculously pastoral, so comically bovine. Well, both of their names would go to the top of the résumé. There was little else there besides le Mareschal's Supermarket. Wallace did help design le Mareschal's Supermarket in Liverpool, off of the A5606. Though critics had described the market as a large unimpressive glass and chrome rectangle, some shoppers had told Butterfield that they had appreciated the large inventory of groceries and home products.

The night before his meeting with the Reverend was a predictably hard night for Wallace. As always, he spent it in his small flat above his slightly bigger office. Wallace was prone to anxiety. He could not remember ever getting what he would consider a descent night's sleep. His dreams, normally vivid and unusual, were positively hallucinatory that night. He marveled at what his brain could concoct when he was asleep. It never showed any signs of creativity or imagination when he was awake and really needed such inspiration. A jellyfish rhinoceros-like creature was hovering over Wallace's bed, reaching down, slowly sticking long gooey tentacles up his nose and down his mouth while intoning an offbeat version of a monastic chant. Chilling, positively chilling— the sort of dream that has you believing that you are awake when you are really not. Fortunately, it all came to an end when one of the beast's tentacles began to prepare Wallace for a ghoulish rectal exam. That did it. That was enough. Wallace already had his annual checkup. No more complicity with this dream. Up he woke— though it did take him a while to steady his nerves to the point that he could convince himself that a multi-tentacled rhino did not exist. It was 3 AM. He spent the rest of the night in fits and starts of almost-sleep, urgently awaiting the return of daylight.

When the sun did finally arrive it made very little difference to Wallace's state of mind because he had all of the day and part of the night to kill before he could even meet Reverend Poda-Pirudi.

It had been a difficult year for Butterfield. His father had died abruptly from a heart attack at the onset of the le Mareschal's project. ***Butterfield and Son Architects*** became for all intents and purposes ***Son — Newly Graduated — Without a Clue — Architect — Maybe***. He had to bluff his way through the onsite meetings, stammered a bit, wrote down a lot of questions, and called up several firms that his dad had been chummy with to beg for advice. Still he had pulled it off. And it was a start. He often wondered why he had even attempted to get started in the first place. His student loans would take him years to pay off and then there was the matter that his father had overextended the business. That's what caused the heart attack. Butterfield had to sell off the family home he had inherited just to get the family business back on its feet. Now he was living in a bedsit just above the office. It might have been easier if he had some family to lean on, but there was no one. His dad had been it.

Butterfield didn't know much about his mother or her family for that matter. Shortly after he was born, she became disgusted with the whole idea of being married, and left. Rumor was that she had gone off to Queensland with some computer techie who had worked for Barclays Bank and left under a cloud of suspicion. Wallace had an aunt who claimed that his mother wasn't suited to care for a child, that she took one look at her newborn boy and got cold feet. But his father wouldn't say much about that or anything else concerning his mother or her people. So, growing up for Butterfield was more or less life with dad: meaning bad food, rugger matches, and interminable meetings at the East Croydon Telegrapher's Society. But now his dad was gone and the torch had been passed on to him, though at times he wondered if it wouldn't be prudent just to take a torch to

Butterfield and Son Architects. Still, he was determined to keep the family business afloat. Obsessing was what Wallace did best. Though he attempted not to remember these things as he filled up the hours till his appointment; it was difficult for him. So, he resolved to cram his head with as much information as possible about Westminster Abbey and worry about the rest later.

—— «» ——

There was a soothing romantic charm about the river walk at night, with its overhanging tree limbs and fanciful park benches. The Embankment had an archaic atmosphere. Behind him was Cleopatra's Needle. Though clearly not Cleopatra's— it was over a thousand years older than Cleopatra— it did come from ancient Egypt. Someone found a way to perch the twenty-one meter high, two hundred and twenty-four ton granite obelisk out over the river, flanking it with a bronze winged sphinx on either side. But to Butterfield, three thousand years of history staring down at him was nothing more than an incidental aspect of this stroll. It wasn't the antique bric-a-brac that he appreciated most. No, it was what was on the other side of the Thames. As he came even with it, he paused to take it in. It had gone up over a period of time during his early teens. It towered. His fathered had often commented on this during their many walks, providing Wallace with the precise figures: one hundred and twenty meters wide, one hundred and thirty-five meters high. It was a lit up with electric diodes that bathed the mechanism in the purest of colors. The London Eye, Europe's largest Ferris wheel and the city's premiere tourist attraction. Butterfield could never resist the temptation of rock back and forth on his heels whenever he stopped to stare at it. But he knew that this evening he couldn't afford to be caught up in it too long.

A glance at his watch told him it was time to move on. He pushed off for his meeting, quickening his pace a bit. It would be wise to be early and unforgiveable to be late.

Butterfield's stride was naturally long. Everything about him was long. He had a long delicate nose, and elongated fingers and limbs to boot. He loped, rather than walked. His skin, especially in the incandescent light from the street lamps, was pallid, and his reddish brown hair drew attention to it. His skin he blamed on his genes and an urban, almost sunless, life. He would confess that he spent far too much time in his office, but he had to make a living, to make his start in his chosen career.

His hair was moderately short and styled in a fringe cut. He had no mustache, no beard. He often worked in jeans and a casual shirt because he had so little contact with clients. However, for this occasion he was out of his denims and in a suit. He looked more like a boy playing dress up in his late father's clothes, rather than the serious businessman he had hoped to be viewed as.

Wallace left the Thames Path and clamored up the steps to Bridge Street. Parliament was to his left and Big Ben loomed high above his head. But he didn't notice, or chose not to notice, the large bronze statue of Boudicca in front of him. Imposing in bronze, her arms outstretched, one holding an upright spear, as she gazed down from her perch above the Thames. Her horse-drawn chariot plunging into battle, with her two violated daughters clutching to her dress. Below her, deep underground, still flowed the River Tyburn. But it was not as it had been. No, the modern Tyburn had been encased in brickwork, diverted, channeled, turned into a sewer. Wallace Butterfield didn't know this.

But there was something else that Wallace Butterfield didn't know— couldn't know: Despite his mild appearance and his pastoral name, Wallace Butterfield was special. He would have been amazed to know how exceptional he really was. Only a select group of observers were even aware of what distinguished him, and even they were baffled, staring at him intently. For Wallace Butterfield was a highly unusual freak of nature. If you could see as those who gaped at him saw, you wouldn't be looking at his wing-tipped shoes or gawking at his rather ordinary worsted suit; his thin face and auburn hair would hold no significance for you. The object of concern was higher up, above his head. It was an ugly bluish head with a pair of big bulging oval eyes—

eyes that were much like those that stared at him, with an ever-changing deep blue pulsating luminescence, like a squid's skin. Every living thing had those eyes or something comparable to them. It was only the dead that could see them. No, not really just the dead... the about to be dead could see them too... that is the unborn souls that incubated within the fleshy walls of the living. All of them could see that Wallace Butterfield was different. Because Butterfield's ghost had become unstuck...

Butterfield quickened his pace. He imagined that he was cutting his arrival a bit too fine. Mr. Bradshaw had explained to Wallace that he was to meet with the Reverend in his office in the triforium and had provided instructions as to how to get there. But Butterfield worried that he would not be able to find his way to Reverend Poda-Pirudi's office by ten o'clock sharp. Big Ben and the Palace of Westminster were now behind him. As Butterfield turned off Saint Mary's Street, he could clearly see the Abbey in her evening glory.

She looked as if she was at a cotillion in a magnificent golden dress, the neo-Gothic grande dame of the ball. Her stone gown was formed from perpendicular vertical runs of yellow limestone, ending in spires illuminated by floodlights. Flying buttresses connected these spires. Circumscribing the upper heights of the ancient monastery was a large rose window, spoked with a stone tracery that held the window's stained glass in place. The whole structure was an ornate layering of stone in a honeycomb of medieval styles. Below, well below the rose window, were three doors, each with a succession of intricately carved arches covered with a multitude of saints.

The largest door at Westminster Abbey was the center door. As Butterfield approached, he worried that someone may have locked it up for the night. Maybe the Reverend was so busy he had forgotten he had an appointment with Wallace, or, he still fretted, maybe his whole trip to the Abbey was just an elaborate joke. Butterfield looked about for a doorbell, wondering how one would announce oneself to such a large and historically significant piece of architecture. Then Wallace remembered what Mr. Bradshaw told him to do, and he opened the door. Even then, he expected to be challenged. There had to be Abbey security on the other side. Wallace had his invitation in hand, and was ready to wave it about, but there was no one there. First he peered into the empty expanse, then, cautiously, he entered like a mouse creeping out of his hole.

It was as he had remembered it from his first school outing. The vaulted ceilings rose high above, adorned with gilded stone floral designs. Huge crystal chandeliers were suspended below. The walls of the Abbey were thick with monuments and statues commemorating the lives of famous and occasionally not-so-famous Britons. Illuminated directly in front of him was another rose window much like the one over the great north door. That was the south transept. To its left was Poets' Corner and that was the direction Butterfield was supposed to head. Still looking about for somebody he would have to explain himself to, he found nobody. Butterfield hurried himself past the quire and sacrarium. Mr. Bradshaw had told him to look for a small inconspicuous door below the bust of Ben Johnson with a small white sign labeled in red, "No Public Admittance." But it wasn't as easy as that had sounded. Poets' Corner was a large area crowded with marble busts.

As he walked about looking for the door, old memories started coming back. When he was a child he found the whole place to be a little creepy. The Abbey had a musty smell back then, and it still did. But it would, wouldn't it? Thousands of dead people filled its cellars, vaults, and tombs, bodies, and ashes were stuffed everywhere. Some were even discreetly concealed beneath the paving. This thought forced Butterfield to look down at his feet. He gulped. He was standing on the grave of Lewis Caroll. Next to Caroll was Henry James and nearby were Rudyard Kipling and Charles Dickens. Butterfield recalled that Chaucer was buried somewhere about here. He turned around, hoping he hadn't stepped on Chaucer. To his relief he hadn't. He had just walked across a memorial plaque for some guy named

Thomas Sterns Eliot before realizing that it was T. S. Eliot. The paving read

THOMAS
STEARNS
ELLIOT
OM
Born 26 September 1888
Died 4 January 1965
"the communication of the dead
is tongued with fire beyond the
language of the living"

Wallace felt a slight chill when he read that, not because the words were exceptionally disturbing, but because, for the first time, he began to sense the quivering mass above his head, and to feel its playfully malevolent intent. Fortunately, at this moment Butterfield saw the bust of Johnson and made a beeline for the door below it.

Chapter Two

The Office in the Triforium

Beyond the door, Butterfield was presented with a dimly lit circular stair that wound its way up inside a stone turret. As he proceeded up, he could see no more than a few steps at a time. He was in the habit of counting steps and could not restrain himself from doing this even when stressed, particularly when stressed. Butterfield grabbed hold of a waist-high iron railing and guided himself up. A millennium of footfalls had scooped out the stone making deep depressions in the treads. Wallace had to be careful where he planted his feet. He didn't look up until step twenty-three placed him on a landing that had two stairways branching off from it.

Mr. Bradshaw had cautioned him to take the stairway to his right; in fact he had told Butterfield that getting to the office would be a series of consecutive right turns. Wallace turned to his right and picked up the count. There was some kind of hammering on metal coming from up above and the stairway was growing warmer. At tread forty-four he could see the source of the heat and the noise. A large steam pipe painted red and stenciled in white with the words *Do Not Touch* had been retrofitted through the building's masonry. He resumed his ascent, sweating and puffing from both the temperature and his deplorable level of fitness. At tread eighty-seven his counting gaze noted that he was about to step onto a wooden floor. He looked up and yelped!

A dozen or so draped, shadowy figures stood before him, backlit by the city lights streaming in through a large monochromatic daisy-shaped window set in an arching Reuleaux triangle of stone. Though he was not fully aware of it, whatever was lurking above Butterfield's head was now moving up and down his spine with glee. There was sufficient light for Wallace to realize that it was just old statuary, the likenesses of discarded saints and notables who were no longer saintly or notable enough to be put on public display. The presence within him wished that Butterfield hadn't gotten a grip on himself. However, it consoled itself with the knowledge that it would do a better job of scaring Wallace by replaying this scene in his head once he had fallen asleep. This was something it did with great regularity. Only last night, in fact, it had created the illusion of a tentacled rhinoceros giving Wallace a proctologic examination with a Gregorian chant thrown in for extra measure— hysterical— absurdly funny. Dreams like this so aggravated Wallace's unconsciousness that his brain would reject the presence like a bad transplant, allowing it to escape the incessant chatter in Wallace's brain.

There were a few abandoned and battered gargoyles on the floor, which Wallace stepped over as he threaded his way around stacks of wooden boxes labeled Royal Wedding, State Funeral, and Coronation. He picked his way through these obstacles to get closer to the window. He had never seen Parliament from this perspective. The window, his schooling had taught him, was made from panes of wavy medieval glass. They were created by ancient glass blowers who had first blown spheres of glass, then flattened them, spun them into circular shapes, and cut them into sections. This glass distorted light, bent it, and softened it. Through this window he could see Parliament's Central Tower. It was so close. Floodlights gave it a tawny yellow glow. Big Ben chimed out a few bars from Handel's Messiah and then rung the hour. It was ten o'clock and Butterfield was late.

Wallace Butterfield turned to his right and headed across the thick planked unfinished flooring. He then took the next right-hand turn offered to him. At last he saw what he had been looking for. There stood a rustic medieval door with weathered bronze strap hinges. He knocked. The door opened. There was a man of average height but sturdily built. He had a great barrel chest and was dark-skinned, very dark-skinned. He wore a clerical collar.

"You must be Mr. Butterfield," he boomed with a sense of self-assured camaraderie.

Wallace was surprised. He had expected the Reverend Poda-Pirudi to be an Italian or maybe an Italian-American. He hoped he didn't show his disappointment. He felt out of sorts, off balance — this wasn't because Reverend Poda-Pirudi wasn't an Italian-American. No, it was because the being within Butterfield had gone into a total state of panic. The sight of Reverend Poda-Pirudi had filled it with dread. His eyes… they had no soul! There were no luminescent blue eyes peering back— just flesh— and, worst of all, that flesh could see it! The creature that lived within Butterfield ran, ran down deep inside him, curled up in a fetal position, tucking itself together as tight as it could squeeze. If there had been a door there, the Reverend and Wallace would have both heard it slam. There it hid where it was born in the pit of Butterfield's stomach.

"Welcome to England's attic. Well the whole Abbey is the nation's attic, but this spot most particularly is the attic, for the nation's history, I mean. Over three thousand notable people buried here you know, seventeen of them monarchs," Reverend Poda-Pirudi laughed. "Come in, come and sit down please."

The Reverend motioned to an elegant red satin couch below another large window. But this one looked into the Abbey. Butterfield was happy to oblige him. He felt very obliging, even light-hearted.

"Can I get you something? Spring water, a cordial?"

Butterfield shook his head.

"Well, please, you are our guest. I can send Bradshaw to the commissary and he can get you anything you need," he said, motioning with his head in the direction of an open office door to indicate that was where Mr. Bradshaw was lodged. Then the Reverend sat himself down at his desk.

It was a massive hand-carved desk, topped with a large pink slab of polished marble. It was an exquisite piece of furniture. In fact, the whole office décor was stunning. It was done all in burnished wood tones: linenfold old oak paneling with richly carved Tudor wooden traceries bordering the hammer beam ceiling. It had a parquet floor of branching ebony and white oak. A huge mahogany bookcase stood at one end of the room, filled with gilt-edged books. The Reverend's desk sat on a deep red oriental rug. Two brass lamps with maroon shades gave off a warm rosy light. The room flowed together seamlessly. Nothing was out of place. Nothing was out of place on the Reverend's desk either, papers neatly stacked, his pen left at a precise perpendicular angle.

"Melanesian Brotherhood, Archdiocese of Melanesia," the Reverend said, as though he was just answering a question.

"Excuse me?" Butterfield was trying to come to terms with where he was and he hadn't a clue what Melanesia had to do with anything.

Seeing his confusion, the Reverend clarified his point.

"Most people are surprised to see me. A man from the South Pacific here in the Abbey and in charge of our illustrious Westminster Abbey Foundation." He grinned. "Well, Mr. Butterfield, let me tell you a little about myself, for I think I know something about you, and we should be acquainted before we discuss our business. First of all you don't know my first name. It is Jae. Please call me Jae. I'm only Reverend Poda-Pirudi at weddings and funerals and such. Okay? And may I have the privilege of calling you Wallace?"

Butterfield nodded but the Reverend gave him no time to respond.

"I am from the Solomon Islands. You've heard of them?" The Reverend's voice was deep, but his words would modulate up to a high falsetto at the end of a thought, as if the ending were a punch line to a joke.

"The Solomon Islands are off of Fiji?" Wallace guessed, knowing he'd be wrong.

"No, they are off of Papua New Guinea and Australia. But no matter, I'm from the Island of New Georgia, specifically the Marovo Lagoon. The world's largest lagoon you know, full of beautiful coral reefs and fishes, tropical birds, huge trees, and lizards the size of large dogs. A marvelous place. A very nice place and a very spiritual place. Everybody spends Saturday getting ready for Sunday. But that is enough of that. When I became old enough I joined the Anglican Melanesian Brotherhood. Later I won a scholarship to the University of the South Pacific in Public Administration. Then I was so fortunate to be asked to attend Saint Stephen's House in Oxford where I trained for the ministry.

"And now here I am before you ready to discuss the future of this marvelous old Abbey. I confess that I have no skills in architecture, but that's why you are here: a member of The Royal Institute of British Architects with a master's degree in architecture from the University of Manchester. I need a vision, Wallace. "

"Vision... excuse me what kind of vision? I don't understand."

"Of course you don't. And don't get nervous, I'm not asking you to have the Virgin Mary appear before me. I want your vision for our own central tower."

"A central tower... Do you mean like Parliament's? I'm not sure..."

"Of course you are not. I haven't brought you up to speed yet. Relax, let me finish. Westminster Abbey lacks a tower. I know you might say that it's just an abbey but come, come, Wallace, this Abbey is the Church of England. It needs to proclaim that. It's not a new idea. Abbot Islip tried to get one built during the Reign of Henry VIII, but there was no money. Henry was a very high-maintenance king— pageants, jousts, fine food clothes, and palaces— that sort of thing. Well during the reign of Charles II, Christopher Wren tried to do something with the crumbling west front, but botched the job with those two pygmy towers of his. "

"Sir, I mean Reverend." Butterfield was flabbergasted. This was madness to consider an obscure grocer's architect to present such an important idea. "I'm not Christopher Wren!"

"And I'm glad to hear it. Look Wallace I'm not asking you to build me a tower. I'm asking you to submit your idea for a tower on paper. If Christopher Wren could make a mistake on the real edifice of Westminster Abbey, why shouldn't you be allowed the same latitude to make a mistake but on paper? After all I'm just looking for some ideas to present before the Abbey Foundation. To get them thinking about finishing the Abbey, the way it was meant to be finished.

"Besides," the Reverend said encouragingly, "I've been shopping at your le Mareschal's Supermarket. And I might say it was quite a treat. I was struck by the architecture. The chrome. The glass. The refraction of natural light. A grocery store that would soar if given the chance. A heavenly structure that ties man and God together in a supermarket. This is why I sought you out Wallace. From your work I could tell that you are a spiritual man. Are you a member of the Church of England?"

"Ahhh, no. As a boy I did attend a Methodist Church in South Croydon," Butterfield sheepishly confessed.

Reverend Poda-Pirudi laughed. "Well, we will work on that, as well as your plans, together. Look, York Minster, Salisbury, Norwich, Canterbury, and Lincoln cathedrals all have commanding towers or spires that proclaim 'here is the place for worship. Here we interconnect God and the heavens with man on earth.' Man has always tried to touch the face of God by reaching for the heavens," he rhapsodized. "The Mayans and the Egyptians had their pyramids, the Babylonians their ziggurats, the Incas, Machu Picchu, and what do we have here where the greatest movers and shakers in British history are buried? What does London's skyline proclaim? Europe's largest Ferris wheel, a gargantuan sybaritic amusement park attraction for a pampered and hedonistic populace, and the Gherkin, that obnoxious 180-meter tall skyscraper fashioned into the shape of a pickle. I think it makes a suitable home for our lords of industry whose greed has gotten us into this pickle of debased values and moral decay. Well, what a pickle they've gotten us into… hah! Sorry," the Reverend chuckled, "I'm a serial punster. I'll control myself— promise."

He then went quiet hoping that Butterfield might have something to say on the topic.

But he didn't.

The Reverend began to feel embarrassed about allowing the conversation to lapse, "Don't you think we need something big in our skyline for our churchgoers?"

"Well there's the dome of Saint Paul's. As I recall it's much higher than any of the cathedral towers in England. Isn't that enough?"

"Saint Paul's dome?" the Reverend said dismissively. "No, no, that was a premonition of Christopher Wren of things to come. Looks like the U.S. Capitol dome doesn't it? That speaks volumes about modern Britain. Saint Paul's is Wren getting things wrong again. You know he's not buried here? "

Butterfield shook his head. He had no idea where Christopher Wren was buried. Never thought of looking it up.

The Reverend laughed self-consciously. "Forgive me. No more haranguing Wren or the worshippers of the Gherkin tonight. I'm sure that you with your architectural sensitivities understand my passion. I don't want to put you on the spot, but do you have any initial ideas, Mr. Butterfield? Any of your creative muses whispering to you? Come, come, share them with me."

Butterfield knew he had to say something. "Perhaps we should keep things light?"

The Reverend clapped his hands encouragingly. "We are here for the light. Yes, yes, light versus darkness. Go on?"

"No, I mean, I'm a bit concerned about the foundation and the weight-bearing capacity of such an old structure. I can't see how you could integrate a tower or steeple unless you used glass and maybe chromed steel. Something like the pyramid I. M. Pei designed to be placed in front of the Louvre. It's sort of comparable in history and grandeur with the Abbey."

Reverend Poda-Pirudi's face went temporarily blank but recovered instantly. He breathed in and then explained. "I have all the soil boring data and those strain and stress structural thingies from our engineers. The project has their green light. No need to stifle your imagination with concerns about whether the old Abbey can carry the weight of your imagination. What I need from you is a vision! Something I can present to the Abbey Foundation. If I can convince them, we should commence work within a year or two.

Wallace hesitated. "But, don't you think the Royals might get upset if we tamper with such a venerated historic building?"

"Oh, my goodness no. It's a royal peculiar you know? It falls directly under the Queen and not under a bishop. The Royals want this. The old Abbey has had many a facelift over time and has had all sorts of indignities committed against it throughout its existence. This will be a major improvement. Consider, if you will, how Henry VIII slighted it. Stripped it of all its gold and treasure. There were golden pillars around Edward the Confessor's altar with a feretory of saintly relics of solid gold and covered in jewels. They were all melted down and the jewels picked out. He grabbed hold of anything he could lay his hands on that had any value. Henry the VIII is not buried here, you know.

"And then there was that Puritan rabble during the Civil War. Cromwell's thugs attacked and badly damaged the Abbey. Unfortunately Oliver Cromwell was buried here. But then there was the Restoration of the Monarchy, and the corpse of this repugnant regicide was exhumed. His body taken to Tyburn tree where he was executed— posthumously— and hanged along with a couple of his confederates, who were also, at the time, buried here. Their heads were placed on a spike."

The Reverend pantomimed sticking an invisible head on an invisible spike, and then added, "He is no longer buried here, is he Bradshaw?"

This was the first time there was any indication that Mr. Bradshaw might be listening into their conversation from back within his office. The Reverend's voice had an edge to it now that Butterfield hadn't heard before. Perhaps he didn't like eavesdropping.

"No, Reverend, he is definitely not buried here," came an almost apologetic response from beyond the door that led into Mr. Bradshaw's office.

"No he's definitely not," the Reverend went on with a chuckle. "Besides all of these indignities, the Abbey has endured hundreds of years of souvenir hunters who have stripped the place almost to the degree old Harry the Eighth did. The armor and silver head of Henry V... gone. The silver cradle of Edward IV's daughter... stolen. Six gilded brass images of the children of Edward III... pilfered by tourists. Queen Phillipa's gilt angels... scarpered off with. Worst of all, a schoolboy ran off with the jaw of King Richard II, as though the old monarch hadn't suffered enough indignities. You see it is time to start putting things right. Prince Charles is very keen on this project, very keen indeed. You, of course, know that he has made a pursuit out of advocating urban renovation— restoring and upgrading architecture that upholds London's traditional ideals."

He lingered here and stared at Butterfield for a second or two; then another big smile blossomed across his face. He got up and walked across the room to where Butterfield was seated.

"Come, my boy, look out this window. I want you to take in the place. This is your grand canvas. "

Butterfield turned to face the double-arched window behind him. The Reverend clasped Butterfield by his shoulder and made a sweeping motion toward the view with his free right arm.

"Wallace, look there." He pointed. "There is the High Altar."

Butterfield stared down into the Abbey. He felt like a pigeon in the rafters, looking down through the window at the scene below: the large golden choir screen, an altar with large golden candlesticks, and a large golden cross.

"On the other side of the screen is the Chapel of King Edward, Edward the Confessor, who built the Abbey. His tomb is there."

Butterfield nodded.

Reverend Poda-Pirudi continued. "When Henry VIII took to looting the place, the monks took Edward out of his tomb and secretly buried him. I guess they felt that his body might be despoiled because he had been canonized by the Church of Rome as a saint: Saint Edward the Confessor. Henry was on the outs with the Catholic Church at the time. Eventually they put Edward back. Well, of course, Henry the Eighth isn't buried here."

Yet again Butterfield felt obliged to nod.

"Oh yes, as per Edward's wish, the high altar is built upon soil brought back from Jerusalem." The Reverend chuckled. "You know some scientists with ground-penetrating radar recently found a slew of old crypts under there. Did you read about the ground-penetrating gizmo Wallace?"

"Yes, I think I did read about that a while back."

"I'm glad to see you keeping up on current events. Bodies are always turning up around here. When they went looking for the body of James the First, they discovered that he was shacking up with Henry VII. Now, why doesn't that surprise me? And when they opened the crypt of Mary Queen of Scots they found her there with her great grandson, a niece, Elizabeth of Bohemia, as well as Arbella Stuart, and a couple babes of James II, and Queen Anne. Over-active maternal instinct, I'd say."

The Reverend held a hand to his chest to stifle a laugh. Then he got serious. "But you know the most wonderful feature of this entire Abbey is right below us. There," he pointed. "In front of the high altar. There. You see? The Cosmati Pavement."

Butterfield looked down and saw in the foreground a large swirling mosaic of geometric patterns made from brightly colored stone.

"It was ordered to be built by Henry III in the thirteenth century. Some say it is a prayer to God; some say it depicts the end of the universe, Judgment Day. The mosaic is about seven and a half meters square. The stone for it was acquired by special dispensation from the pope. They chopped up ancient Roman and Egyptian antiquities to make this. It's comprised of semi-precious stones like green serpentine, purple porphyry, and red- and blue-colored glass on Purbeck marble. Do you see that central roundel?"

Butterfield pointed to it.

"Yes, that one. Well, it is onyx, and it is also the very spot where Edward the Confessor's throne is placed for the royal coronation. You know, the throne that is encased in glass and on display downstairs?"

Wallace had seen and nodded.

"Well, almost every monarch who has been crowned in England has been crowned in that chair over that roundel. Funny thing is that for almost two centuries the pavement had been covered over by a dirty oriental rug. Nobody paid much attention to it. Well, the Abbey Foundation has recently thrown that old rug out and restored the pavement. We do good work you know."

"I can see that."

"Odd thing. There are brass letters around the border of the paving. Some are missing, but we know it's a formula for the end. The medieval end of the world based on the multiple life spans of men and dogs and hedges and sea serpents, some sort of Ptolemaic system for prognosticating such a cataclysm. Well, I'm sure you want to know. The magic year for when the apocalypse is to take place is 19,683 years from the time the pavement was built. So Wallace, don't sweat it. We have more than 18,000 years left to go.

"Wallace, I can't wait to see your drawing— just don't mess with my paving. "

Butterfield knew that he was supposed to say something, but what? It wasn't a dream come true because he wouldn't have ever dreamt it. The silence was awkward. Finally, he spoke. "With all due respect, Jae, I'm not your man. Shouldn't you put this out for some kind of architectural design competition? Get some really qualified people who know all about the Gothic architecture in here?"

"Well, perhaps at some point. Let's see what you can come up with first. My money is on you for now. I've cut you a check as a retainer." He handed an envelope to Butterfield. "Give it try, won't you?"

Butterfield opened the envelope and glanced at the sum on the check. He stumbled on his first few words in response. "I... I... w-w-w-will get right to work. Clear my desk. I'll give my best shot. I assure you."

"Of course you will. We'll be in touch. How I envy you. This is such an historic moment for the Abbey. Go home and get a good night's rest and then have at it."

The Reverend escorted Butterfield to the door of his office and waved farewell to him as Butterfield began to work his way back around the packing crates piled about the triforium.

Reverend Poda-Pirudi shut and locked his office door and then walked over to the open door of Mr. Bradshaw's office. He leaned in. "I'm going to need a couple of first class noggins. Get me the ghosts of Newton and Darwin."

Chapter Three

During the Night

When Wallace got back to his bedsit above his office, he was walking on Cloud 9. Sure, he knew that he was totally unprepared for the job he had been given, but for the first time in his life he felt that he was significant. He liked the feeling. It made him strangely calm. With all the excitement of the evening, you might think that he would be up all night, his mind racing. But no, he was sleepy. He told himself he would advertise for a secretary with Jobcentre Plus in the morning. His office would be a proper office now. Then Butterfield fell asleep, confident that he was going to have good dreams. And he did because deep down inside him behind his pyloric valve, curled up like a hedgehog, was Wallace's unborn ghost. Who was quite content to forgo any playing in Wallace's brain this night.

Butterfield's ghost came into being when Butterfield was born... though strictly speaking his ghost hadn't been born yet. Ghosts hatch out upon the death of their host. In the interim, they matured by soaking up the life experience of the living. It is a parasitic relationship. Incubating this way, the unborn soul strengthens, absorbing the abilities and personality of the mortal rind.

However, at the time of Wallace's birth, the center of his spectral pupa's being was way down in his stomach. The stomach acts as sort of a yolk for the development of a proto-ghost. As an unborn ghost grows older it rises upward and upward, till eventually they are crammed into that incessantly chattering hunk of meat, the frontal lobe.

If you asked Wallace Butterfield in what part of his body his consciousness was located, he would point to the middle of his forehead just above his eyes. So would most people. So would his maturing ghost. But his ghost would do so with less enthusiasm. It was a place he hated to visit, unless it was to give Butterfield a nightmare; it was always buzzing, always changing, never the same, neurons discharging willy-nilly like the randomness of fireflies pulsating in the dark.

But there was a time when Wallace's consciousness wasn't located there, in the frontal lobes. When the ghost and Butterfield first started out, they hung about together in a lower region of the brain, an older section, the amygdala, a nice cozy spot that humans had inherited from some reptilian ancestors. Butterfield's ghost had been fond of this place; little chatter there except perhaps on Christmas morning ... or later on in Wallace's adolescent life when a pubescent girl drew near. Then his neurons did do a lot of chattering then, sparking and discharging all sorts of mental images, conjuring up hopes, possibilities, and anxieties. But nothing much happened beyond that. And adolescent girls so rarely came close to Butterfield that it was hardly a problem.

It was when the larval ghost moved with Wallace into those frontal lobes, that area just over Wallace's eyes, that things got rough. This was about the time that Butterfield's head started to get stuffed with facts, definitions, treatises, opinions, values, encyclopedic articles, and textbook piffle... nonsense layered upon nonsense. And worse, this nonsense fed Wallace's insecurity, inhibitions, phobias, and all those other things that make human beings such pathetic creatures.

Butterfield's ghost hated it there and hated being forced to stay there. So, one night he chose to rebel. He had long ago discovered that whenever Wallace slept, his thoughts would become diffuse and sink down into another region of the brain, the hippocampus. The hippocampus told him stories while he rested. On the evening of the rebellion, as things started to calm down in Wallace's head, his ghost pounced, seizing the moment, he forced his way into the hippocampus and hijacked a dream. He filled the hippocampus with his ghostly thoughts, frightening things, bizarre horrors, cruelty, and death; and that's when the miracle occurred. Just as Wallace Butterfield was losing his balance and about to fall into a pit full of gigantic tarantulas, Butterfield's brain forcibly expelled the ghost. Rising upward, the ghost's head, so to speak, suddenly surfaced, coming to rest just above Wallace's head. What a delightful it was up there! No annoying thoughts; Wallace Butterfield's consciousness was well below. The silence was wonderful!

His ghost wished he had discovered this phenomenon earlier. He began to utilize this technique every evening. Every day Butterfield's ghost spent Butterfield's waking hours searching for a new idea that would scare the crap out of Wallace while he tried to get some sleep. What he concocted during the day he would parade about Butterfield's hippocampus at night. The result was always the same. The ghost would be kicked out of the brain and surface a good ten inches above Wallace's head.

Up there he would survey the outside world without any of the lame distractions that came from his host. Butterfield's ghost did find it to be strange that none of the other ghosts seemed to know how to do this. As he surveyed the outside world from his lofty perch, he could see their eyes peering through the eyes of their hosts... how tortured they looked trapped within those brains, their existence confined to a human straight jacket, all of them anxiously awaiting the liberation of death.

But tonight was the ghost's night to be scared. There would be no repeat performance of a tentacled rhinoceros giving Wallace a proctologic examination with a Gregorian chant thrown in for extra measure. Butterfield's ghost lay hidden in the small intestines just on the other side of the pyloric valve shivering in fear, as he tried to make sense of what he had just seen.

— «» —

While Wallace Butterfield was experiencing one of the best night's rests he had had in a decade, miles away a voice could be heard booming throughout the dimly lit Abbey. And though there were no lights on in the triforium, the voice was coming from there.

"What do you mean, you won't do it? What are your excuses now? Crohn's disease? Lupus? Migraines? Allergies? Athlete's foot? Oh no, not chronic fatigue syndrome? You're spirits! You get plenty of rest, besides you can't get ill anymore! Why are the intellectual types always such babies?"

There must have been a reply, but it was not audible to the specters rising up in their crypts down below in the north and south transepts and in the naïve or in Henry VII's high chapel. But those same specters certainly did hear the indignant first voice continue.

"It's beneath you? You said it's beneath you? You're dead! Sometimes I think that the ascent of man— Yes, yes, I mean the ascent of spirits— is just a quest to see how stupid we all are. What is it with the two of you? Oh don't tell me, you are only going to be satisfied when you have analyzed the world into total immobility? All ones and zeros, is that it? Positives and negatives, black and white, everything must have perfect mathematical symmetry, like the latticework of some humongous crystal? You have it all down don't you? Facts in their succession— one after another in a nice long row— a big chain of interrelated causal events. Of course, what hasn't yet been discovered will have space allocated within your great continuum. If not, someone will write a new theorem to nudge it into place. You've got it all figured out. Well, of course you do because you have simian brains. Well, listen up my fine pair of monkey eggheads. Do you want to end up like Bradshaw's ghost over there, spending eternity packed in with disposable diapers and kitty litter at the Mucking Marshes Landfill? And it will take more than an army of your fellow scientists with ground imaging radar to locate your bodies!"

The Reverend Poda-Pirudi gave the threat a little time to sink in so it could be fully appreciated. But just in case the shades of Sir Isaac Newton and Charles Darwin had any further doubts, Poda-Pirudi further clarified their situation.

"Bradshaw come here. Tell the mega-brains how much fun it is down below the Mucking Marshes Landfill with a smell of rot far worse than your own."

The response was inaudible, but a new voice began talking excitedly and quickly. It was that of John Bradshaw.

The Reverend interrupted him.

"I imagine me Johnny boy, that you are enjoying the fact that I've allowed you back here at the Abbey. How does it feel to be home again?"

A frantic explanation followed. Then the Abbey went silent for a while. You had to be in Reverend Poda-Pirudi's office in the triforium to make out what was being said.

"Of course I understand. Just a bit of nerves, that's all. A bit of a panic attack. It has been a while since you've been out and about in London. No, no, I'm not mad at you. Now, chop-chop, off you go, and remember I want daily reports."

Chapter Four

Tipsy Dolls

Tipsy Dolls Fine Dining in Mayfair was built near where an 18th- century gingerbread baker hawked obscene gingerbread men and women to the crowds watching the executions at Tyburn tree. The restaurant was close to the spot where his ovens once stood. It thrived here for four decades, advocating traditional British fare, beef Wellington, tripe and onions, fried smelts, bubble and squeak, lamb's tongue in raisin sauce, beef collops with pickled walnuts, baked jam roly-poly, and of course gingerbread.

The restaurant had frontage on Samlesbury Avenue. It was a five-story stone building with a wooden facade on the street level. Countless windowpanes were confined in what was once dark blue sobering woodwork with the name Tipsy Dolls carved across it many times in gold-leaf script. The gold-leaf was long gone, the royal blue paint had chipped off to reveal white primer underneath, and there was no trace of the blue and yellow awnings that once protected the windows. The window boxes, once full of purple lobelia, had crumbled long ago.

At one time, Tipsy Dolls was so exclusive that you had to have a recommendation to get in.

You still couldn't walk in. Though Tipsy Dolls had the look of a foreclosure, it was paid up in full, and, for those who knew its secrets, it still served a purpose.

A rumpled-looking woman with dull brown hair, exhausted from too many applications of coloring, came to the old musician's entrance door of what was once the Tipsy Dolls Restaurant. She pulled out some keys from her purse, fumbled around with several, and finally let herself in. A few minutes passed before another woman, wearing pink Crocs and an untucked T-shirt that hung below her brown wool sweater, did the same thing. Then came a jogger in her mid-thirties who dipped into her fanny pack for her key to the old restaurant. Over the next hour several more women went through this same routine. For a while it seemed that anyone who was going to enter had and that those inside were no doubt proceeding with their business.

Then a white limousine pulled up. A long-legged woman in a short black dress with large silver polka dots stepped out in the most fashionable high heels. She was slender. Her skin was creamy. Her hair was dark black and long with a high gloss to it. She was alluring. And it was apparent by the angular overstated way that she had stepped onto the street that she knew that she was the sort of woman men wanted.

Behind her, tumbling out of the limo, came quite a different fashion statement. She too was very conscious of her appearance, but hadn't a clue as to what kind of image she was trying to project. To any observer, it was obvious that she was a girl in flux between two dissimilar poles. Unlike the elegant woman who had preceded her, her apparel was all about contradiction. She wore a light blue jersey with a red and yellow neckerchief. Her arms were heavy with silver bracelets. Her eyelids and lips had been blackened with makeup. She had colored her hair blue-black, except for her bangs, which were dyed to match the silver of her bangles. A Girl Guide sash covered with badges completed her outfit.

The elegant woman in the short black silver polka dotted dress moved towards the door to the musicians' entrance. She didn't have to fumble for her keys. The door was opened for her. As she entered, her young companion eagerly followed at her heels. The woman, wearing pink Crocs and a brown sweater, was there to greet them.

"Maeva most of our sisters are here. When shall we start?"

Maeva Wolusky turned to the woman, who for the purposes of this club was known as Artemisia.

"Oh Artemisia, just in a minute or two. But first I'd like you to meet a special guest. This is Emma."

Artemisia held out her hand, which was shyly received by the teenager. "Always pleased to meet a sister," she said. Then, turning her attention back to Maeva she added with a slightly puzzled look, "Will she be staying for the meeting?"

"Oh, no. I would like to give her a brief tour. Just before we begin, she should go upstairs with the other young ladies and start her studies. Her mother says that Emma hasn't been quite herself lately. So, I suggested that a trip to our ladies club might help her find herself... that is in addition to the wholesome experience of being a Girl Guide."

Artemisia couldn't suppress a grin and was about to say something when Emma chimed in. "We've just come back from indoor skydiving." she announced.

"There are these big fans underneath you and it gets really windy and you get pushed up above a net. You float up just above the net like you're really skydiving. Ms. Wolusky took our group of Girl Guides there this morning."

"Well, I'm sure that you got proper instruction from Ms. Wolusky. I'm sure you know that she's a champion sky-diver."

"Oh yes. When we're a bit older, she promised to take us up in her plane and watch her jump."

"I'm sure that she will. Soon you'll be jumping out of planes yourself." Artemisia turned to Maeva. "When you're done with your little tour give me a shout and I'll take Emma upstairs and introduce her to the other girls." Artemisia then left the entryway and walked through a door that led to the old dining area of Tipsy Dolls.

Maeva was about to follow her in when Emma gushed, "Why it's you. Look it's you Ms. Wolusky."

In the hallway, hung just above Emma's head, was a French poster in a golden frame. "La Fée Verte, The Green Fairy," it read. The poster was a bit washed out and tinged by cigar smoke. "Absinthe," it proclaimed in a long snaking Art Deco script. Below the script was a nude, a beautiful and seductive green fairy with dark butterfly wings, partaking of the alcoholic distillate from grande wormwood.

Maeva was pleased that the girl had picked up on the likeness. Many had. And the similarity between her and the green fairy's looks was the main reason why she had had it hung there.

"Yes Emma, some have said that. But more importantly, absinthe is the theme of this most private club. And you must start calling me Maeva. Oh and we are all sisters here. Ms. Wolusky is fine when we're out Girl Guiding. Speaking of which, Emma what is the first rule of a Girl Guide?"

"Rule one," she said, a little surprised to be asked such an easy question, "A guide is honest, reliable, and can be trusted."

"That's right. I will emphasize the reliable and trusted aspect of that sentence. Today you are going to see and hear about things that few people know about. Most of those who do are your sisters. The reason you are here is that you have much in common with the women beyond these doors. You've been hearing things in your head haven't you?"

"Uh huh," Emma sounded embarrassed. "I hear things... whispers."

"How often do you hear whispering?"

"Not often," she apologized.

"Well, as you get older you will hear the whispering more and more and it won't be just whispering after a while. It can get pretty loud inside our heads. I don't mean to scare you but you must know that someday those voices will try to tell you what to do and try and take hold of your life. That's what this club is mostly about, controlling those voices... or learning to live with them. Emma what's the third rule of being a Girl Guide?"

"A Girl Guide faces challenges and learns from her experiences."

"That's right. Today you are going to see the challenges that you face and you must learn from these experience."

With that, Maeva threw open the French doors that opened up into Tipsy Dolls main dining room.

The old dining area of Tipsy Dolls was divided into two halves. Several rows of silver satin brocade wing chairs faced one way, behind them, several rows of emerald green satin brocade wing chairs faced in the opposite direction. The women seated in the chairs had a variety of appearance and came from assorted backgrounds. One woman wore a long pink dress made of flamingo feathers. She also sported an enormous beehive hairdo, which her beautician had dyed platinum. But her look was rather tame compared to the woman sitting next to her. She had wired and glued her hair to resemble an enormous black claw, seemingly reaching out to pounce on the head of the woman who was seated directly in front of her. Who was rather ordinary in appearance— looking like somebody's granny— except that she was puffing on a meerschaum pipe that was carved into the likeness of a skull with horns. Still, there were many who had been able to look fairly normal despite the jumble of bizarre ideas that coursed through their heads. Seated in the front row of the green chairs were members of the coven who had managed to fit comfortably into a variety of walks of life. Some of them had their work attire on— a stewardess in a British Airways uniform who had oversized her mouth with deep red lipstick, a dental hygienist who was reluctant to take off her blood splattered smock, an auto mechanic who felt the most comfortable in greasy coveralls, and a game warden who would dress in oak leaf camouflage only when visiting London.

One difference between the two groups segregated by colored chairs was that the women in the silver satin chairs sat erect and rigid and chanted in incomprehensible tongues, while the women seated in the green satin chairs preferred to drink and become incomprehensibly drunk.

The green-chair women were always seated facing a fancy mirrored bar with several very large and ornate glass-and-silver absinthe water fountains, cradled by silver-plated nymphs. In the center of the bar was a silver statue of Diana the Huntress with a drawn bow. Below Diana's statue were bottles labeled Lucifer's Delight, Green Man's Own, Escobas de Brujas, Hexenkessel and Before Morning Imperial Absinthe. Whereas, the silver-chaired women were always seated facing a large yellow sandstone carving of the Wedjat eye, the left eye of the Egyptian sun god Ra.

As she entered the room, Maeva spun about with her arms in the air. Then, facing a very bewildered looking Emma, she said, "This is all my creation. It's called WITCH. It's a feminist support group. Do you know what a feminist support group is?"

Emma was having a hard time focusing on what Maeva was saying, the chanting in the background was so loud. But she ventured a guess, "Something that helps feminines?"

"Yes, exactly! WITCH is an acronym… a bunch of letters that stands for something." She hoped that she was getting through to the teenager.

"As I was saying, it's an acronym and it stands for Women In Therapeutic Chemical Healing. Of course it is true that the group wanted our organization to be called WITCHes before we came up with the name Women In Therapeutic Chemical Healing. Fortunately, it all fits marvelously together. You see Emma, everybody in this room suffers from a condition that psychiatrists would call schizophrenia, but they would be wrong. We Witches preferred to call our condition by an earlier term: 'precocious madness.' Now, I know this may come as a bit of a surprise to you— and maybe a bit scary too— but you are a witch. And before I tell you more, remember that we are all here for one another. We are sisters."

"You mean I'm a witch… like because of the whispering and all? You don't mean like ride a broomstick?" Emma's face conveyed her growing uneasiness.

Maeva began looking about the room wondering where Artemisia might have gone to.

"Here dear, sit down for a moment." Maeva motioned to one of the satin chairs. "You are with the green chair sisters today. I'm a member of the green chairs."

Emma started to sit in the chair but then became very distracted by the chanting from the women in the silver chairs.

"Ra, god of light, decided to punish mankind.

He gave his daughter Sekhmet, the woman lioness, his left eye.

The Wedjat eye.

Lady of Slaughter. Lady of the Flame!

Robed in scarlet she took the left eye of Ra
And burned mankind with it
Till Ra begged her to stop
Lady of Slaughter. Lady of the Flame!"

Maeva had to take her right hand and beat the seat of the chair to regain Emma's attention. Emma sat down compliantly.

"Now don't be alarmed dear. I'll explain all of that. It is a bit unnerving at times, even to me, but you'll get used to it."

But not only did Emma regain her composure, she became exuberant. "No. No. I'm fine... this is so cool Ms. Wolusky... I mean Maeva! I know those words! I know what they're saying. I've heard those words whispered in my head."

"You have? You're not just saying that to please me and then plan to go running out of here the first opportunity you get?"

Emma smiled, "Never. Never. I'm at home here."

Maeva appeared relieved to hear this. Though this was the way things normally went. An inductee seemed to become at ease with the place within minutes upon entering it. Maeva had a theory that this was because their ghosts were helping to steady them. Her past experiences had taught Maeva that it would be smooth sailing now. Emma would fit in well.

Though just to be on the safe side, Maeva wasn't going to go into too much detail with Emma as to what being a WITCH meant. There would be plenty of time for her to learn about such things upstairs with the other girls. It was sort of a Sunday school for the younger witches. Emma would be in an environment with other young women who would be exploring this newfound truth about their peculiar state together. There they would learn about the mishmash in their heads... how a witch's brain is all scrambled up with neurons that misfire into unworldly ether. Over time, the girls would be educated on how witches and their larval ghosts often become a dysfunctional schizophrenic mess, in a constant flux between the human and the nonhuman.

It was a pathetic state that had cursed their people long before there were even words for witch, sorcery, or magic. So many of their sisters had been doomed to be drowned, hanged, pressed to death under rocks, or set on fire just because their ghost's influence had taken too strong a hold upon their personalities. It wasn't till the medicinal beverage absinthe was discovered in Switzerland by Dr. Pierre Ordinaire, in the late seventeenth century, that they had any hope of concealing their bewildering state. It was more than coincidence that the execution of witches ended at the same time.

"Emma, you see all the bottles about?"

Emma nodded enthusiastically.

"That's absinthe. The French named it La Fée Verte, The Green Fairy, green for the color of the liquor. It's made from the plant grande wormwood, *Artemisia absinthium*."

"Green fairy like the poster in the hallway ... and Artemisia like the lady you introduced me to?"

"Yes. The one is distillate and the other a great drinker of the distillate," Maeva chuckled. "You see, wormwood is an herb. It has psychoactive properties that come from the chemical thujone. I mean it sharpens your wits."

"Can I have some?" Emma asked hopefully.

"No... not now. You are too young. But bear in mind that as the voices get louder it will be available here to help you. You'll be able to keep them quiet. However, it will be several years more before you are old enough to join the green chair ladies at the absinthe fountains. We'll have a big coming out party for you then. Witches from all over Britain will be here for the event. However, till then, you must apply yourself to your studies."

"Oh I will... I will."

"Emma, you are going to fit in so well. Do you like to draw or put on little plays?"

"No... no I don't do that."

"Oh, well, many in our membership are of an artistic persuasion. I'm sure you'll find them to be so interesting. We have many, many illustrators and painters, writers and poets, potters and glass blowers. But don't feel you have to be an artsy sort. We have all types, a taxi cab driver here and a welder, a crossing guard, and a physical education teacher and many other occupations as well. But there are a lot of artists. Did you know that Vincent Van Gogh drank absinthe?"

"No, is he a member?"

"No. We are exclusively a woman's organization. Men who are in our condition must fend for themselves. Mr. Van Gogh is long dead but he was a very famous artist. He painted a still life of a bottle of absinthe with a glass."

Emma didn't seem to be very impressed.

"Well there are other famous absinthe drinkers. Have you heard of Pablo Picasso, Ernest Hemingway, Edgar Allen Poe, Mark Twain, Alfred Jarry, Henri Toulouse Lautrec, Paul Verlaine, Jack London, Oscar Wilde, and Arthur Rimbaud, Charles Baudelaire, Amedeo Modigliani, and Aleister Crowley?"

Emma shook her head.

"Hmm, I see your point. Why should you know about them? Just another long list of men. Whenever anyone speaks of the past all it ever is men... men... men. There would have been lots of famous women who partook of the brew but frightened men no doubt burned them all. That's what happens when women dare to show their superior intelligence. But let me see... how about Mata Hari, she was a famous exotic dancer and a spy and a sister in the pursuit of our beverage? Certainly you know of her?"

"I'm sorry Ms. Wolusky... I mean Maeva. Should I know of them?"

"Well, apparently not if you attended our local grammar schools. Anyhow, Mata Hari didn't live long enough to be truly memorable."

Maeva then grimaced. "Men took her out and shot her... but don't worry. That's not going to happen to you. You're a member of WITCH now. Though we've been oppressed for centuries we've come together here. Nobody is ever going to mess with us again. And I'll tell you Emma that it won't be long before every Girl Guide will be able to recite a list of names of prestigious women absinthe drinkers."

Artemisia now came back to join them. Looking down at Emma she inquired, "So have you been learning from our president about our little group?"

"Oh... I didn't know she was the president. Yes, she told me so much. I know about your name too. Are you going to be my teacher?"

"No, but I certainly can answer any questions that you might have."

"Oh then... why are the ladies in the silver chairs chanting and have such odd voices?"

Artemisia glanced at Maeva as if to say, "What am I supposed to do?"

Maeva shook her head almost imperceptibly.

Artemisia picked up on her signal. "Oh that's a complicated question. I'd best take you up to meet Zoraida. She's going to be your teacher. I'm sure she'll fill you in on all the things that are important to know."

As Emma and Artemisia walked off to meet Zoraida, Maeva breathed a sigh of relief. It was too soon for Emma to hear about the silver chair ladies. Nor did she want Emma to know very much about the green chair ladies. She just wanted to touch lightly on the subject of the green chair ladies' consumption of absinthe. She didn't want to tell Emma that Van Gogh drank too much of the stuff for so long that it produced a state of temporal lobe epilepsy in his brain. And that this was why the green chair witches drank it. Her ladies club treasured this convulsive out-of-body experience. It was cathartic and put things right for them for a little while. Their heads were almost normal for a short time after a seizure. Maeva and many of her sisters at WITCH tried to stay just under the influence of absinthe. It never dulled their attention but gave them the necessary focus to control their constantly chattering ghosts. It gave them human dominance. As long as they drank it, they were fine. Their troubles began when they stopped drinking it. Then, their ghosts pushed forward and the witches were driven by their ghostly hybrid personalities into the occult.

However, it would have been far worse for Emma to have heard about the chanting of the ladies in the silver chairs. They rarely went to the absinthe fountains. They preferred maintaining a close relationship with their ghosts. The silver-chair women and their ghosts sought answers, not through the convulsive fits of Vincent Van Gogh, but through the aberrant lifestyle of another absinthe drinker, Aleister Crowley.

Crowley was a nineteenth-century mystic. He was the wealthy son of a brewer from Plymouth. He was also a hedonistic magician who was said to have killed his pet cat as a boy. Crowley had many labels that could be affixed to his name. He was a poet, a libertine, an occult philosopher, an Egyptologist, a publisher, a chess player, and devotee of the notion that light is found in the depths of darkness. He invented the word "abracadabra," a word Crowley may have used often while engaged in rumored acts of cannibalism, infanticide, and human sacrifice.

However, it was the belief of the silver-chaired women that Aleister Crowley's brilliance and understanding of the occult only came about when he spent time with his dark angel— his ghost. They were sure that this could only come about when he had abandoned any attempt to control or subdue his ghost with heavy dosages of absinthe.

When a witch refused to take her absinthe, she would seat herself in a silver chair. There she would let her ghost, her dark angel, take charge. Before the Wedjat eye, the left eye of Ra, she would then worship.

The silver-chair women believed the Wedjat had the power of the lunar force, that it governed menstruation and had certain healing qualities. They were sure that it was the embodiment of the power of women. That it held dominion over intuition, magic, and things non-linear, knowledge that is felt but not reasoned. But all too often when ladies of the club seated themselves in these chairs things got out of control. All too often the result was an attempt at some kind of sorcery.

Artemisia now came down the steps from the second story of Tipsy Dolls. At the landing, she turned to Maeva and gave a wink as she made an okay sign with the fingers of her right hand. Maeva breathed a sigh of relief.

It was now time that she turned and addressed all of her sisters, those seated in the green chairs as well as those seated in the silver chairs.

"Ladies. Ladies, please. We have to commence now. Could I have a bit of quiet? We have the minutes of last Friday's meeting to be approved and a report from the Advisory Committee, then there's the budget to go over. Ladies, please!"

The incessant chanting of the silver-chaired women wouldn't stop. Maeva was patient by nature but knew her people all too well.

She shouted to Artemisia, "I think we should start the meeting with refreshments first. Don't you?"

"It would seem best," she yelled.

Artemisia then shuffled off to the bar a little unsteady in her clogs. As she did so, she motioned to a few of the other women in the green chairs to assist her. They had all been drinking for a while and becoming a bit unsteady on their feet.

At the bar, they began to quickly fill some green cut crystal goblets with three or four ounces of the strongest absinthe, the 175 proof. After this the glasses were placed under the fountains that had been filled earlier with water and shaved ice. Slotted spoons with sugar cubes on them were then placed on top of each goblet. The faucets to the fountain were opened to allow for a steady drip of cold water onto the sugar cubes. The sugary slurry dripped down into the green liquor in the goblets, changing its color to a milky opalescence. The crystal goblets were then placed on silver trays and carried to the women in the silver chairs by the women who had been reclining in the green chairs. The process took a long time. There had to be several trips to the bar and then back to the silver chairs. There was at least one mishap where a tray fell to the floor. But the mess was cleaned up and the goblets kept coming.

Initially, many of the women in the silver chairs were reluctant to take their absinthe. They had to be restrained by a couple of the green chair women, who were then forced to pour the elixir down their throats.

Maeva watched approvingly as she sipped a cocktail of absinthe and champagne, called "Death in the Afternoon."

Eventually all the women who had been seated in the silver chairs had got up and re-seated themselves in the green chairs.

Maeva then announced, "I call this meeting of WITCH to order."

"Thank you, sisters. I really need all of you in the green chairs today. We have some very interesting news to discuss. Normally, I don't like to forgo the appropriate sequences in our agenda, but we have something so exciting to discuss that I feel we should get right to it. Do I have a motion to table today's agenda and take up this new matter?"

"I motion that we… we take up this new issue and worry about today's agenda next Friday."

"Anyone to second Artemisia's motion?"

"I'll second Artemisia's motion," said a woman who had just recently been cashiered from the Royal Navy, and who now went by the Wiccan name of Hecuba.

Maeva took another sip from her cocktail and asked, "All in favor?"

Those who voted all said, "Aye."

"Good, we have a report to discuss. Hecuba, will you please tell our sisters what you saw on Wednesday?"

The athletic-looking middle-aged woman stood up. "As you all know, I prefer the silver chair. Absinthe keeps you pretty focused, but I don't like exercising with a drunk on. I was visiting a friend a few days ago, in Croydon, and took a little time to jog down Walpole Road. As I was jogging behind the Holiday Inn, I saw this man walking toward me down the sidewalk. The sight of him stopped me full in my tracks. Again, I'm telling you that I hadn't been drinking, but this guy was the most unusual person I'd ever seen. A lanky guy in his late twenties who looked more like a kid than a man. But there it was. I was dumb struck… his ghost."

Murmuring went about. "What do you mean you saw his ghost?" someone said.

"I'm not delusional. I saw it… all blue and luminescent. It was sticking out of the top of this guy's head. What's more, it wasn't anything like Crowley's ghost. It was a really ugly looking thing…"

Maeva interrupted her, "Perhaps that's because it's a larva. I don't think any of us have seen a larval ghost. Larva is pretty ugly."

"Well?" Hecuba said snidely. It was apparent by the sarcasm in the tone of her voice that she didn't appreciate having her report interrupted.

Hecuba took no joy in Maeva. She frequently told the women of the silver chairs that she thought Maeva was a stuck-up rich bitch. And Maeva didn't care much for Hecuba as well, despising the way she had just become a member of WITCH and within a short time bulldozed her way into being the spokesperson of the silver chairs. By being pushy, she'd made inroads among the green chairs as well. Especially after she had concocted a ceremony that actually managed to summon up the ghost of Aleister Crowley.

Maeva gave an exaggerated nod to Hecuba, who smirked and continued on with her account.

"So, I turned myself around and followed him. A few minutes later I saw him enter a small office located on Bedford Park. I stood outside for a few minutes. I could see in. This man seated himself at a desk and didn't come back out. I didn't see anybody else in there with him. The office window said Butterfield and Son Architects."

The women seated in the chairs now turned to one another, looking for some kind explanation. As they turned their attention back to Hecuba, none of them noticed that the shaved ice in the two absinthe fountains was slowly drifting and rearranging itself into patterns. Perhaps it was because translucent shapes of ice in water are hard to pick out, or because everyone had had far too much to drink, or maybe it was the excitement of Hecuba's news that was keeping them focused on her. In one of the fountains a high forehead formed and then a pair of mutton chop sideburns. In the other, the ice transformed into a pointed chin and a long sharp nose. Eyes followed and peered out at Hecuba as intently as the eyes of everyone else assembled there.

Maeva took the floor again. "I've consulted all of our literature, including the old tracts. I went to several psychiatric hospitals and nursing homes and talked about this with several of our senior sisters. Nobody has a clue as to what this means."

"Well, I think I do." Now it was Hecuba's turn to interrupt. "I've backed way off the booze and have been spending a lot of time talking with myself— my spirit and I— and we agree that this guy— I'm guessing his name is Butterfield. This Butterfield guy has managed to get his spirit pushed partly out of him. Don't know if it was intentional, but we sure do need to find out how it happened."

"Do you think it will leave him on its own?" asked Maeva.

"The best I can glean from my ghost is that there has been some kind of break with the soul. I think we should consider kidnapping him to learn from him how to unscramble our own souls. Kick his ghost all the way out of him. Hey, if we fail we're only messing with the mind of a man."

Other people were agreeing with Hecuba, but not Maeva.

"That would be premature, I think. Let me have a little more time to look into this. We've been living with this mishmash in our heads all of our lives; we can give it a bit longer I believe."

"This Butterfield," said Hecuba, "if that's his real name, is still young. We have time. But he might be hit by a lorry or fall off Millennium Bridge or something. So what do you have in mind?"

"Let me research the subject a little longer, and if he still remains a mystery, we'll bring him in. Then Hecuba, you might wish to talk to him in your very special way. As you said, he's just a man."

Normally, it would be unkind to describe the laughter of a group of women as cackling, but not in this case. When the last shriek subsided, Maeva put the issue to a vote. Everyone endorsed the proposition at hand. This time there was a vigorous "Aye!" from all of the women seated in the silver chairs.

Chapter Five

The Dean of Westminster

Reverend Poda-Pirudi had been seated at his desk in the Triforium when the ringer box of his 1915 office telephone rang. Grabbing the upright candlestick phone by the Bakelite shaft, he raised it up while removing an Ignatsio Gaudelupe maduro torpedo No. 2 cigar from his mouth. Leisurely exhaling smoke, he placed his cigar in a vivid green malachite ashtray on his desk. Uncradling the earpiece from the hook, he placed the receiver up against his ear, while bringing the mouthpiece up to his lips.

"Hello, Reverend Poda-Pirudi speaking. Ah, Newton it's you. I was hoping to hear from you. And how are you and Chuck getting along?"

The diaphragm in the Reverend's receiver vibrated frantically with Sir Isaac's words.

The Reverend spoke tersely. "I see. Well, the two of you have been only a few feet apart for the past 130 years; it's quite understandable that you might be feeling a bit of a strain. But Sir Frederick Herschel is buried right next to him and I've never heard a bad word about Darwin from him."

He backed the earpiece away from his ear to distance himself from Newton's shouting. "Sir Isaac… Sir Isaac…"

The Reverend attempted to interrupt, but decided to let Newton vent.

As the irritability in Newton's harangue softened, Reverend Poda-Pirudi decided to again hazard a conversation. "Well perhaps I should have considered sending him and

Herschel out on this but I have the highest confidence in you."

This opened the door for another long-winded tirade, which like its predecessor ran its course in a minute or two.

"Yes I know that he has a few issues, but, to be frank with you, I'd forgotten all about his agoraphobia. I guess London isn't really the place to be out and about in that sort of condition. He's doing what? Well is it working? So then what's the problem? It's embarrassing? No one can see the two of you unless you want them to. How can you feel embarrassed? Look, just get used to it, and please get along with your assignment."

Sir Isaac's ghost didn't want to get along with his assignment. He gave even freer rein to his feelings. The Reverend reached down for his cigar. Taking it to his lips he took in a long luxuriant drag of Dominican tobacco before replacing it on the ashtray. He was now prepared to speak.

"Sir Isaac I'm getting cross with you. Please let us focus on the little task I've asked the two of you to do for me. I promise in the future I will have Sir John Herschel accompany you and not Charles... no, not Herschel too? Honestly you're just upset with him because he named seven of Saturn's moons and four of Uranus's. I'm sure that you could have seen them in your Newtonian telescope. He just named them, that's all. Come on, you did very nice work with your prism and the visible spectrum. That's right, everybody appreciated it. Yes, yes, they still appreciate it. And the Laws of Motion, too. Please Ike, let's get on with this! What do you have to report?"

The Reverend could now bring the receiver closer to his ear. He listened intently as Sir Isaac related the day's events. Not until he had finished his story and was taking an extra jab at Darwin, did the Reverend interrupt.

"So it's some kind of secret society? A cult based on absinthe and the Egyptian goddess Sekhmet? You say some of them are followers of Aleister Crowley's ghost? Reverend Poda-Pirudi laughed. "You know Isaac that absinthe is made from the herb wormwood don't you? And the ancient Egyptians used wormwood to drive out their intestinal parasites. These witches have latched on to a dewormer and coupled the teachings of that nut Crowley with it and made a cult. Ha! That's a good one! What? What was that? Oh that's too funny. I'll have to use that one. *What is life but carbon acting strangely?* Very good. Very good. Did Darwin think of that? No, no, no, just kidding, just kidding."

The commotion that was taking place outside the office of Reverend Poda-Pirudi was not normal. Over the centuries he had made every effort to teach people to keep clear of the triforium. He couldn't imagine what was going on now.

"Sorry Ike, something has come up and I've got to get off of the phone now. Do give me a buzz when you've got more to report and do keep an eye on Chuck. Yes, yes, I know I know. Bye."

A bespectacled, goateed man wearing a single-breasted black cassock strode through the Reverend's mahogany bookcase. He was followed by a group of ladies in their Sunday best.

"This is the window I've told you about. Come over here and take a look." The Dean of Westminster gestured with a welcoming flourish of his hand.

The ladies gathered around the Dean as he triumphantly pointed down.

"There, didn't I tell you that this was an exceptional view? There's the high altar and below us, the Cosmati Pavement. Of course, on the other side of the altar is Edward the Confessor's Chapel, which contains the tomb of the Abbey's sainted founder, King Edward the Confessor. Whom, I'm sure you all know, founded the Abbey, which was consecrated on the 28th of December in the year 1065. That was just a week before King Edward died. And exactly nine months to the day from this official consecration, William the Conqueror invaded England."

There was a polite murmuring among the ladies in response to these facts.

The Dean knew his audience well, and he reckoned that now was the moment for his final sales pitch.

"So you see how important it is to open this entire area up to the general public? It is vital that the West London

Women's Civic Association support our plans to turn this attic into our new museum."

That remark brought Reverend Poda-Pirudi to his feet as his desk chair tumbled backwards onto the highly polished ebony and white oak parquet floor.

"What was that?" blurted out a woman in a teal satin suit jacket.

The Dean looked a bit puzzled, but he quickly volunteered, "Well, I suspect that something in storage has just fallen over. But a building this old makes all sorts of noises." He laughed and added, "Of course there are all those old legends about the triforium being haunted."

"Haunted?" asked the woman in teal. "Do you believe in ghosts Dean?"

He chuckled, "Oh no. Though I'm sure some of our employees do. As for me, as it should be for us all, it's Hebrew 9 verse 27, *"And just as it is appointed for men to die once, and after that comes judgment." Ladies, there is no in between* death and resurrection... no ghosts. But I assure you, what the staff thinks it sees is no doubt due to the gullibility of some and their over-active imaginations. I've been about this place for several years now and I swear that the only thing scary about it is the electricity bill."

The Dean did not get the laugh with that joke that he had hoped for. The women of the West London Women's Civic Association were apparently a serious group.

"Oh, even though there are no ghosts, do tell us about them. I mean... the stories," insisted the woman in the teal jacket. "No harm in telling a story. Even though the Abbey isn't haunted, it still must have lots of good ghost stories."

"I love ghost stories," added a woman in a white silk pantsuit.

"Oh, well, in that case I'd be glad to," the Dean said, clasping his hands together, hoping that a good tale might produce good donations.

"Well, as you may know, back in the day of Oliver Cromwell, King Charles I was put on trial by the Rump Parliament. This was during our Civil War in 1649. Well, the old tale for this part of the Abbey involves a judge, a regicide judge. His name was Jonathan Bradshaw. He was the First President of the Council of State and presided over the high court of justice that tried the king and then sentenced him to death by having his head chopped off."

"Uhhh… a decapitated monarch. That's a good start," chimed in the woman in the white pantsuit.

"Yes, of course. We have nothing but top-drawer spook stories at the Abbey. You see Bradshaw was the presiding justice of this court, but he showed up three days late for the trial. Then he claimed that it didn't matter that he hadn't heard the earlier testimony."

"A true bureaucrat. A man who was apparently ahead of his time," added the woman in teal.

"Why yes, he must have been because he ignored the king's objections and pressed on with the remaining evidence. He made his judgment based on what little he had heard. He condemned the king to death for treason."

The Dean's chat about John Bradshaw was making Bradshaw's ghost somewhat uncomfortable. He stood next to Reverend Poda-Pirudi round-shouldered and hangdogged.

The Reverend gleefully took this opportunity to jeer at him and wag a finger of disapproval as the Dean continued with his story.

"Well, for his trouble Bradshaw got a lease on the deanery of the Abbey and a small office up here in the triforium. But it wasn't all beer and skittles for Mr. Bradshaw. Ten years after he had condemned King Charles to death, he himself passed away from what they think was malarial fever. Of course the roundheads had him entombed here in the Abbey as were his co-conspirators, Oliver Cromwell and another parliamentarian named Henry Ireton."

"But this is just a history lesson. Where are the ghosts you promised us?" insisted the woman in teal.

"Oh it gets better. You see when the restoration occurred, King Charles' son, Charles II, was crowned king. Of course the son wanted revenge over his dead father. But he couldn't execute Bradshaw, Cromwell, and Ireton because they were already dead. So, what he did do? He had their corpses removed from the Abbey and then taken to Tyburn in open ox carts. They were treated just like criminals who were still alive: they were hung up, still wrapped in their funeral shrouds. Once they were taken down, their heads and hands were chopped off and placed on spikes in front of Parliament as a warning to others not to defy the king.

"Legend has it that Bradshaw's ghost is still up here, where his office used to be. Perhaps that noise we just heard was a special treat?" he added with a bit of a giggle. "Supposedly he walks about this place on January 30th, the day of the execution of the king. A few claim to have heard him over the centuries, and even fewer have claimed to have seen him. In recent times, our organist and choir director were up here for some reason... let me see... rummaging around in some boxes of old sheet music. Yes, that's right. And while doing so, they claim that they saw Bradshaw. But please understand that they came up here just after the Abbey's mid-winter carnival. They'd been celebrating a bit too much with a bottle of cognac and got it into their heads to go and poke about some old containers that are stored up here in hopes of finding a copy of Handel's *"Gloria in excelsis Deo."* Did any of you notice the composer's crypt in Poet's Corner? It is just by the stairs we took to come up here."

There was silence.

"You see, a copy of *"Gloria in excelsis Deo"* had been recently found at the Royal Academy of Music and that's like finding gold to a musicologist. I'm sure you can see why our organist and choir director were ever so keen on..."

"Yes. Yes. That would be of interest to them. What about the ghost?" said the woman who had absolutely no desire to listen to the Dean discuss rare sheet music.

"Of course, the ghost story. Well, these two members of our musical staff said that what they saw was Bradshaw. They insisted that the apparition matched the portrait of him at the British Museum... long gray hair, puritan style dress... but there was one curious difference... his skin was blue."

"Blue?" several ladies responded.

"Yes blue. But again I must emphasize that they might as well have been seeing pink elephants. As I had said, they had been celebrating. Anyhow, even though they confessed to being tipsy at the time, they insisted that they saw the ghost of Bradshaw hunched over a small desk, holding a quill pen in his hand, while being taken to task by some fat dusky imp, who was leaning over him."

"Imp?" questioned the woman in the pantsuit.

"Fat!?" stammered Reverend Poda-Pirudi, permitting only John Bradshaw to hear him. "Johnny, am I fat?" he said, again making sure to screen his voice from everybody's hearing but Bradshaw's.

"No Reverend … perhaps big boned? Surely not fat. It must have been the cognac."

The Reverend nodded and turned his attention back to his uninvited guests.

It was apparent that the dean's ghost story was falling a little off the mark. It wasn't quite meeting the supernatural standards of the West London Women's Civic Association. Since properly entertaining these ladies was key to his fund drive, he began to embellish a bit.

"Yes an imp. With long tusks and a tail."

The Reverend was now very agitated and was taking deep drags on his cigar as he stared menacingly towards the Dean.

"They said he did a jig around Bradshaw as he held up the head of King Charles. Then the imp reached over and plucked off Bradshaw's head from atop his shoulders and then danced about the room."

"I mean Johnny, did you ever?" the Reverend exclaimed as he gestured in the direction of the Dean.

"You can imagine how alarmed our organist and choir director were when they came running to find me. I did indulge them and did listen to this rubbish. But believe me, I've kept a close eye on the use of distillates around here ever since. I'm sure that some would ask me why I didn't discipline them. But you must appreciate the dilemma I was in. Both men were members of the Public & Commercial Services Union. You may recall that a few years ago the PCS had threatened to picket the Archbishop of Canterbury's residence over a minor wage dispute. These gentlemen's inebriated treasure hunt had occurred about this time. And truly we mustn't judge our staff too severely. I confess that I let them off the hook too easily, but not before extolling them to heed the words from Ephesians 6:11 *"Put you on the armor of God, that you may be able to stand against the deceits of the devil."*

"Devil? Did he call me the devil?" The Reverend was puffing so furiously on his cigar that the paper band was beginning to be singed by the ember.

"Well, that's a wonderful story," said the woman in the silk pantsuit, "but did this Bradshaw fellow smoke cigars? Because this place stinks of cigar smoke."

The impertinence, to claim that an Ignatsio Gaudelupe maduro torpedo No. 2 cigar could possibly stink was beyond all the other insults that the Reverend had endured. He moved across the room and planted himself eyeball-to-eyeball with the offending woman. But of course she couldn't see him.

"You know, now that you've mentioned, it does smell a bit like cigar smoke up here. Perhaps we just surprised a member of the cleaning crew? I keep after them not to smoke on the premises. The Abbey is in complete compliance with the Smoke free England laws. All of our entrance doors have the mandatory 70-millimeter international no-smoking signs attached to them. I don't know what I'm going to do with our staff though. I've handed out brochures and offered them free attendance to a smoking cessation clinic. I've even sponsored noontime fitness walks for a smokefree Abbey."

The Dean then moved on. He had solicited all the sympathy he was going to get from this group of would-be donors. Ghost story over, he pushed on with his reason for inviting them up here in the first place. "Any questions about the proposed museum?"

"Yes," a woman said, as she raised her hand.

"Go on, please. I'm here to answer all of your questions."

"It was some walk coming up all of those steps to get up here. I can't imagine anyone who is handicapped or elderly or who has small children making their way up here. How are you going to accommodate them?"

"Excellent question. I'm so glad you asked that. It is almost as though you read my mind. I was just about to get to that bit. Near where you came up, in Poets' Corner, we have this lovely design for a circular glass elevator that will bring people up and down."

Reverend Poda-Pirudi was now facing the Dean and blowing smoke rings at him. The Dean started to cough.

"It will be," he wheezed "on the outside of the masonry so we will not have to make any major structural changes, sort of like those glass elevators that you see in the lobby of some fancy modern hotel that can take you up thirty stories, but in our case it will just be a couple."

The smoke rings intensified, and the Dean went into another coughing fit.

"It's so easy to retrofit it into the existing architecture," the Dean coughed. "The Abbey will be in full compliance (more coughing) with the Disability and Equality Act. You know I really must get security up here. This is not a smoking lounge. Just not acceptable. Ladies, I assure you that we won't have any closet smokers up here when the museum is built. In fact we will have an ultra-modern air purification system suspended from the... cough... the hammer beams. Would you please follow me to the other end of the triforium? We passed a wonderful window with a splendid view of Parliament. I'd so like you to see it," he said after another spasm of coughing.

The Dean of Westminster Abbey motioned and his troop of prospective benefactors followed him back the way they had come, through the Reverend's bookcase.

Reverend Poda-Pirudi was very distressed. He picked up his chair and again seated himself at his desk. He even extinguished the little that remained of his cigar in his malachite ashtray. He then turned toward the doorway that led to John Bradshaw's office. "Bradshaw!"

"Y-e-s, Reverend," the ghost of John Bradshaw stammered.

"Bradshaw, I want to see Edward the Confessor in my office now!"

Chapter Six

The Office in Croydon

It was curious how this fellow seemed to know that sleep had always been a preoccupation with Wallace.

"I have a theory," he had gently intoned. "Could I explain it to you?"

Butterfield didn't really want to hear the theory. After all, the man was in his office because he had applied for the job that Butterfield had posted. Wallace hadn't even had a chance to ask the guy about his secretarial skills and here he was offering up opinions. Theories weren't being solicited; just the routine organizational abilities needed to help get an anemic business back on its feet again.

"Well, sure. I have on occasion had a hard time getting some shuteye," Butterfield lied. It was only during the past couple of nights that he could ever recall getting his full eight hours. Only since Reverend Poda-Pirudi had handed him that check had he been able to have an anxiety-free evening snooze. Maybe that was because there was now a chance to save the family business.

"You see, sleep is very important to our health. You must get plenty of it to be healthy. Yet you mustn't get too much."

Butterfield nodded as he decided that this kook obviously wasn't going to get the job. He would humor him and then show him the door.

"Yes we need our sleep." It was a subject Wallace could relate to.

"We need sleep to dream. Dreams are what everything is about. Dreams have played a vital role in evolution. You see, if a species that dreams, like, let's say human beings, has wondrous dreams all the time, they would never get out of bed. Life would be fulfilled through dreaming. There would be little or no attempt to work at survival. The creature would starve to death while in bed or be gobbled up while napping. Any creature with consistently good dreams would go extinct."

"I see," said Wallace. Maybe it was this guy's retro-muttonchops that were straight out of the 1960s, but something more than this theory was out of whack here. Butterfield felt a cold shiver go down his spine as his ghost came out of hiding for the first time in days.

"But if your dreams are too bad, then you wouldn't get any sleep. No sleep, and your health falls apart. You become sluggish and slow-witted and you are either chased down or eaten or you die from an illness caused by sleep deprivation. So, you see, then your genes wouldn't be passed on."

The ghost rose up to the spot where it normally stood, just above Wallace's head, and, perplexed, looked out and immediately became spooked by what it saw. Wallace was talking to nothing— to thin air.

The man with the mutton chop whiskers stopped, stared intently at Butterfield, and then resumed.

"You need to have the right balance, you see. You need your good dreams to make you want to go to bed and some bad ones so you don't grow overly fond of being there."

"Yes, of course. One can't get too much sleep," Though he had never known the experience, Wallace hoped by blurting in he would end the man's babbling and then could see him on his way. "Mr. Berwyn have you ever been employed as an office assistant?"

Mr. Berwyn was unflappable. He ignored the question and continued with his discourse about sleep. "The best dreams are the so-so ones. Man and other animals have evolved to have mostly so-so dreams. They don't make much sense, they don't make you feel good, nor do they scare you, but they do let you get the right amount of sleep. The survival of the fittest means having boring dreams."

Of course, Wallace's ghost knew what was going on, but he had never seen a spirit that had been liberated from his host. The ghost knew that they must be all about, but also knew that no embryonic specter, like himself, or any living creature, could see them unless they wanted you to. What Wallace's ghost didn't know was why this apparition from some long-dead person was making its presence known to Wallace. Things were getting to be very unsettling around Wallace Butterfield. First there was that creepy Reverend with no spirit at all, and now a spirit had come calling on him.

Butterfield placated the applicant with another nod and more feigned interest. He knew what was bothering him about this guy, not that he was some nutter, but that he looked ill, physically ill. He struck Butterfield as the sort of person who kept inhalators, EpiPens, and nitroglycerin tablets in every drawer of his house. He imagined that he might be a terrible sick-time abuser, and no doubt Jobcentre had sent him down to do this interview just so that he could keep his jobseeker's allowance. Obviously no one expected him to be hired.

"Well, thank you very much Mr. Berwyn, I've enjoyed listening to your little theory but I have to press on right now. I have a tight schedule today. There are several more people to interview, you know. So, when I've finished, you will be hearing from me."

Mr. Berwyn smiled faintly and appeared thankful. He seemed to be pleased that the interview was over and that he would now be allowed to leave. Butterfield moved to the office door and opened it, hoping to help the fellow on his way and get him out of his hair. But as he did so, Mr. Berwyn stopped and looked at Wallace without making eye contact. Wallace assumed that Mr. Berwyn was bashful or had some self-esteem issues. So, he stuck out his hand to show his friendly intent.

Berwyn didn't notice the invite to shake hands, but stared upward, to a spot a little above Wallace's head. He then continued with his obsession upon the subject of dreams.

"You know now my dreams are quite delightful, but then again I am no longer concerned about my survival."

Mr. Berwyn then noticed Wallace's proffered hand, and clasped it weakly. "Mr. Butterfield, I so enjoyed meeting you."

As he shook Wallace's hand, a mist seemed to clear so that Wallace's ghost was able to see Mr. Berwyn for the first time. It was a shock. The ghost had never seen a disembodied spirit. There it was, a manlike creature all shimmering in blue, young, yet old. At first the specter had muttonchops, then a long beard. The face became deeply wrinkled and then it was a child's face. A baby floated in mid-air with its life's history streaming behind it, then it was a middle-aged man again, with every garment that it had ever worn passing into view within a few seconds. There was a flickering of muted shades; buff, brown, grey, and green, upon fabrics of wool, cotton, and linen. Clothes suddenly fanned out as though a magician was displaying all the cards in a deck and then folded back into place. Suits, waistcoats, dressing gowns, and nightshirts collapsed into a dusty black frock coat. Just below the brim of a threadbare top hat, Mr. Berwyn's eyes pulsated iridescent blue. These eyes locked onto those of Wallace's ghost, gripping it hard with a mesmerizing gaze. Wallace's ghost had had no way of knowing what being on the outside of Wallace could be like. The ghost wanted to know more. The ghost had oh so many questions... years of questions. But then the frock coat and top hat disappeared and a rather ordinary man in a soft yellow windbreaker was being led out the front door of Butterfield and Son Architects.

Wallace Butterfield crisply snapped a door lock into place, just in case the old tramp tried to wander back in and tell him about how he had just devised a theory about how dogs domesticated man.

Butterfield's ghost was not happy with Butterfield. He was not happy with Butterfield at all.

— «» —

Between interviews, Wallace groped for ideas, something to show to Reverend Poda-Pirudi. He needed to come up with one quickly. He liked having the money. He didn't want the Reverend to sue him for return of the funds. Ideas were needed, but ideas were just not there. His brain was a sponge. It could sop up other people's ideas. It could parrot back architectural treatises from textbooks, but making something truly good and his own was just not his specialty. But, then again, Reverend Poda-Pirudi must have realized during their conversation that he couldn't expect something that was truly good from Wallace's head. Maybe mediocre was all that was necessary?

Clutching to this hope, Butterfield booted up his computer and searched the Internet for photos of cathedrals. His idea was to cut and paste various towers and steeples onto a downloaded image of Westminster Abbey. Perhaps one of them would fall into place— But none of this proved to be inspirational. In desperation, he narrowed and elongated an image of his le Mareschal's Supermarket and the placed it atop the roof of the Abbey. Of course, it looked horrible. Butterfield knew it would. All this Photoshop exercise proved was that he was woefully inadequate for the task.

As had happened so many times during his career as an architect, Butterfield felt compelled to clasp his head in his hands and question his sanity and that of his late father's for choosing such a frustrating profession.

He stroked his temples to try to ease his tension. His face felt flush. He knew that with his fair coloring he must have been turning red. Just above him, his ghost looked down at the computer screen and sneered.

— «» —

A few streets down from the office of Butterfield and Son Architects, a white limo pulled alongside the curbing. The limousine door opened and long legs stretched down to get firm footing for a pair of black patent leather pumps with 14 cm stiletto heels. A slender yet shapely woman in a short sea-green dress with small silver polka dots began walking down the sidewalk. At first her stride was determined and purposeful. She was a woman on a mission, a woman who was not going to brook any interference. The heels of her shoes announced this as they clattered on the concrete. But when she caught a glimpse of a white gold-leaf sign that announced the place of business of her quarry, the clipped staccato sound of her footfall slowed to a gentle dolce.

Her movements became exaggeratedly feminine. Her body swayed tenderly. The small purse that she had been dangling at her side was now raised and perched by her left breast.

Her normal scent of alcohol and wormwood had been doctored. That was because Artemisia had doused her with a special perfume. It was a pheromone-based concoction containing vomodors and androstenone. Potions were Artemisia's specialty. She had made this one specifically for Maeva Wolusky's undertaking; it contained a quantity of pine pollen, some sow's urine, and a little vaginal aliphatic acid from a couple of rhesus monkeys. But the main ingredient was axillary sweat, which Artemisia had collected from the armpits of some very over-worked Bulgarian whores in an East London knocking shop. Of course, all of these malodorous scents had been masked with the sweet fragrances of vanilla bean and tonka bean infused in ambergris. Maeva was primed for the kill.

As she approached the door to the office, she could see a young man with red hair engrossed with an image on a computer terminal. She stopped for a second to examine him. Butterfield was a fidgety sort of person. He was banging the sides of his head with his hands, first with the left then with the right. He alternated this pattern back and forth as he hunched forward. This was the man that Hecuba had described; there was no doubt. She stared for a few seconds. It was amazing. What an odd-looking soul this Butterfield had and it was truly unstuck— or rather partially unstuck— more like its head had gotten caught in a door that life had slammed shut before the body could decompose.

Maeva was walking a fine line. She hadn't wanted to drink too much of her Green Man's Own. Too much and she'd be looped. Too much and no matter how powerful Artemisia's musk concoction was, she would never get the job. Maeva was traveling in the silver chair side of her psyche. She had had just enough absinthe to guarantee her mental clarity but not enough to deaden her own ghost's influence upon her frontal lobes.

Butterfield was banging out "Shave and a Haircut Two Bits" upon the sides of his cranium when Maeva pounced.

The door to Butterfield and Son's opened with a decided creak. "Porn?"

"What? Excuse me?" Wallace was taken aback.

"Just kidding, do forgive me. I can't ever pass on a joke. I'm your three o'clock appointment, Maeva Wolusky."

"No, no just dealing with some plans." He felt a need to declare his innocence. "Oh yes, Ms. Wolusky. Do come in here. Please sit down." Wallace moved a second-hand office chair forward as Maeva extended a hand.

Butterfield clasped it in politeness, still concerned that she might think he had been googling naked women.

Maeva held his hand firm. She wanted him close enough so that this whole interviewing process would be swayed by Artemisia's pheromone-based love potion. As she clutched Butterfield's hand, she looked up briefly at his ghost. She wasn't playing coy with Butterfield, but with his ghost.

This unsettled Butterfield's ghost, for it liked being the thing hovering in the periphery, liked seeing but not being seen, liked influencing Butterfield through nightmares and shivers down his spine. Maeva apparently saw the ghost and knew it for what it was. There was no shriek. No "Oh my god! What is that? What is that?" No, there was just a mischievous twinkle in her eyes.

It was the second time that day that this had happened. And it was the third time in a week that the ghost had been confronted by something it had never seen before. In the 28 years he and Wallace had been together, nothing out of the ordinary had happened. Now, all sorts of craziness... The ghost was growing very nervous.

Maeva's head was flashing on again, off again, indiscriminately, higgledy-piggledy, like a malfunctioning traffic signal. Her eyes were most peculiar too. The large blue bulging eye of her ghost would come and go, on and off. She was a freak!

"So, Maeva please be seated." Butterfield gestured to the chair, which Maeva pulled closer to him, so that her exposed knees were nearly touching his trousers. At first Wallace wished she hadn't done that. It was awfully cheeky of her, Wallace thought.

True, she was an exquisitely beautiful woman, but having perfect creamy white skin, lustrous dark hair, and deep dark brown eyes that smoldered with intense sexuality did not give her license to flirt her way into a job.

Butterfield's ghost tried to amplify Butterfield's concerns by flashing negative images into his cerebral cortex. First the ghost tried a depiction of Wallace in a wheelchair being pushed over a cliff by a scheming Maeva. Oddly, this didn't work. Wallace had a fear of falling. It was a standard ingredient in the goulash of horrors that the ghost served up every evening as nightmares. Then, the ghost presented an image of Wallace dumping buckets of cash into a bathtub that the naked Maeva was bathing in. This proved to be a miscalculation on the ghost's behalf. Wallace was pleasantly receptive to the vision of a naked Maeva: Maeva naked in the interview, Maeva naked in the shower, Maeva naked in bed. The ghost tried to counter the fantasies that it had inadvertently promoted: Maeva covered in spiders, Maeva with no hair, Maeva as a man, but it was to no avail.

Wallace took in a deep breath and sighed, "Would 15 pounds an hour be sufficient to start you out on?"

Chapter Seven

A Haunting We Shall Go

Only one of the five bedrooms of a Georgian townhouse near Belgrade Square was occupied. The Dean of Westminster enjoyed solitude. His days were always too filled with people. His duties brought him into contact with an endless procession of glad-handing politicians, overly pious parishioners, and irredeemable and recalcitrant staff. But here in his oasis of solitude, the only staff he dealt with were contractual. No need to worry about unfair dismissal claims, workplace grievances, or the interminable disciplinary hearings. At home, Upstairs Care on Wheels, Ltd. took on all his problems. The Dean only needed a cook and a cleaning lady and rented them by the hour through this admirable domestic workers service. So, his house was cleaned long before he came home, and dinner was left for him in a large well-stocked and air-purified refrigerator. There were no smoking issues here. If he ever suspected that even a whiff of burnt tobacco had made its way into his laundry room, he would be immediately on the phone with Upstairs Care: end of problem. No trade union grievances at 748 D Ipswich Mews.

It had been a particularly bad week at the Abbey. It started with the West London Women's Civic Association tour of the smoke-filled triforium and ended with an elderly woman in a walker sinking down to her hips in muck where a broken sewer main had erupted on the south lawn. The fire brigades and the ambulance service were called in on that one. It was mortifying. The old woman's family had said that she was not all together there; they had apparently turned their backs on her for just a minute when she decided to bull her way through the yellow caution tape. Tourists and reporters snapped away on their cameras, documenting every misstep, as the old girl struggled to inch her way up and out of the smelly ooze.

But it was over. Another week of tumult had passed. Tomorrow was Tuesday, his day off. And now he was home, several miles from the Abbey, and safe within his retreat; his sanctum sanctorum, his cloister, an isle of sanity removed from all those cares of having good public relations. The cleaning lady had done her duty. There was a glass and an opened bottle of cream sherry on his bed stand. His bed sheets had been starched and ironed and the Dean slipped between them like a child exhausted from play and awaiting his mother's goodnight kiss and a bedtime story. Then sleep would carry him away. On the bed stand was the bedtime story. The Dean sipped a little sherry from his glass and then opened to the first chapter of "A Lady Never Surrenders."

Well before midnight, the Dean dozed off. His half-frame reading glasses, in due course, inched down the bridge off his nose far enough to disturb his slumber. Mechanically, he removed them and placed them and his book next to the reading lamp, which he groggily switched off. Once again he was fast asleep. As he lay in his slumber, dreaming of scantily clad missionaries' daughters converting the heathen tribes of Westchester County, New York, a strange sensation began to insinuate itself into his darkened room.

At first it was only a vaporous substance suspended in the air. It thickened and began to coalesce into a faintly pulsating blue glow. The longcase clock down in the foyer began to strike twelve. As it did so, the temperature of the bedroom grew colder. The coverlet atop the bed frosted over with a thin layer of ice crystals. The glow intensified and an image flickered, a silhouette, gaining proportion and detail. As the Dean slept, static charges of electricity discharged about his room. Positive ions and free electrons spit and sparked above his head. A golden aura formed within the confines of a human shape. Then, through this cosmic fire, strode a king.

He was a great and angry spirit. He tossed his long grey hair about as he jerked his head in agitation. His face was contorted with so much pain that he could have been wearing sackcloth and a crown of thorns instead of royal raiment. Upon his head he wore a crown of golden oak leaves, with white pearls and blue sapphires, yet this crown was less regal looking than the head it adorned. The king's ermine robe heaved and expanded with each of his ghostly breaths, as the point of his broadsword twitched in the nap of the Dean of Westminster's shag carpeting. Then the gauntleted hands that gripped tight the bejeweled hilt, lifted this sword high above his head.

"O God! God! How weary, stale, flat and unprofitable, Seem to me all the uses of this world! Fie on it fie! It is an unweeded garden that grows to seed; things rank and gross in nature!"

"Ahhhhhhhhhhhhhhhhhh!!!!!" The Dean of Westminster had awoken.

"No, I'll not weep. I have full cause of weeping, but this heart shall break into a hundred thousand flaws, or ere I'll weep. O fool, I shall go mad!"

With this, the king brought his broadsword down. It sliced through the coverlet, crashing into the box springs of the bed. The sword lodged, hilt gently swaying, between the dean's knees.

If the Dean of Westminster had had any illusions that all of this was part of some phantasmagorical dream, such misapprehensions had now been dispelled.

He cried out again in absolute panic.

"Silence!" the king bellowed. "Art thou not my servant? Dost thou not attend to our Lord's flock at my sacred Abbey? Art thou not the guardian of my bones, steward of high tombs and warden of blessed sepulchers of those most worthy remains that have in their brief span made glorious the name England?"

The Dean no longer had a scream in him but sat at the far side of the bed, huddled up and hyperventilating. He could not even look in the direction of the king. He just moaned as the king watched patiently. But in due time the Dean's breaths became less labored. He gripped his arms around his knees tightly and then stole a furtive glance in the direction of his spectral visitor.

The king took this as an overture to renew their acquaintance. "Oh I have watched thee in thy daily course presiding over the affairs of thy congregation. Thou art a good man. A true man of God and I crave thy service."

"Whooo are you? Ah, what are you?" the Dean said with the little strength he had left.

"Why come hither man and know me better. For I am the king who had laid the foundation of thy Abbey."

The words took a while to find a resting place within the Dean's brain. The fact that he was a minister of the Church of England had momentarily escaped him. The fact that he was the 41st Dean of Westminster Abbey was nowhere to be found. But things began to drift back into place.

"You… you are saying that you are King Edward— Saint Edward— Saint Edward the Confessor?"

King Edward indicated his assent with a slow and gracious tilt of his head.

The Dean's mood now swiftly changed from abject despair to sublime exhilaration. He was not losing his mind or being haunted by some devilish monarch. Oh no, he had been blessed by a holy visitation. He was experiencing a miracle.

"Oh, my lord. What have I done to deserve such trust for you to come to me?" The Dean scrambled off his bed and knelt before the pulsating blue feet of the king. He raised his hands in prayer.

"Come now rise up. Greet me as a fellow Christian for we are both in the service of God and equal unto his eyes." He grabbed the Dean about his shoulder and helped lift him to his feet.

"Please tell me how I may be of assistance my Lord?"

"I need thee to help right an ancient wrong."

"How? How?"

King Edward stepped backwards, turning away. In a moment he faced back again, sweeping his ermine robe before him with a flourish, and pointed to heaven.

"Time has unfolded what plaited cunning hides. Harken, there was this priest, a false mendicant, who swore to renounce all worldly possessions, but in due course perjured that oath and robbed our Abbey of its greatest possession. There is no more faith than in a stewed prune than was in this perfidious priest. Thou hast heard of the martyred saint, Saint Cyriacus?"

"Saint C-y-riacus. Oh yes, the Roman Christian nobleman who gave away his wealth and ministered to the needs of the slaves in Diocletian's bath. As I recall, the Romans had burning pitch poured upon his head."

"Aye! Tis true. Tis true. His soul now rests in the bosom of our Lord, but not his arm. That magical arm, wrought with silver and gold, transformed into a reliquary, fashioned with such art and cunning that like the living limb it did so appear. Nuns from far off Strasburg brought this divine appendage to Westminster upon the day of the Abbey's sacred consecration and placed it upon the high altar. There it abided for over 500 years, a sacred arm clothed in precious metals uplifted toward the heavens in a benediction for all mankind. Lepers were cured by its touch, evil blood was purified, demons were driven out, and sight restored by it. But then that accursed priest, Father Benedictus, stole it!"

"Father Benedictus?"

"Aye, thou hast heard of the knave?"

"Well, there's a silly ghost story..." The Dean checked himself and began again. "Yes, I've heard tales of a ghost named Benedictus. They say he floats about the Abbey and chats up visitors."

"Truly this is the same Benedictus. The wretch must be looking for accomplices."

"Accomplices?"

"During the Reformation, one of those regrettable times when the Abbey was being sacked and looted, this dissembling cur, Benedictus, grabbed the reliquary, telling all that Saint Cyriacus had just spoken unto him and commanded that he hide the sacred arm lest it be stolen. None could stop him. He dashed forth from the Abbey with it and was never seen— that is, as a living priest— again. Benedictus was murdered that day while attempting to sell the arm to some thieves.

"He had been too coy with them and they'd resorted to torture, hoping that he would tell them where he had hidden his treasure. But Benedictus showed resolve and died silently, his greed worth more than his own life. That very greed still liveth in his spirit and still doth covet the reliquary. But alas, he needs corporeal aid to dig it up— a living accomplice. But such a fool is hard to come by, for our Lord reveals to all that are tempted a vision of their lives in hell!"

"Torments of hell? Saint Edward, my own soul is very dear to me!"

The Dean was again close to hyperventilating himself into a swoon.

"Calm thyself. The fiery pit is not for you, but to be shoulder-to-shoulder for all eternity with the angels up above. Nay, God shall be heartily pleased with thee for thy labors this eve. For I have found where Benedictus hast buried the sacred relic and we shall restore it unto his church."

"It's been buried? You've found it?"

"Aye. For over 400 years my eyes have searched from beyond my crypt, beyond where I lie within my chapel within my great Abbey. Here I have seen many doings and the doings of Benedictus have never escaped me."

"And what have you found, uhh, good king?"

"A broken sewer main! A broken sewer main has rewarded my vigil! When it cracked, Benedictus fell into a panic. His specter flew to it, fretted over it, hovered over it and would not be content till the main had been patched and the work crews had gone. Thou know what that means?"

The Dean shook his head.

"Saint Cyriacus's arm is buried near the sewer main! Have thee a spade?"

"A spade? Why, I think so. Yes, I keep one up in the shed. I have a small garden up on the roof." The dean pointed in the direction of the bedroom ceiling.

"Excellent! We will get it and be off."

"Be off?"

"Yes, as I said the corporeal is needed for this task. All that lives must die, passing through nature to eternity. I am but a thing of what has once been. I cannot wield a spade. But who better in my stead that the Dean of my own Abbey?"

The Dean of Westminster looked down to where the king's sword had cut through his mattress. And then looked back at King Edward.

"Come not between the dragon and his wrath. I am a king and a saint!" the king bellowed.

Then he tempered his tone, and politely added, "It is not becoming for me to go a-digging in pus-filled putrefaction. Mend your speech a little, lest it may mar your fortunes."

The terrified Dean nodded repeatedly.

"I see you stand like greyhounds in the slips, straining upon the start. The game's afoot: Follow your spirit; and, upon this charge go get thy spade and meet me in thy Audi. 'Tis the champagne-colored one out front?"

The Dean again nodded.

"Good. Men of few words are best. In peace there's nothing so becomes a man as modest stillness and humility; but when the blast of war blows in our ears, then imitate the action of the tiger! We are off!"

"Yes of course..."

"Why then art thou not imitating the tiger?"

"Oh... sorry... I just hadn't realized it was you who had said that."

"What? Of course. Who else?"

The Dean seemed bewildered for a moment, but then, as instructed, imitated the tiger and hurried off to his rooftop to get the garden spade.

—— «» ——

It was doubtful whether any of the residents of Ipswich Mews were awake at the hour that the Dean of Westminster entered his Audi, spade in hand. If they had, they no doubt would have wondered what his need for a digging tool was and why his task necessitated his going out in his bathrobe.

Every turn of the Audi was second-guessed. There could be no tailgating of taxicabs, though they saw only two. Rolling through a stop sign was strictly forbidden and the speed limit had to be observed. As the Dean drove to his Abbey, his blood pressure was whizzing, his heart was palpitating, his stomach was churning, and his brain was spinning. This rapidly deteriorating physical state was not helped at all by the fact that there was a 1,000-year-old dead king seated next to him. Nor, was it helped by the fact that this long-dead king insisted on telling him how to drive.

The Dean of Westminster Abbey was relieved when he finally parked his car in front of the south lawn. He grabbed his shovel and followed the floating apparition of King Edward to the fenced-off area where the sewer line had fractured and created a deep dark smelly depression.

Looking down into the five-foot deep sinkhole, the Dean hesitated. King Edward slid near him, clasping him about his shoulders as he whispered into an available ear, "Now it is the time of night that the graves, all gaping wide, every one lets forth his sprite, in the church-way paths to glide."

Grinning, he pointed into the hole.

The Dean saw no humor in the remark. He climbed down into the hole as any man would who knew his duty. He was afraid, but resolved.

— «» —

It was a long grisly night of digging, shovelful after shovelful of vile smelling grey muck and no glimmer of gold or silver from the sacred arm of Saint Cyriacus. But King Edward skipped and capered about the edge the sinkhole offering regal encouragement and advice. When the Dean had dug down well beyond the depth any thief would consider appropriate to hide his loot, the King would point to a new section of the hole. He would exclaim enthusiastically that, most assuredly, the arm was buried there. Back and forth all night, the Dean went from one spot to the next, excavating one new site after another. His dressing gown and pajamas had long since become indistinguishable from the earth he had been working in. He was giving up hope on ever finding the holy relic as the sun began to rise.

Then, the king looked down upon him and gleefully exclaimed. "But, soft! Me thinks I scent the morning air. Whether in sea or fire, in earth or air, the extravagant and erring spirit hies to his confine."

"What? You are going?" the Dean asked panting. He sank the point of his spade into the ground and used it to steady himself. "Why? Why are you leaving?"

King Edward pointed to where the morning fog was lifting near a cluster of trees. The Dean then clamored up to the rim of the sinkhole to get a better look. Two constables were walking straight towards him. In horror, he turned to the king to ask him what they should do but King Edward the Confessor had vanished.

Chapter Eight

The Performance

Bradshaw, have we heard anything from Sir Isaac and Charles yet?"

The ghost of John Bradshaw had just entered Reverend Poda-Pirudi's office, his arms loaded with the day's mail.

"Why no, Reverend. It's been some time hasn't it?"

"You know, I expressly told them to keep in touch."

As if it were haunted, the electromagnetic bell clapper in the telephone ringer box went off. It was as though the device sensed the Reverend's frustration.

Reverend Poda-Pirudi removed his telephone's receiver from the hook and placed it against his ear as he brought the rest of the phone up close to his mouth to speak.

"Reverend Poda-Pirudi speaking. Oh, Sir Isaac how strange that you should call now," he said with a smirk.

On the other end of the telephone, in a red telephone kiosk on the Walpole Road, the ghost of Sir Isaac Newton began to make up for lost time by giving Reverend Poda-Pirudi a long and exhaustive report concerning the events of the preceding day.

"Well, Sir Isaac, so things went well then?"

It was apparent that the Reverend knew that he had miscalculated by asking the question. Even before Newton's ghost started to reply, Reverend Poda-Pirudi pulled the earpiece away from his ear, as though he expected to be burned by its heat.

"Yes Ike. Yes, Ike I know. I really didn't expect Charles to be hired, but I confess I hadn't expected that polka dot lady. What's her name? Maeva. For Maeva to get the job. That was good thinking on behalf of Women in? Oh, yes thank you. Women In Therapeutic Chemical Healing. I think I've got it now. Oh yes, did Charles get the message through?"

As Reverend Poda-Pirudi braced himself for the next response, John Bradshaw slipped a copy of *The Sun* onto his desk, just under his nose.

"Excellent!" the Reverend exclaimed. "Simply excellent. No, no, not you. I mean I'm very glad that Chuck got the point across, but something has just come up and I've got to ring off. Thank you so much, and please do keep in touch."

Reverend Poda-Pirudi picked up the copy of *The Sun* and began to read the featured article on the front page. The banner headline read: "Dean of Westminster Abbey Surprised by Police While Digging for a Lost Reliquary Near Ruptured Sewer Main." Under a photograph showing an indignant Dean lecturing two constables, the caption read "Claims he had instructions to do so from the spirit of Saint Edward the Confessor."

"My, my Johnny, you certainly did a good job of timing on that one. I assume that you called in the police and the press. Waited for daylight, did you, then called everybody up?"

The Reverend had to pause a minute to chuckle. "He certainly got himself covered with mud didn't he?"

"Yes Reverend, he did. Thank you. It all came together rather well."

"Indeed it did. Well, I think our office will be safe for a little while. No museum here. Where is the Dean now?"

"Here in London, Bethlehem Royal Hospital."

"Well good job all around! Tell King Edward that I really appreciate his work."

"Oh, sorry. I'm afraid—" Bradshaw stopped himself in mid-sentence.

"You are afraid what?" quizzed the Reverend.

"Well, Saint Edward did intend on going. He really gave it a lot of thought. But then Sir Larry somehow found out about what was going on and then he saw the king—"

"Are you telling me that Laurence Olivier portrayed King Edward?"

"Yes, Reverend."

"And why did you two find it so difficult to adhere to my instructions?"

The Reverend's right eyebrow arched up along his brow ridge to form an anatomical version of an exclamation mark.

"Oh, please, Reverend, don't send me back to the Mucking Marshes Landfill!"

"I'm considering it, but do go on."

"But Reverend, it was most therapeutic for Olivier. Sir Larry said the chance to act again put him in high spirits."

"Oh he's trying to soften me up with a pun, is he?"

"And he said that it lifted his soul."

The Reverend began to guffaw as Bradshaw's ghost continued with the story.

"He was so jubilant when he came inside. He said his performance was a merry romp through King Lear, Hamlet, and Henry V. He said that he had reprised many of his favorite roles at the Old Vic. And he even enlisted a little aid from Charles Dickens for directional advice."

"Don't tell me—*A Christmas Carol*?" the Reverend asked with a groan.

"Yes, Sir Larry wanted a very dramatic entrance."

"Not the ghost appearing at the stroke of midnight at the foot of the bed? That sort of thing?"

John Bradshaw's ghost nodded.

"Well, he got the job done. That's all that matters. Actually, an audience of one was perfect for him. He does suffer from stage fright so. Anyhow, no worries, a good job all around! But say, what's this reliquary business they mentioned in *The Sun*?"

"The arm of Saint Cyriacus."

"Oh yes, the arm of Saint Cyriacus. I remember now. Where did that go off to? I recall Cyriacus's head is in a reliquary at Santa Maria in Via Lata, in Rome, right?"

"Yes, you are correct Reverend."

"It's coming back to me. His head turns blood red on his birthday. No, that isn't right— on the day of his martyrdom.

Got it now. So, Bradshaw, whatever happened to this arm? I do recollect it being on the high altar. I confess that I haven't had much time to pay attention to these things lately. But I do recall seeing it a couple of centuries ago. Wait, that was just about the time— it was your lot that pinched it, wasn't it Johnny?"

"No, Reverend, it was Copper-Nosed Harry and his crew that pinched it."

"What a bald-face liar you are Johnny. Still trying to point the finger at Henry the VIII and the Reformation for all the looting done by you and Cromwell?"

"No sir ... seriously Reverend, we'd have taken it if it had been about— but it wasn't."

Chapter Nine

Maeva

Maeva admitted she had never put together an Excel spread sheet or a PowerPoint presentation, and that she had no secretarial experience whatsoever. In fact, she had never worked a day in her life. But she did say that she would be willing to field calls from clients, keep a journal, and make travel arrangements. More importantly, she had suggested that Wallace take her out so that they might get better acquainted. Ah Maeva, he so delighted in that name. During the night he'd dreamt of her.

As Wallace recalled, his dream began with him sauntering down a street in Croydon. The sun was out, the birds were chirping, and he had a pink heart-shaped candy box covered in polka dots in his left hand and a bouquet of huge hibiscus flowers in his right. Suddenly a mariachi band, with guitarrón, vihuela, violins, guitars, and a trumpet struck up a polka and began to follow him. Then Butterfield's suit became a purple mariachi costume, with a sombrero richly embroidered in gold and white polka dots. He was just passing the Mecca Bingo Club on Tamworth Road when the sidewalk became alive with blue hands. Hundreds of them were rising up through the concrete and laying banana peels about. The chocolates and flowers zipped out of Wallace's hands, and a pair of maracas flashed into their place. The band set up a new rhythm— a samba! Butterfield took up the beat with his maracas and nimbly danced around all of the banana peels.

Then, the mariachi band's trumpeter sounded the fanfare to a bullfight. This time two gigantic blue hands emerged on either side of the street. Between them, they held a monstrously big banana peel. The hands proceeded to drop the mammoth banana peel in front of Butterfield with a ceremonial flourish. Wallace couldn't keep his balance. Slipping and sliding he went down Tamworth Road totally out of control. And then the road opened up into thin air— a void— just blue sky.

As he began to fall, he managed to reach out and to get hold on something. It was a blade of one of the three large wind turbines atop Strata SE1 apartment complex. Unfortunately for Wallace, the wind began to pick up. Soon, it was blowing a gale. Butterfield couldn't maintain his grip. He was spun off into the air again. Once more, he began to fall. A roof appeared. Butterfield went crashing through it, falling into an ice skating arena in Brixton. But he didn't go splat on the ice. No, he landed perfectly and, with a pair of ice skates, proceeded to execute a camel spin. He followed this with a Salchow, a double axel, and a back flip. The crowd of penguins went mad. With so much cheering, Butterfield took a victory lap around the rink, his arms outstretched. Then a blue Zamboni ran over him, embedding him under the ice. It might have gotten worse, but Maeva suddenly appeared above him. She had an acetylene torch and she was wearing protective dark blue welder's goggles. Soon, Maeva had him thawed out and seated on the ice. She placed a gold medal around his neck, gave him a hug, and then kissed him. All in all, it was not a bad dream. In fact, it was probably the best dream Wallace Butterfield had ever had.

— «» —

The Reverend Poda-Pirudi was again troubled by the lack of communications between himself and the outside world. So, he stuck his head into Bradshaw's little office and said. "You know it's been several days since we interviewed Butterfield. He seems to have gone to ground. You'd think he would be excited over his commission. Johnny, get Wallace on the line for me."

Obediently, the ghost of John Bradshaw picked up his telephone and dialed the office of Butterfield and Son.

"Mr. Butterfield? Yes, this is John Bradshaw. The Reverend Poda-Pirudi was wondering if you had a free minute. Oh, very good. I'll transfer you to him."

John Bradshaw's ghost then handed his phone to the Reverend.

"Ah Wally, been meaning to speak to you. Thought you needed an explanation for all that bother in the press— the stuff in the tabloids."

There was a brief response from Butterfield, which puzzled the Reverend.

"You haven't seen it? Well I'm sure that's for the best. You see, our Dean has had a hard time of it lately— you know, the preparations for the Queen's Diamond Jubilee and all. There will be a big shindig here ... sixty years as our sovereign. That means lots of ceremony. I'm afraid the stress has been a little too much for him. He has a medical issue, which, as always, the newspapers have blown way out of proportion. He just needs some rest; he's at a religious retreat regaining his old vigor as we speak. Just wanted you to know that this momentary lapse in our leadership will by no means affect upon our plans concerning the design for a central tower. By the way have you made any progress? I bet you've got the whole thing sketched out by now."

The Reverend covered the mouthpiece of his phone. Rolling his eyes, he turned to Bradshaw's ghost. "He's chattering away like a schoolgirl."

"Yes, of course you've got to get your office in order first. I do appreciate that. Oh, she does sound like she's just the woman for the job. I might add that it's wonderful what you've done on the computer so far. Perhaps in a couple of days we should touch base again. Yes, we'll do that. Oh thank you, that's very kind of you Wally. I'm sure that the Dean will be so pleased to hear that you wish him well. I'll pass that on to him. Well, be talking to you. Bye."

Reverend Poda-Pirudi shook his head as he placed the telephone down.

"I'm afraid this Maeva is going to pose a bit of a challenge to us."

"Should I get Sir Isaac?" asked Bradshaw's ghost.

"No, let's let her play her hand. She may be of some use, unwittingly of course. For now we'd best monitor the situation... wait and see which way it breaks."

Chapter Ten

The London Eye

It swam, almost slithered, down the dark channel. Occasionally the light from a street lamp would filter down through a catch basin grating, but beyond that there was no light. The vaulted brickwork overhead prevented that. The creature's alligator-like head had a pair of eyes that could poke through the murky surface. It knew that there were more storm drains downstream to the river. It had counted them. It had spent considerable time here and liked this place. To the Tiktaalik, it was almost home. It was so quiet and pleasant below the street level. This was a secret layer of London, devoid of hustle and bustle and the throngs of tourists. The shallow fresh water that formed this channel was not unlike that of the Devonian swamps it had grown up in and hunted fish in 375 million years ago. Here too, like in those swamps, there were snags in the flow of water, not from the fallen trunks of giant ferns or the roots of immense club mosses, but from chunks of wood and concrete, soft drink bottles, and candy wrappers. When confronted by these obstacles, the Tiktaalik used its spade-shaped tail and fin-like legs to push its long body through whatever blockage barred its descent to the river.

The Tiktaalik could taste a change in water chemistry as the tide pushed in from the River Thames. Up ahead was the opening, near the bronze statue of Boudicca. Here, what was once the Tyburn emptied into the River Thames and the Tiktaalik followed its course. When it reached the Thames, it used its lobed fins to struggle out of the water onto the grassy bank by the Thames Path Trail.

Tiktaaliks never could survive out of the water long. This one rested on the riverbank and gulped in air. The night sky was dark and moonless. Across the Thames on the South Bank, the long ornate Edwardian London County Hall was lit by colored lights. The spacious wings of the old steepled stone building appeared golden, while its curved columnated center went from purple to salmon in response to the ever-changing illumination. Next to the hall was the London Eye, radiantly red against the night sky. All of these colors reflected on the surface of the Thames, turning the river into a watery neon sign. This light show invited the public to cross the Westminster Bridge and join in on the fun on the other side.

Tiktaalik's pulse was slowing; its crocodilian eyes were drying in the chilly night air. It was failing. It was dying. But then, just before it expired, it faded away, transforming itself into another creature. A large lizard with feet, not fins, a Proterosuchus occupied the spot where the Tiktaalik had been.

The Proterosuchus immediately put its tail and four feet into motion. Up a stairway it moved onto the Westminster Bridge. It waddled with confident terrestrial mobility, passing through holidaymakers, businessmen, married couples, and tourists of every shape, size, and nationality.

But the Proterosuchus didn't last long. It transitioned into a bipedal Theropoda with huge carnivorous jaws. Then— poof— it was gone and there was something that looked like an ancient mouse. Poof— that was gone and replaced by a wooly mammoth, then a saber-tooth tiger, followed by a tree shrew. Animals, existing and extinct, were coming and going in rapid succession, one after another. Suddenly the focus was on the metamorphosis of great apes. One followed another, knuckle-dragging their way across the Westminster Bridge. First there was a chimpanzee, then an orangutan, then a gorilla followed by Ardipithicus ramidus, Australopithecus, *Homo habilis*, and finally by *Homo erectus*. It was *Homo erectus* that neared the end of Westminster

Bridge. Apparently, it would be the last in the chain. It held its form as it marched toward a thirteen-ton white stoneware statue of a British Lion: the South Bank Lion.

A strange-looking fellow was sitting on the top of the South Bank Lion's pedestal, just beneath the lion's jaws. He was a slender man sporting two days' worth of stubble. The long locks of his hair were matted. His clothes were of an odd old style and dirty. One of his leather shoes was buckled but the other was not. His hose sagged below his britches. His appearance could be explained by the singularity of his concentration. His sense of things going on around him often went numb when he had an idea. He had lots of ideas— astounding ideas. His ideas received his scrutiny, not the state of his appearance.

He had just had one of these ideas. It came to him in a flash while he was deep in thought. The idea was considered earth-shattering, revolutionary, beyond the reach of the greatest minds, but it had been driven from his head by the distraction of the extravagant parade of animals that had come across the Westminster Bridge.

Homo erectus sauntered up to the South Bank Lion and looked up. Its hairy face brightened with a toothy smile.

This smile was not pleasing to the scholar who was perched atop the lion's pedestal.

"Darwin! You know I will not talk to apes!"

Charles Darwin's ghost acquiesced and allowed his form to move back into his usual gentleman-of-the-nineteenth-century shape.

"Bah! Sir, this is not but mummery— a pageant of idolatrous images of antediluvian flesh— mere manifestations of the devil and contrary to the love of god! You shall repent Mr. Charles Darwin. You shall repent as it is said in the Book of Mathew, 'Just as the weeds are collected and burned up with fire, so will it be at the end of the age. The Son of Man will send his angels, and they will collect out of his kingdom all causes of sin and all evildoers, and they will throw them into the furnace of fire.' Besides, you are very, very late! Well, sir, this watch is now yours. They are heading to the Ferris wheel."

Then the ghost of Sir Isaac grinned and added, "I bid you a goodnight."

With that, he dropped an apple that he had been holding in his hand. The apple exploded into pieces on the pavement at the feet of Charles Darwin's ghost.

Floating up off the pedestal, Sir Isaac Newton's ghost landed gently upon the sidewalk. He then turned and started to walk back toward his cozy tomb in Westminster Abbey. As he did so, Newton's ghost turned briefly to see if his remarks had made any kind of impression upon Charles Darwin's ghost. What he saw was that Darwin's ghost had once again transformed himself into a chimp and was waving goodbye to him.

"You have a vegetable's soul." Newton's ghost muttered before moving on.

—— «» ——

Maeva Wolusky and Wallace Butterfield had made it through security and were being herded through a turnstile into a glass pod. Twenty-five people could fit into each pod. Attendants held the doors open and motioned with their arms as people obediently picked up their pace to fill the Ferris wheel on schedule. The ghost of Charles Darwin just made it in before the doors were secured shut. Each pod was attached to the exterior skeletal of what looked to be a humongous bicycle wheel. The pods and spokes of the wheel were lit in bright red.

People took their places around interior periphery of the pod. There was no view left unclaimed by a sightseer. Each window was filled with a line of heads, with more heads behind them, craning for a better look at the emerging vistas.

As Ferris wheels went, it was a slow ride. One lap took thirty minutes. And that's what you got for the price of admission, one lap. But that didn't bother Wallace Butterfield. The architecture of London would soon be his, displayed below him.

He was so excited, and it wasn't just the repressed kid in him; he was excited because he had by his side the most beautiful girl he had ever come within arm's length of.

As the wheel began its slow turn upward, he glanced down at her. She was smiling at him attentively, as though she didn't really mind being on a souped-up kiddy ride with a man who was wearing one of his father's old suits. He had at least forsaken the white shirt with obligatory tie for a black T-shirt that made him look dangerous. But, as always, he didn't feel dangerous around women, nor did he know where to begin. It was such a big task to get someone to like him, a task he was woefully unprepared for. What should he say and how should he say it? How could he make her feel comfortable around him? If she wanted to be around him.

They had met, as planned at Westminster Bridge. Not much was said, but "Hello," "How are you?" "We should be off." It was nervously formal, almost mechanical. After that it was pay for the ride and get on board.

However, now there was no activity beyond rising upward and staring out at the night vistas of London. It was time to really talk. He had to say something, and it had to be witty and charming, not dorky and lame.

"So, do you come here often?" It was the best he could do.

"No," she said with an embarrassed grin, which he interpreted as meaning that she normally wouldn't be caught dead in this place. But he'd hoped that he was wrong.

"Gwell," he said. Butterfield wanted to say "great" and then changed his mind in mid-word to "swell." It came out as "gwell." This made him even more anxious and he began to spew out a lot of other words after "gwell" hoping to distance himself from this mistake. So, what he said was, "Gwell. This is a great place to see the city's architecture. A Ferris wheel ride can be educational."

Maeva laughed and, with a mischievous smile, said, "Go ahead educate me."

"Well, obviously there's Parliament and Big Ben in front of us and of course our project, the Abbey right behind them."

She glanced down at the gold lights around Parliament and the green ring of light around the old clock tower. "Where exactly is the Abbey?"

"Oh," he pointed, "there. When the Abbey has a steeple it will be a lot easier to pick out."

"My, you must be so excited, having your plans presented for such an important spot in our country's history and culture!"

She sounded enthusiastic, which gave him a tad more confidence. "Oh my, I hope. I mean, I hope they accept my plans," he gushed, though he knew he didn't have any and most likely wouldn't have any soon.

The crowd in the pod pressed Maeva a little closer to Wallace. He breathed in her alluring fragrance and began to forget how nervous he was.

"Yes, there is a lot of big modern architecture that you can take in from up here."

"But it's dark," said Maeva.

"Oh but that's part of it— how a building presents itself to the public at night. In some respects, is more important than in the daytime. The silhouette of a structure or how it is illuminated often portrays more of the architect's original concept. In the daylight his genius can be lost in the jumble of shapes that surround his creation. Besides, imperfections like cracks, staining, posters, and graffiti are masked by the dark."

"So, if I follow your reasoning. That's why a date looks better in a dimly lit pub?"

"No!" he said apologetically. "I think of the night as a sea and buildings like great ships afloat on it. You know how pretty the shabbiest looking street looks when everything gets covered in fresh snow. It's like that. The night is cleansing like fresh snow. The snow and the night tie everything together making it one big design. Does that make sense?" He wasn't sure if it would. It would to his father. It was what he used to say.

Maeva nodded, and said, "Tell me about these ships of yours."

"Of course there are the venerated old ones like the Abbey and Parliament over there and you can see Saint Paul's off to the far right. Christopher Wren's masterpiece— of course he's not buried at the Abbey."

"What?" she asked, not because she was confused over what he had just said, but because Wallace's ghost was coming into focus and she could now see him sneering down at her.

"Oh, nothing... just something the Reverend said. He doesn't approve of most of the architecture about town. But I do. You see over there, past Saint Paul's is One Canada Square and 30 Saint Mary Axe, known as the Gherkin. They are two hundred and thirty-five meters and one hundred and eighty meters tall and just across from them, on this side of the river is a new building. It is only two-thirds done: the Shard. When that building is finished, it will be three hundred and ten meters tall. It will be the tallest building in Europe. Our skyline is becoming a mountain range of glass and lights. You have to look at it all together, not individually. So that's why it's so nice to see it up here, especially at night."

"I see. What's the building over there by the river with the large clock?"

"Oh that's a marvelous old Art Deco building: the Shell-Mex House. I frequently go for walks over there. It's in front of Cleopatra's Needle. That's the oldest structure in London."

Maeva's face became flat and lost expression. "The crowned Horus— Bull of victory— Loving Ra," she said under her breath, as though in a trance.

"Excuse me?" Wallace asked in bewilderment.

Maeva gave an embarrassed laugh. "Oh, for some reason I've heard that's what a bit of the hieroglyphics on the obelisk says. At least that's what I think I've heard. Isn't it strange what obscure bits and pieces of information people choose to remember?"

Wallace was intrigued. "So then, you know something about Egyptology?"

She quickly rebuffed this suggestion, "No, no hardly anything." Maeva distracted him from this line of questioning by asking, "What's that purplish lit building over there that looks like a bunch of concrete bunkers?" She gestured to their right, where several people were looking out.

"The Royal National Theatre. And that bit right there is the Olivier Theater," Wallace replied.

As Maeva stared out in the direction she had just pointed to, a shadow was forming within the crowd. First a top hat was visible. Then, the form of a man began to emerge from within the group of sightseers. A pulsating blue Victorian man was condensing out of the vapor around him.

Apparently the ghost of Charles Darwin had been momentarily distracted. Evidently, he had let his guard down when he saw the large bronze statue of Sir Laurence Olivier in front of the Olivier Theater. Olivier's statue portrayed the actor in his role as Hamlet, wearing a cape holding up a sword. Darwin's ghost chuckled to himself, for that costume was very much like the one Sir Larry's ghost had worn when he'd paid a visit to the Dean of Westminster.

No one else in the pod could have seen him unless he wanted him or her to. But Maeva's ghost was all scrambled up in her brain, and she hadn't consumed enough absinthe to prevent her from seeing him. Darwin's ghost slid further into the crowd, attempting to get as many people between him and Maeva as possible.

"Excuse me Wally," Maeva said. "I think I see somebody I know. I'll be right back."

Butterfield was so pleased that she had called him Wally and not Wallace that he didn't mind so much that she was leaving his side for a few minutes.

Maeva began to push her way through the other tourists in the pod. When she got to where she had seen Darwin's ghost she found that he was no longer there. She looked about the pod, and then glanced out the window. Darwin's ghost wasn't there either, but something else was. A paratrooper, all blue and ghostly, was tumbling out of the sky. He waved to Maeva as he passed her pod, and then crashed into the Thames.

She knew this paratrooper and also knew that her blood chemistry was getting way out of whack. Maeva Wolusky reached back under her suit jacket and pulled out a glass hip flask from where she had tucked it beneath her pink lace panties and black slacks. To the amazement of the group of people around her, she knelt down so that Wallace couldn't see her, and began to chugalug the green contents down. The people beside her muttered and pulled away. Maeva dropped the now emptied bottle onto the floor and then reached for a second smaller bottle, which she kept in her jacket pocket. Uncorking it, she dosed her earlobes and her neck with the fragrance the little bottle contained. Then Maeva turned about and worked her way back through the crowd to where Wallace had been patiently standing.

"Everything all right?" he queried, a bit puzzled by the crowd's behavior.

"Oh yes… just a case of mistaken identity. I thought I knew somebody over there, somebody from long ago— but, no. Just a close likeness, that's all."

Maeva Wolusky pressed closer to Wallace Butterfield. The ride had come to an end. The pod was on ground level. Butterfield breathed in the deep heady fragrance of pheromones and wormwood that he had come to know as Maeva's scent. She teetered, almost falling, and then grabbed his arm to steady herself.

"Shall we be off?" she asked with some enthusiasm.

The next part of their evening was Maeva's idea. Now, she would show Wallace a bit of her world.

Chapter Eleven

High Times At The Brocken Specter

It was an inconspicuous street that was kept in perpetual shade by a five-story parking garage that occupied one whole side of it. On the side that was not dedicated to the automobile, there were a few homes, but no shops. The overall appearance was of stark utility. The sort of place where you could almost hear the residents think, "Here we come to go to sleep. Here we leave to go to work." There was also a dead area among the houses, an abandoned tube station. You might think that it had once given life to the area, pumping people in and out, sending them all over London and bringing them back again. But the terminal had been an ill-conceived appendix to the Piccadilly line. It had had little use and was eventually abandoned.

The night was still young when the lady cabby let Maeva and Wallace off in front of the forgotten terminus. Maeva insisted on paying the fare. This was her treat. It struck Wallace as a bit odd that she took her change from the cabbie and offered no tip. He thought that perhaps she was cheap by nature. But the cabby didn't seem to care, which was even stranger. The street where she had instructed the driver to let them off was not well lit. They were in front of a red brick tube station with a large multi-paned half-moon window taking up the entire second floor. On the street level were two padlocked doors, above which were large exit and entrance signs. The dreary appearance of the place had Wallace wondering why on earth Maeva had taken him here.

Where was the nightclub she had been speaking of in the cab?

Apparently, she could read the confusion on his face. "Not these doors. Over here."

Maeva motioned Butterfield to a third, smaller door that had been stenciled with the words "Fire Escape." She winked at him and asked, "Are you ready?"

"For what?" he asked in bewilderment.

Maeva didn't reply but pounded on the metal door of the fire escape.

The door opened partially. A woman stuck her head out.

"Oh Maeva. Come on in." She said.

The fact that he was about to enter a fire escape leading down to an abandoned railway station was not as disturbing to Butterfield as the woman who had just let them in. She was huge, a female bouncer, no doubt, and certainly capable of handling any man he knew. Her overdeveloped steroid-induced musculature was well oiled and deeply bronzed by a tanning salon. She had muscles that he didn't know existed— at least they didn't exist on him. The few parts of her that didn't have any muscle tissue were only barely covered by the skimpy fabric of a yellow thong bikini.

"You're the first tonight. A bit early aren't you?"

"Oh we need some quiet time together before it gets rowdy. How's it going Paula?"

"Quite well, you know. I've scraped up enough money to get a flat of my own—"

She stopped mid-sentence and stared in amazement at Wallace.

"Come Wally," Maeva ordered, as she grabbed his left hand and pulled him toward the white tile-lined stairway that led to the platform below. Industrial-grade florescent lamps starkly illuminated the series of steps.

"One... two... three... four..." Butterfield started counting them beneath his breath as he worked his way down to the platform below.

Step number sixty-four was the last step in his descent. Beyond where the stairs ended was a solid white wall with a simple white wooden door. Next to the door was a black version of the Amazon they had encountered on the way in. Above the door was a blue neon sign. The Brocken Specter, it said.

"Maeva, how nice to see you this evening," the woman said, as she opened the door for them.

"Nice to see you too," Maeva responded as she tugged Butterfield through the doorway.

Cobalt, azurite, indigo, lapis lazuli, electric blue, Egyptian blue, and Mayan blue, multiple shades of blue were merging, ebbing, flowing, swirling about the walls and ceilings of the old train station. What once was a dual platform tube station had been gutted, and the circular tunnel that used to convey trains had been retrofitted with countless light-emitting diode tiles, embedded in the arched vault of the abandoned rail system. Like a shock wave, purple suddenly erupted at one end of the tunnel and was projected by the LED system down the length of the passage to where Maeva and Wallace stood.

"Wow, that's some light show. It's a giant computer screen," Wallace exclaimed, as he began to take in the physical details of the psychedelically retrofitted tube station.

At the far end, where the trains used to come in, was a bar encased in mirrored glass and rising up over two stories. Hundreds of liquor bottles were displayed on glass shelves behind the bar. There was nothing in the center area where the tracks had been. The railroad platforms had been converted into a series of private booths.

"Why is there nothing in the middle?"

"It's a mosh pit," Maeva said, laughing. She was clearly enjoying Wallace's astonishment. "Don't worry, it will soon fill up. This place gets quite wild. I wanted you to see before they started the show. Besides, it gets so loud we won't be able to talk to one another. Let's grab a table."

They moved over to the nearest booth and sat down. A waitress appeared immediately and waited as Maeva took off her black blazer, revealing a cream-colored top with a rounded neckline. There was a large silver circle in the middle. The circle caught Wallace's attention.

"You wore a polka dot dress to my office. Is that just one polka dot?" He laughed.

"Yes. How sweet of you to remember. It's my shtick. I love polka dots. I'm Polish you know?"

"Yes, so I've gathered. Should I order you a drink with Polish vodka?"

"No, no. I don't touch the stuff. But let me order for the both of us. This place has quite an interesting collection of booze. Are you game for something different?"

He nodded.

"Good," she said as she turned to the waitress. "A fountain and a bottle of Green Man's Own."

"What an appropriate name. What is it?"

"Absinthe. I have a passion for it." She said as she winked at him suggestively.

"Well, I've never had it. Isn't it hallucinogenic?"

"Maybe, if you drink a lot of it." Maeva leaned forward across the table, as Wallace subconsciously began to breathe in as much of her aroma as he could take in. "You do want to try some don't you Wally?"

"Why yes, of course."

The waitress returned with the bottle and the fountain and curiously with more glasses than were needed. Maeva nodded to her appreciatively, then picked up an absinthe spoon and placed sugar cubes on it. She mixed their drinks and handed Butterfield his. "Now Wally, I must hear all about you. Now that I'm part of your firm."

"Not much to tell. From Croydon. Father was an architect. I'm an architect. End of story."

"Oh there has to be much more to Wallace Butterfield than that." She glanced up just over his head. Due to her intake of wormwood, Wallace's ghost was just visible but she could see that he was still sneering at her. Maeva had been a bother to him all evening and he was desperately trying ways to make Wallace aware of his presence but it was proving to be hopeless. Every time he sent a chill of foreboding down Butterfield's spine, a rush of pleasure welling up from his groin counteracted it.

"Not much," he added. "My father passed on last year. Heart attack. I took over the business."

"What about your mother?"

Butterfield was amused by the question. "She ran off when I was a babe with a data engineer for a bank. Went off to Australia, I've been told. Guess I might have some boomerang-throwing half-brothers and sisters. Don't know."

"How about hobbies— bred fancy tail guppies? Kept ferrets?"

"No. I had a terrier, Mutsy. I also had a train set that I was keen on. Still have it, but it's packed away. My dad was into radiotelegraphy. He had a citizen's band radio— you know with a telegraph key. We'd spend hours typing out messages to people all over the world. But I want to know about you," he said, breathing in deeply.

Maeva mixed him a second glass of absinthe. As she handed it to him, she said, "Well, my family had a textile factory in Hertfordshire. They sold it a few years back. I've been out of school awhile and living in London. But you've read my résumé, haven't you?"

Wallace emphatically nodded that he most certainly had. "But what sorts of things were made in your factory? Don't tell me polka dot prints?"

"No. Ladies clothes and, during World War II, just military stuff."

"Uniforms and blankets, that sort of thing?"

"Parachutes."

The LED light show went totally black. Then, like glowworms on the roof of a cave, bottle green maggot-like images appeared in the darkness and slithered down and around throughout the system. Pictures began to flash up on the curved sides of the former rail tunnel. Prehistoric cave paintings were now the theme. Bison, lions, antelopes, horses, and scores of human handprints etched in ochre and charcoal.

"Parachutes?" Butterfield asked firmly, attempting to put the visual distraction out of his mind.

"Parachutes are how we Woluskys made our money. Big demand for them during the war."

A rock group of five blonde women in red patent leather cat suits began to tinker with their mics and amplifiers in front of the bar.

"So did your family come over from Poland and set up a factory here?" He was raising his voice now, so he could be heard.

"No. Not quite." Maeva was almost shouting. "It was on my father's mother's side, the Ridleys. My grandma Ridley joined the Women's Auxiliary Air Force during the war, and, since the family was into parachute-making, they determined that she could best serve by packing parachutes at Spitalgate. It was an RAF training facility. My grandpa Wolusky was in the First Polish Independent Parachute Brigade. She met him there."

Maeva poured Butterfield a third glass and slid it next to the one she had just poured. She was forming a tabletop conveyor belt of drinks, which she hoped Butterfield would keep hoisting to his mouth.

People were beginning to crowd the nightclub but Butterfield ignored them and the fact that they were all women. He was trying to have a conversation. The fact that these women were in outlandish attire and had more makeup on than circus clowns was not registering with him.

"So your grandfather was a war hero. Nothing like that with us. We were clerks and cooks and technicians, that sort of thing. But your family history sounds like great stuff for a romance. War hero meets WAAF who packs his parachute. They fall in love. They marry and raise a family."

Butterfield's speech was beginning to become very deliberate. He was trying to keep control of what he was saying, but the absinthe was taking hold of him.

"Well, it was that way for a little while. My father was born shortly after they got married. But then things got nasty when grandma discovered, from one of his army buddies, that grandpa had another wife in Lublin," Maeva said as she finished her third drink and poured the two of them their fourths.

The band had completed its tuning and now was blasting death metal to a mosh pit full of screaming, undulating ladies.

Butterfield had to yell. "That's too bad. Did she divorce him? Take him to court?"

"No, he died shortly after that."

"Oh. In combat?"

"No, during a training jump. His shoot didn't open."

"Oh… too bad. I mean too bad for everyone." Butterfield muttered as his head came to rest on the table.

Maeva moved to his side of the booth and handed him another glass of absinthe. She made sure that he drank it down before speaking into his ear. "Wally, I hope you don't mind me asking but were you ever very sick as a child?"

"No, I don't mind." He slurred. "Odd question. No, not sick."

"No close calls with death?"

"Noooo." He raised his head up off the table and stared into her eyes. "Maeva— what a pretty name. Irish?"

"Why yes Wally. It's Gaelic."

"Does it mean beautiful princess?"

"No Wally. It means intoxicating."

"Yes, yes, of course." Butterfield murmured as his head collapsed back onto the table.

The walls of the nightclub now appeared fiery red as images of ancient mother goddesses flashed into view. First came crude looking bits of clay that had been molded to show off the oversized buttocks and breasts of some prehistoric woman. Then, the naked and winged Ishtar of Assyria was displayed. Next, came a bare-chested woman from ancient Crete, holding up two snakes. Then, a fifteen-breasted Artemis was revealed. The last image wasn't of a mother goddess, but it was female. It was part woman and part lioness. It was Sekhmet,

"Mistress of Dread."

"Lady of Slaughter."

"Lady of the Flame."

The crowd in the mosh pit went wild.

A tall woman with large three-dimensional linen gorgon heads sewn onto her shoulders, chest, and back, making her look like she was covered with tormented spirits, looked down upon the now unconscious Butterfield. Next to her was a short pudgy woman in a Raven costume.

"Well?" demanded the taller of the two women. This was followed by a less imperious sounding, "Well?" from the shorter woman.

Maeva looked up at Hecuba and Artemisia. "I don't know. I've got too much Green Man's Own in me to still see it. Has his ghost gone away? Is it back in him? Or has it disappeared?"

"Neither," Hecuba said tartly. "It appears to be as out of it as Butterfield is. His ghost's head has crashed on the table just above his. So, did you find anything out?"

"No, not really. Beyond that he's awfully cute... Wally that is. You know, I know it doesn't matter much but I don't think I could bear it if my ghost were that bad looking."

Hecuba and Artemisia knowingly rolled their eyes at each other.

The drink had made Maeva too uninhibited around her sister WITCHes. She hastened to return to the relevant topic.

"But he never had a near-death experience. So, that rules out him almost dying and his ghost somehow being trapped in him on his way out."

"Maeva, this isn't a date. Obviously, there is no point in having you continue looking into this matter. We'll be taking him now. And I assure you that we will find out what's going on here one way or the other."

She gave Maeva a menacing stare as she reached for Butterfield's shoulders.

"No you won't!" Maeva slammed both of her palms into the table as she raised herself up. She quickly reached over and snatched Hecuba's hands off of Wallace. "I'm the president! It's my call. Leave him alone!"

Hecuba reluctantly backed away. "Okay you're the president. That is until our next election. Which I assure you will be soon."

— «» —

Sometime during the middle of the night Wallace woke up to discover that he was in his bedsit and that Maeva had taken the liberty to crawl into bed beside him. He couldn't remember how any of this had happened. But there she was. He examined her naked body through a drunken haze and then nodded off to sleep again. However, in the early morning, chance would have it that both of them opened their eyes simultaneously. What happened next, during those few minutes, when Maeva and Wallace were conscious together, disgusted Butterfield's ghost. It confirmed his belief that humans were nothing more than sacks. Certainly they were sacks for ghosts, but their culture was about sacks too. Everything important had to go into a sack— food, liquor, sperm, and dog's droppings, even their children raced about in burlap versions during their family reunions. He had developed this theory that humans measured the significance of their lives by the number of sacks they had filled. Once again he had witnessed another sack filling, and though this variety might provide for some more ghosts, the whole thing was just so tedious that it appalled him. He figured that the only reason humans died when their ghosts left them was because they were no longer useful as sacks.

Chapter Twelve

Coffee Possession

It took Butterfield hours to wake up. When he did so, it took another full hour to get out of bed. He felt so weak and frail. His ghost felt the same way. Butterfield's condition was far worse, for he was nauseous. Ghosts never suffered from that. So, Butterfield's ghost looked on disapprovingly as Wallace Butterfield hurled into the toilet. Everything that Wallace had taken such care to place into his food sack the night before was now being thrown out and flushed away. Butterfield's ghost had learned this lesson about human hosts a long time ago. They were never satisfied with what they had.

At some point, late in the morning, Wallace Butterfield began to piece together his evening. It occurred to him, despite his hangover, that he had had quite a wonderful time. He searched his room hoping to find a note, an article of clothing; perhaps an earring had been inadvertently left behind. But he found nothing. No note. No token. There wasn't a trace of the woman he had become so attached to. Then he grabbed his pillow from his bed, placed it to his nose and breathed in deeply. It was true! His nose confirmed it! Maeva had been here!

This post-inebriate realization did wonders for him. His vital signs improved. The sticky sweat that clung to his skin and had saturated his bed sheets and underclothes started to evaporate. His skin temperature decreased. He developed goose bumps and felt refreshingly chilled. His stomach then reported in and grumbled for another chance at food. Soon,

Butterfield could move his head from side to side without causing himself any injury. His brain was once again comfortable sloshing about in his brainpan. His legs were a little unsteady, but they were fit enough for service. It was time for Wallace Butterfield to rejoin the living.

Though the heel of one sock was twisted and his shirt buttons were fastened in the wrong order, he managed to get his clothes on and approach the narrow stairway that led down to his office. One step at a time, he lowered himself down, making sure that both his hands were pressing firmly on the walls on either side of him. As he stood on the ground floor, his bloodshot eyes swept about his office, just in case there might be something there. Maybe she left a note in his office? He was right. There it was taped to his computer screen. Butterfield lovingly coaxed the taped note from his computer, then read it.

"What a wonderful evening. Went home to freshen up. Can't wait to get started on Monday morning. Loved the Ferris wheel. Let's have coffee. I noticed a place just a few streets down the road from the office. Though I don't get about Croydon, I've been there before. The place with all the paintings. Excellent green-eyed coffee. Be there elevenish.

Love you Wally,

Maeva"

"*Be there elevenish*." How charming he thought. So cute that she was giving him orders. It didn't matter, after all, she was coming back, she liked the London Eye, and she said love. Maybe she just used the word casually, but to him it was so nice to read it in association with his name. What a wonder, he was starting a romance with Maeva and had a commission from Westminster Abbey. His life had become too good to be true. And though he could feel a faint ghoulish chill running up and down his spine, he chose to ignore it.

Wallace Butterfield was becoming a success story! He threw open the door to the street and stepped outside and onto the sidewalk as though he owned it, as though he were a conqueror: Wallace Butterfield the Hernando Cortez of Croydon. Outside of his office, Butterfield normally felt like a snail without his shell, but not today. And though the sun beat down upon his fragile pale skin, as colorless as a cave dwelling salamander, he refused to shrink from the sunlight. Instead, he breathed in several lungs full of crisp Croydon air, which had just been rated 88 on the London Air Quality Index, and set off to find the coffee shop.

— «» —

Even though it wasn't usual to have a meeting of WITCH during the morning hours, Hecuba had summoned most of the membership to the old Tipsy Dolls Restaurant for an emergency session.

"How can you be sure that she's betrayed us?" demanded Zoraida indignantly.

"Because I followed them back to his office and saw the lights go on then off in his upstairs flat. She was there all night. I saw her come out around seven this morning."

"So what on earth does that prove?"

"That she's been sleeping with this guy." Hecuba continued with her argument, though she knew it was a weak one.

"Well, sleeping with a man is commonly done. I've been known to do it myself. It might not always be the wisest thing to do but the only thing that might be betrayed is your own personal standards."

"Zoraida, you weren't there last night at the Brocken Specter to see how lovey-dovey the two were."

"No, I don't go to that infantile nightclub for immature Witches. Again, it's a matter of standards. Hecuba, you must have hated your time in the Navy with all those men about you. Again, having a relationship with a man is not an abomination. You certainly have no qualms about Crowley now do you? I've seen you groveling before him. Yes master this and yes master that. Some adherent to feminism you are. You act like his pet hamster."

Hecuba's voice became shrill, "No wonder Miss Fancy Britches put you in charge of the youngsters, you're as much of a snob as she is. You should be educating the kiddies about the works of Crowley. If you knew anything you'd know that he was a champion of women."

Zoraida began to laugh, "This is far too silly. If you have any complaints as to our president's conduct feel free to bring them up at the next general meeting. I would ask all of you; especially you silver-chair gals to come join me for a drink at the bar. And Hecuba, let me treat you to a bottle of something that is 175 proof. You certainly could use it."

Hecuba had a sly grin on her face as Zoraida walked over to the bar.

"Where are our supplies?" Zoraida said as she turned to confront Hecuba.

"Why, in the dumpster out back. It's about time that you realized that there has been a revolution going on around here. The absinthe has been removed and no one is leaving. In a few hours there will be a lot more silver-chair women than green-chair. Then we will take a vote on who our president is. Don't look so alarmed Zoraida. It will be a legal vote held in accordance with our organization's bylaws. There will be a new order around here. Out with absinthe! Out with the green chairs! I think all of us are sick of spending our miserably short lives with our brains jumbled up with ghosts. They will have all eternity without us once we are dead. We need our mental freedom now to enjoy what little time we have left without being annoyed by ghosts or avoiding them by being perpetually drunk. If that means sucking up to Crowley for help, then I'm for it."

She then turned to Artemisia, who had been standing nearby.

"Assemble a team and get all of this green chair rubbish out of here."

"Of course Hecuba," Artemisia said with deferential enthusiasm.

"Oh, Artemisia, that includes our schoolmarm. Take her upstairs, chain her to one of her pupil's desks... and give her a copy of Crowley's Liber AL vel Legis to read. Maybe it will bring her to her senses... if not, the withdrawal from the booze will."

"Of course Madame President... almost-nearly," she laughed at her own joke as she and two silver-chair ladies began manhandling Zoraida up the steps to her classroom.

—— «» ——

There was only one coffee shop close by and, though he had only known Maeva a short while, he was pretty sure that it was the one she meant. It was unusual and everything about her seemed to be immersed in the unconventional. That would suit her. He was having a hard time remembering the name of the place: Coffee Passion? ...Coffee Compulsion? ...Coffee Preoccupation? ...Coffee Obsession? ...No. Coffee Possession! He'd been in it once— didn't care much for the atmosphere. An artsy place with the walls covered with the works of some artist. Again he tried to pull up the name. "ZDZISLAW BEKSINSKI!" the name echoed through Butterfield's head. It hurt. He chalked his pain up to his hangover but still he felt proud of himself remembering a foreign name like that, especially since it had been many years since he had last stepped foot into Coffee Possession.

It was Butterfield's ghost who remembered the name, and couldn't believe that the idiot he was forced to travel with had forgotten it. Butterfield's ghost had long wanted to return to the coffee shop so he could once again gaze at the beautiful pictures. They were so inspiring – so uplifting. But of course his host didn't care for them and was only motivated to return to the place by the temptation of having another go in the sack with Maeva. It was disgusting.

As Wallace walked he found that his balance was improving. He felt stronger and steadier. Soon he was briskly on his way, passing the Six Way Poultry Bar, the Grateful Boar, and McMillan's Garden Pools and Aquariums. His stomach had stopped punishing him. The queasiness that he had felt earlier had all but gone. His confidence began to match the vigor of his stride. Maeva was just down the street. Coffee Possession was up ahead.

Though it was true that he hated the interior of the place, he rather admired the exterior. The building was classic Victoriana. It had a recessed doorway, with off-white pilasters that had been repainted so many times that they truly gave a sense of antiquity to a relatively recent knockoff of an ancient Greek temple. Decorative corbels, like ones from ancient Athens, supported an ornately carved cornice running along the eaves. It was a shrine to commerce.

The place originally must have sold fine lady's shoes, or pretty parasols and hats— something like that— probably had withstood around a hundred and fifty years of retail commerce— from high fashion to comestibles. Perhaps it was once a bakery or a butcher shop, then was transformed into a bicycle repair shop— probably sold hookahs as a head shop in the 1960s. Now, only the façade of the building was dedicated to beauty, and that was just incidental. In today's world it was only the location of the building that had any real value.

As was frequently the case, Butterfield's ghost always found himself disagreeing with Butterfield. Wallace had no idea about what true beauty was. Stepping into Coffee Possession was like stepping into a nightmare. What could be more beautiful than a bad dream?

Coffee Possession featured no other artist's works but Beksinski's. You could hardly see the old pressed tin walls due to the pervasive presence of his ghoulish paintings. Butterfield's ghost was convinced that the café owner had a great appreciation for the finer things in life... which would be anything that was grotesque. The ghost rejoiced in the dark lurid skeletonized humans that occupied the canvases. He admired the crablike creatures that were depicted crawling amongst the painted ruins. He adored the rotting faces. The artist's world was a world populated solely with hellish escapees from a morgue. So enchanting. So uplifting. But it was his depiction of architecture that the ghost liked the most. It crumbled burned and exploded. What a delight!

As Butterfield opened the door to Coffee Possession, an old fashioned bell above the door tinkled. His ghost remembered that sound. It was like he was coming home. He eagerly looked about from wall to wall, trying to take it all in for tonight's dream.

Maeva had seated herself in a far corner with her back to the wall. This provided a clear view of the shop entrance. She was relieved that she couldn't see his ghost resting his chin above Wallace's head. This assured her that her late morning libation of absinthe was the proper dosage. But then she thought she might have drunk too much. Maybe he would smell the alcohol and think her to be a morning boozer. Maeva reached down into her white leather clutch bag and placed her hand on the bottle of love potion that Artemisia had provided her with the day before. She was tempted to put some more on to mask her scent, but too much might make Butterfield go out of control. She really couldn't imagine him ever getting out of control, but this wasn't the place to have him dancing on the tabletops.

"Wally. Over here," she called out, as a mime walked up to a neighboring table, blocking her view of Butterfield.

He had heard her voice, stopped to look about, then spotted Maeva as the mime went off to fill an order. Mime waitresses were something new, another aspect of this place that made him feel very uncomfortable. But there was Maeva, and she was beckoning to him to come over.

"Lovely Maeva," he thought, "What a contrast to everything in Coffee Possession. So cute in her pink polka dotted dress."

He hurried over to be with her.

"Wally," she said as she held out a white-gloved hand for him to kiss. Which he obediently kissed before he seated himself.

This was just the reaction she had been hoping for, no hesitation, no questioning her as to why on earth would any woman be wearing opera gloves to a java shop and who kisses a woman's hand today? He just showed passive devotion. Maeva now knew that she had applied the correct amount of love potion.

He was about to tell her how lovely she looked when a mime showed up at their table. All the waitresses were dressed like Marcel Marceau, with white pancake makeup on their faces and their eyes and eyebrows painted black. It gave them a cadaverous look like bloodless corpses in sailor suits.

A wooden menu board was propped up on the table by the waitress-mime.

Maeva politely and exaggeratedly nodded to the mime, then she pointed to a line on the menu that said green-eyed coffee.

The mime held up her a hand as which to say, "Anything else?"

Maeva shook her head.

Now, it was apparently Wallace's turn. The menu was turned to face him.

"Tetley tea with cream and sugar," he said.

The mime pantomimed horror. Shaking her head, she waived her hands about while making a shish sign across her mouth with her right index finger.

"Sweetie, you point and never speak to the mimes. It's part of the ambiance of the place."

Butterfield felt momentarily annoyed, but Maeva had called him sweetie, so he decided to go along with it. By pointing to where it said orange pekoe. But this wasn't good enough for the mime, she drew a finger along the board where it said orange pekoe, Gorreanna, orange pekoe Ceylon, Chester broken orange pekoe.

He pointed to one of the offerings thinking he was done but the mime continued on with her silent interrogation. She traced out the sweeteners; brown sugar, stevia, New Zealand honey, and turbinado sugar, followed by the types of creams; Ayrshire, Guernsey, Jersey, and goat.

Butterfield perfunctorily placed a finger on two of the choices and was relieved when the waitress brought two fingers up to the edge of her lips, made a smiley face and then went off to the barista station.

"I know," Maeva giggled. "This isn't your cup of tea."

Butterfield chuckled. "You should save puns like that for the Reverend."

"Oh I would like to meet him. He sounds like an interesting man."

"Yes, interesting. He's interesting." Butterfield wanted to say so much more but it had nothing to do with Reverend Poda-Pirudi. He started to tell her about how much he cared for her. "You know about last night ... I'm mean I feel..."

Maeva wasn't listening. She seemed to be distracted. Her attention had become fixed on a painting that hung on the wall behind where Wallace sat. She hadn't noticed it before, but it now seemed to be pertinent to their conversation. It was of a cathedral. Not dissimilar in shape to that of the Abbey. But instead of being made of masonry it appeared to be organic and growing, more like interconnective bone tissue than block. It glowed too, a rust-like color. The composition of the painting directed the eye towards the central feature, a large rose window, which did not look like it had been made to let in the light of God. It was more like a lair for a giant spider. Maeva's face went blank.

She lowered her gaze a bit and saw that she had been ignoring Wally and that he looked concerned.

"Oh sorry. Sometimes I get caught up in the paintings." Then she added in a more serious tone, "I've been meaning to ask you. How are you coming with the project? Any new ideas today?"

"No not today." Then he drew in his breath and whispered, "All I've been thinking of is you."

Maeva was touched and was going to return the compliment but Butterfield wouldn't allow for that. Embarrassed he moved on, "I think I might have been assigned an impossible task. Though the Reverend seems to be confident in his hiring of me, I'm not so sure I can come up with any ideas that will make him happy. Mucking about with such an historic structure… I'm not sure it can be done. Take a genius to plop a tower in the middle of the Abbey without ruining it. I thought perhaps plopping it to one side. There's a grassy courtyard in the middle of the cloister. Maybe there?"

"You see, you are a genius. The Reverend has chosen well."

"No, he hasn't. But he said that he was just looking for ideas. So it's not like I'm going to be in charge of bringing in a wrecking ball or anything like that. I just can't think of anything that would look appropriate."

Their waitress returned with their order. Placed it on the table as Maeva made a motion for a check.

Butterfield looked hurt. "I'm sorry," Maeva said quickly, "I can't stay too long. I've got to take one of my Girl Guides on an outing today. She's having problems at home and I thought it might do her some good to get out."

"I didn't know that you were a troop leader."

"Wally, there is lots you don't know about me. But perhaps we will learn a lot more about one another. I'd like very much to help you with this project. Is there anything I might do?"

"No. I can't imagine what you could do. It's up to my brain I guess."

"Well, I've been thinking," Maeva said, using that serious voice that Butterfield had just heard for the first time. "It might be helpful if I come to work a little prepared on Monday. Would you mind if I take my Girl Guide to the Abbey? I'm sure it would be a good experience for her and might help me to understand what we are up against."

She paused for a second then added, "Might even bump into that Reverend of yours. I'd like to meet him."

"Oh. Yes… of course. If you can think of a solution to my dilemma, I'll put Wolusky before Butterfield on the family sign."

She laughed. "That would be lovely— Wolusky Butterfield and Son."

"I'd like it too."

"I'm surprised you've been to this place," he said, trying to steer the conversation away from his problems at work and back to just her. "Do you come to Croydon often? You must know your way around to know about this place."

"No, I don't often come to Croydon— just occasionally. I have a friend— Zoraida— she's the owner. Strange, I thought I might have had the opportunity of introducing you to her. She is normally about. Not today… I guess. Well, since she's not here, I'll let you in on my little secret. I can't stand the mimes either. I only come here because she's my friend. Guess you can tell that she's a bit of a collector. She's a painter too— paints garbage. Unfortunately, she's too embarrassed to show her own work on her coffee shop walls."

"Well, if you think her work is garbage, maybe she's doing the right thing?"

"Oh… sorry," Maeva exclaimed, realizing that she had just led Wallace astray. "She paints garbage. Real garbage.

She once told me that it was about starting with the basics and working your way up from there."

"So, this Beksinski guy is her idea of fine art?"

"You don't approve do you?"

Butterfield would be willing to agree to anything if it made Maeva like him a little bit more. "I'm an architect not an artist." Then he added, "But I'd love it if you became my guide to appreciating art."

Maeva smiled, realizing that this was the best that Wallace could do when it came to being flirtatious. He was so charmingly pathetic. Though she found this quality to be exciting in a man, she had no time to encourage it today. Today she must go into this reverend's lair and find out why on earth he had hired Wallace Butterfield as his architect.

"I'm no connoisseur of these thing," Maeva said, politely pushing off Wallace's invitation to become his personal art guru. "I just have a soft spot for Beksinski. A fellow Pole you know?"

"No I didn't know that. Actually, I came here once before. I'm embarrassed to say this— his pictures gave me nightmares."

"They'd give anyone nightmares. Still, there's something that draws people to them. Beksinski was a fascinating fellow you know? No formal training in art. He was a sweet shy man with a great sense of humor and yet he painted these magnificent gothic horrors. Even stranger was that he died like he was a subject of one of his paintings. He was found murdered in his flat a few years back. Stabbed to death. Seventeen wounds."

"Seventeen stab wounds," Butterfield said, in wonderment that she would remember the exact number of stab wounds.

"Seventeen stab wounds!" thought Butterfield's ghost. "Murdered in his flat. How delicious!"

It had occurred to his ghost long ago that Butterfield might take too long in dying. He might end up in an old folks home and die on a respirator. He remembered Butterfield reading an article about an old woman who lived to be a 110. That was unconscionable! Her poor ghost must have felt like she was in a seedpod that refused to burst. If Butterfield's ghost could have figured out a way of killing Butterfield, he would have done so long ago. Butterfield was just too damned resilient. All the ghost's nightmares only made him lose sleep. He'd never be driven to suicide over having bad dreams.

The waitress placed the tab on the table and again drew a happy smile across her face.

Butterfield was tempted to draw a sad frown on his face and not leave her a tip. But he could never be that rude. In fact, he left a big tip. He didn't want Maeva to think he hadn't enjoyed himself.

Maeva thanked him for picking up the check in the appreciative style that women, who are used to having men pick up the check, feign. She then added, "Working with you will be so much fun. Can't wait till we start sharing the office together. I'll see you there. Now it's off to get myself educated about that Abbey. Thanks again for the coffee."

She gave him a peck on the cheek, walked to the door, turned, waved, and was gone.

His heart sank as she went out the door. It took him a little while to pull himself together. But he finally consoled himself with the fact that he would soon be seeing her almost every day back at the office. It occurred to him that back at the office was where he should be. If he was going to win the heart of Maeva Wolusky, he was going to have to make something of himself. The Reverend had given him an excellent opportunity to do so and he'd best get back and start applying himself.

Butterfield had exited Coffee Possession and was just passing McMillan's Garden Pools and Aquariums when it happened. A middle-aged woman in jogging attire came running up behind him. She was quite a sight, her elbows and hips moving wildly from left to right as though her intention was to walk, not run, as fast as she could. Nearing Butterfield, she slackened her step and moved up to his side. This made Wallace feel a bit uncomfortable but his good manners compelled him to nod and smile politely at her. She did the same. It all seemed friendly enough, but it became disconcerting when she didn't move on. Then, another woman, a short dumpy woman who didn't look very athletic, moved up right next to her. She was also dressed in jogging attire and walking briskly beside him like the first woman. She also gave him a friendly smile, as did a third woman who came up and kept pace alongside her. Butterfield thought this was a bit alarming but then decided that he must have absent-mindedly blundered into some sort of ladies walking competition. It was odd that he couldn't recall any kind of race or charitable walkathon that had been announced for the neighborhood this weekend, but he never paid much attention to that sort of thing. It became apparent to Butterfield that it would be best to move to his left and give the women a little more sidewalk room. But when he tried to do so he discovered that on his left there were three more ladies in jogging outfits. They were all grinning at him.

This was getting to be a bit much, so he attempted to extricate himself by announcing, "Oh, I'm terribly sorry. I had no idea; let me get out of your way."

As he said this, he attempted to come to a full stop, then move onto the street and let them pass. But the thing was they wouldn't let him stop or move in any direction but forward. Completely engulfed by a crowd of fast-walking women, he was now being rudely pushed from behind.

"I mean really! What do you think you're doing?" He protested, as he was rushed along.

"You'd best let me out or—"

As he said this, the women in front of him suddenly peeled off to the sides, leaving a narrow gap in front of him. He could see that ahead of him, where the sidewalk ended for an intersection, was a parked cab with the rear passenger door being held open by the same cabby that had chauffeured Maeva and him around London the night before.

"Help!" he screamed as he was pushed into the back of the cab. Several of the joggers followed him in and piled on top of him as he started to struggle. Someone slammed the door.

Wallace Butterfield attempted to struggle. He really did. Especially when multiple sets of handcuffs were pulled from numerous fanny packs. To his credit, it took several minutes of thrashing around with loose cuffs flailing about before someone succeeded in getting both the left and the right cuff to click firmly around Butterfield's wrists. Once that was accomplished, it was easy for the other women to fasten whatever free cuff they had to an appropriate wrist. The whole operation had been performed with almost military precision. Hecuba's career in the Royal Navy never had given her the chance to show off her natural skills, but this had gone down like a commando raid.

Poor Butterfield. His hands were now held behind his back with five pairs of handcuffs. He was secured from his wrists to his elbows. But still, he didn't give up. He screamed as loud as he could as the taxicab raced through London traffic. However, Hecuba was prepared for such an eventuality. Off came her jogging shorts and her military-issue flame retardant antimicrobial booty shorts. With the aid of her confederates, she managed to pry open Butterfield's mouth and stuff her booty shorts into it. Artemisia had been designated for the next task. Producing several rolls of silver-sided duct tape that had been previously purchased by the cabbie, Artemisia began to wrap Butterfield with the unyielding tape.

By the time the cab arrived at the old Tipsy Dolls Restaurant in Mayfair, Wallace looked like a handyman's version of an Egyptian mummy. Only his eyes and his nose weren't covered with silver tape.

The cab pulled directly in front of the old staff entrance door. Artemisia hopped out first, scanned the street for prying eyes, then gave the go ahead. The women gleefully lifted Butterfield up and out of the cab. Many jokes were made at his expense as they carried him into the defunct restaurant. The clubhouse had gone through some minor renovations since Women In Therapeutic Chemical Healing had last met to discuss the peculiar state of Wallace Butterfield. The French poster in the hall of the green fairy had been removed, so had the green brocade wing chairs, as well as the silver absinthe fountains, the fancy mirrored bar, the statue of Diana the Huntress, and all the cut crystal glasses. Even the bottles of Lucifer's Delight, Green Man's Own, Escobas de Brujas, Hexenkessel, and Before Morning Imperial Absinthe were gone. Anything that had been associated with absinthe was now absent. WITCH was no longer concerned about chemical healing.

But the silver brocade chairs were still there. In fact, there were many more of them. The meeting room of the coven was now solely dedicated to the large yellow sandstone carving of the Wedjat eye, the left eye of the Egyptian sun god Ra. Burning torches now flanked the carved eye. On either side of them was an honor guard of members of the coven. They stood at attention with their arms folded, almost nude, except for a skimpy covering of simple white loin clothes.

Hecuba hurried ahead of the rest and fell to her knees in front of the massive stone eye. She then bowed to the floor before it.

"Oh lunar force! Oh great destroying eye! Eye of Ra, God of Light! Wedjat eye! We come in supplication to thee," she intoned almost mechanically. There was a strain in her voice. It had been a long time since she and the others had dosed themselves with wormwood and the confusion caused by her ghost pushing into her own consciousness had taken its toll.

Artemisia hurried to Hecuba's side. She fell to her knees and began chanting as she repeatedly bowed before the stone eye.

<blockquote>
"Oh Wedjat eye,
When Ra decided to destroy mankind
He gave you to his daughter the great
lioness Sekhmet.
Mistress of Dread!
The Lady of Slaughter!
Lady of the Flame!"
</blockquote>

Artemisia then turned to Hecuba, as though she was hoping for an approving glance. There was none. So, Artemisia laid it on even thicker.

<blockquote>
"Mine is a heart of carnelian,
Crimson as murder on a holy day.
</blockquote>

Mine is a heart of corneal,
The gnarled roots of a dogwood and
the bursting of flowers.
I am the broken wax seal on my
lover's letters.
I am the phoenix, the fiery sun,
Consuming and resuming myself.
I will what I will.
Mine is a heart of carnelian,
Blood red as the crest of a phoenix,
the fiery sun, consuming and
resuming myself.
I pace the halls of the underworld
I knock on the doors of death.
I wander into the fields to stare at the
sun and lie in the grass, ripe as a fig.
The souls of the gods are with me.
They hum like flies in my ears.
I am.
I will what I will.
Mine is a heart of carnelian,
blood red as the crest of a phoenix."

Artemisia glanced again at Hecuba. She had recited the Hymn to Sekhmet perfectly.

Hecuba nodded her thanks, then rose to her feet and addressed the room. "Sisters," Hecuba croaked. "Let us make ready. We now have the mutant man Butterfield. So, we must beseech the ghost Prince Chioa Khan, the Great Beast of Revelations, the Baphomet, our dead mystic, Aleister Crowley."

Her voice was now a painful whisper. "The ancient Egyptians embalmed their bodies to maintain their flesh in hopes of finding everlasting life. But our great magus pursued flesh and embalmed his soul. Only he can speak to us from beyond. Only he can give us hope. We must beg him for guidance. Go prepare."

They stood Wallace Butterfield before the Wedjat eye, but not for long, for, it was impossible for him to maintain his balance all wrapped up in duct tape, and he kept on falling to the floor. Finally, Hecuba ordered the guards to leave their posts and hold him up while she went off to get dressed in her ceremonial garb.

Chapter Thirteen

A Trip to the Abbey

It took some convincing but she finally was able to persuade the car park attendant to allow her to pay for two spaces in the underground garage — though her metallic green Mercedes SLR McLaren roadster, retro-styled in the fashion of a 1950s Sci-fi rocket ship, was small enough to fit within the confines of just one parking area. The gullwing doors rising upward while opening in tandem were certainly meant to give the impression that the occupants were from an orbiting mother ship, however extraterrestrials never wore polka dots.

The boot of the Mercedes popped open, as two women in polka dot dresses stepped out on to the macadam of the parking garage.

"Emma dear, would you mind helping me with this?"

Emma was more than happy to. Her visit to Tipsy Dolls had made quite an impression upon the young lady. Her lips and eyelids were no longer blackened with makeup. She had recolored her hair from blue black to Maeva's shade of dark brunette, removed the silver bangles from her arms, and replaced her Girl Guide uniform with a dress of white polka dots on pink.

And though a bit unsteady in this, her first attempt, at wearing high heels, Emma made up for any awkwardness with insuppressible enthusiasm. She walked quickly to the rear of the car, reached in, and began to lift up a case of Green Man's Own.

"No. No. That's for the club. I made a stop earlier at Marley's Fine Spirits on my way to pick you up at your house. We were getting a little low on this brand and Marley's always gives us a good deal. You see his late mother was one of us… though he doesn't know that. For some reason he has the impression that she and I belonged to some sort of absinthe connoisseur's tasters group. In his mind Tipsy Dolls is a modish version of a sewing circle. Of course he's right." Maeva gave a knowing wink, which got Emma giggling. "We'll take this stuff to the club when we're done with our business at the Abbey. For now would you mind helping me stretch this dust cover over the car? The fleece side touches the paint."

"It was so nice of you to ask me along." Emma said as she pulled the fabric over one of Maeva's high intensity headlights. "I've never been to any place old and historical with kings and queens and such."

"Don't get your hopes up. The kings and queens are all dead and if you are looking for prince charming, you'll find him as a bag of bones in some crypt."They both laughed. "Still it was good of your mother to let you come. I need a sharp pair of youthful eyes and ears… in a head that's sober. That would be you." She pointed a long slender finger downward at Emma. "That looks perfect. Shall we be off?"

"Yes… but what are my eyes and ears going to be doing?"

"I don't know yet. But we're on a mission. Let's say it may have something to do with a prince charming… or maybe just a charming head case. We will see."

"Ooh… romance."

"Maybe… No… Official club business."

Maeva said as she pressed down firmly on the button of her car key. An encrypted signal shot out with an emphatic beep immobilizing her car's engine.

—— «» ——

"Johnny!"

John Bradshaw scurried out of his little office and ran over to where Reverend Poda-Pirudi was.

"Yes Reverend?"

"Polka dots."

"Polka dots, Reverend?"

"Indeed. I see polka dots coming through the tourist entrance. As I recall, polka dots were fashionable in the 1920 through the 1960s. We saw lots of women in polka dotted dresses rummaging about our tombs back then. Am I right Johnnie? Didn't Minnie Mouse wear a polka dotted dress in Steam Boat Willie?"

"I'm not sure if I remember her outfit in Steam Boat Willie... but I do remember,
It was an itsy, bitsy, teenie, weenie
Yellow, polka dot bikini,
That she wore for the first time today..."

"Stop that."

"Reverend?"

"In the three hundred and some years you've been my secretary, I've never heard you sing before. It is not an all-together pleasant experience. Don't do it again."

"Of course, Reverend. Never again."

"Good. What was that jingle?"

"Paul Vance wrote it in 1960. It's not a jingle it's called Bubblegum pop. But if I may correct you..."

The Reverend nodded.

"Polka dots came back in fashion in 2006. A local girls pop band, The Pipettes, made wearing colored dots fashionable again."

"Johnny you astound me. Most spooks hang out in their crypts and go walkabout in their dreams. But you really pay attention to the fads and fashions of the living. Look at you, an expert on lady's fashion, pop music, and polka dots as well. I have not truly plumbed the depths of your knowledge, Jonathan Bradshaw. You are far more attuned to what's going on around you than I am. For me, the centuries often go by in a blur. I look out of our office window and down into the Abbey and see people milling about in a variety of costumes. It's like one day they are all wearing wimples and armor, the next gowns and tuxedos, and by sunrise of the next morning they're all in shorts and t-shirts. I'm afraid it quite often doesn't register with me. I have to make a conscious effort to watch myself or the antics of human beings would become like the background noise of fan humming in a room. But here you are taking it all in. But then, you are still very young.”

“Thank you Reverend.”

“Stating that somebody is young is hardly a compliment. I’m just pointing out that you still have a… you’ll have to excuse my next pun… but you still have a lively interest in things.” The Reverend guffawed. “Oh, I see you’re not amused. I imagine I’ve been punning you…” he snickered, “to death… over these many centuries, an unintended aspect of your punishment. And I thought that forcing you to spend all of your free time in the Mucking Marshes was bad enough.”

“No Reverend… I mean yes the marshes are awful… but I really do enjoy a good pun. Will there be anything else?”

“You are a stoic one Johnny. Yes, there is one more thing. Please let us return to our topic of polka dots for a minute.” The Reverend said, pressing his face against his office window. “Can you explain to me why that person in the polka dotted dress… the one next to the girl in a similar garment, is causing the alarm bells to go off in my head? I find her to be most disturbing.”

Bradshaw looked out the Triforium office window and down onto the Cosmati Pavement. “Oh… I know who she is. She’s exactly as Sir Isaac described her, an elegant brunette with a penchant for polka dots. That’s Maeva Wolusky, the president of Women In Therapeutic Chemical Healing. She’s been trying to vamp Mr. Butterfield.”

“Yes, I suspected that was who it is. She does fit Newton’s description and from what he has told me… and he does like to gossip about these things… she’s gone far beyond trying to vamp Wally. She must be looking for information on him. We could invite her up and give her a run down about the tower but she’s a sharp cookie and might see through all of that. Besides, Ms. Wolusky just walked over to a security guard. She’ll be up nosing around here soon. Johnny, just to be on the safe side, we’d best make ourselves scarce.”

“Back to the marshes?”

“Afraid so… but just until she’s gone.”

— «» —

A man in a dark blue blazer, with the coat of arms of Edward the Confessor embroidered over his pocket, was having a difficult time trying to appear as though he was not losing his patience.

"Mam, I'm sorry, but as I told you, there is no office for a Reverend Poda-Pirudi located anywhere in the Abbey. I have never heard of any pastor of the church with that name. I assure you, if I had, a name like that would have stuck in my memory. I'm in charge of dayshift security, so that does afford me some insight into diocesan affairs. No one has ever even intimated to me that there were any plans for building a central tower here. I'm not an architect mind you but I just don't see how that would work."

"Well, as you said you are no architect."

Maeva was beginning to believe him but she wasn't quite ready to accept the idea that Wallace Butterfield was nothing other than a loon who liked to play architect in his father's old office.

"Who is in charge of renovations around here?" She said imperiously, with an edge to her voice.

"That would be the Clerk to the Dean. But his offices aren't here."

"Where would I find them?"

"They're off of Victoria Street. But you can't just walk in on him. You'll need an appointment."

"Oh, I'm very resourceful."

The Chief of Security was now sensing that this lady had the potential to get him into some kind of trouble with his superiors. He regretted telling her the whereabouts of the Clerk to the Dean.

"You know, you might save yourself the walk. I bet you are confusing the Dean's glass elevator with a tower."

"Glass elevator?"

"The Dean wants to make a museum up in the triforium… our storage area. He's looking to have a glass elevator built to make it accessible. He's got a fund drive going on right now to try and get it done."

"Oh, you may be right. I heard something about a triforium. Perhaps I should be talking to the Dean? Where can I find him? I assume that his offices would be located in his abbey?"

"They would be… they are. He's just on leave for the moment. Why don't you try back in a few weeks?"

"Oh, I will. Might even help him out with some funding for this museum of his. But I would like to see this space he wants to transform. How would I get to it?"

Emma had been silent standing next to Maeva watching her in action. She now felt it might be a good time to throw in with her.

"Ms. Wolusky drives a Mercedes McLaren roadster. The cost of one of them could build your elevator."

Maeva was not happy that Emma had just given her name and the make of the car she drove to security. But she didn't let on. As for the Chief of Security, he wasn't impressed.

"You'd get to it through a door in Poets' Corner," he said warily. "But I'm afraid the Dean will have to take you up. It's not permitted for the public to be up there alone."

"Yes of course. Could you take me?" Maeva said, switching from intimidating to sweet.

"No. I'm afraid not. You'd best make an appointment with the Dean's secretary."

"And where might I find her?" she asked adding a smile.

"The deanery is off the west cloister. Go down the south transept and take the entrance to Saint Faith's Chapel. That will take you to the cloisters. Go around the cloisters to the deanery. I hope you have a guidebook?"

"Oh, I'll have to purchase one but thank you. You've been most helpful."

Maeva pivoted on her high heels. "Emma, let's go to the bookstore shall we? We'll find a guidebook there."

A few minutes after their encounter with the Chief of Security, they happened on him again. He nodded at Maeva and Emma politely but with a weak smile. However, they elected to ignore him and instead acted as though they were engrossed in the details of their newly purchased guidebook.

"Great," Maeva said. "Poets' Corner is the way we would take if we actually were on our way to speak to the Dean's secretary. So he shouldn't be too suspicious."

"We're not going to make an appointment with the Dean?"

"No. We are going to get to the bottom of this mystery today not whenever the good Dean decides to see us… or more likely— not see us."

"Oh… we're going find the office up in the triforium?" Emma asked excitedly.

"No… I am."

"Please take me with you. It sounds spooky. I won't be any bother. I promise."

"As I said, earlier, I need your sharp pair of eyes and ears. And I need them right here."

They had just walked the length of Poets' Corner and were standing in front of a small door with a sign that was clearly marked, "No Public Admittance."

"I'm going through this door and will attempt to locate Mr. Butterfield's imaginary Reverend and his mythical office. I doubt if it will take too long for me to determine that they only exist within the confines of Wally's brain. But I feel uncomfortable with that security fellow. I need you to keep a lookout here. If he starts to head over here, come looking for me. We'll find someplace to hide till he goes away."

"Oh, but I do wish I could come."

"Emma, you are a fledgling member of WITCH." She smiled. "This is your first assignment. I'm counting on you to keep me out of trouble. Do you understand?"

"Yes, I'll run through the door if that guy starts to walk down this way."

"Perfect, see you soon," Maeva said, as she opened the door that led up to the triforium and disappeared behind it.

Chapter Fourteen

Tom Parr

It seemed to Emma that she had been standing in front of the dusty old monuments for hours. She seriously regretted sneaking off wearing her mother's high heels. Her feet were hurting her so. The only relief she could find was by half wearing them. Though her toes were in the shoes, the rest of her foot was on the cold Abbey pavement. The shoes were being wrecked. Her mother would put two and two together and realize that added up to Emma borrowing them. For a minute she feared that she would no longer be allowed to go off with Maeva. But then again, she knew her mother all too well. With a new boyfriend and the chance to be alone with him, having a pair of heels crushed by her daughter's oversized feet was a good deal.

Emma had stared at every effigy of every famous person buried or memorialized in Poets' Corner. There was Robert Browning and Geoffrey Chaucer and John Dryden and lots of other people who weren't poets buried here. She didn't know who any of them were but she was learning their names while she waited for Maeva. She figured that would please Maeva. Emma had taken the time to look up all the famous people who Maeva had mentioned had used absinthe. Being cultured was evidently part of being a witch and Emma was taking her newfound specialness seriously.

There was no security hanging around this section of the Abbey. They all seemed to be busy elsewhere. In fact, at the moment, there was nobody but her in Poets' Corner. She looked down at her blistered feet and read for the second or third time the inscription of the burial inscription she was standing on.

> THO: PARR OF YE COUNTY OF SALLOP. BORNE
> IN A: 1483. HE LIVED IN Y REIGNES OF TEN
> PRINCES VIZ: K.EDW.4. K.ED.5. K.RICH.3.
> K.HEN.7. K.HEN.8. K.EDW.6. Q.MA. Q.ELIZ
> K.JA. & K. CHARLES. AGED 152, YEARES.
> & WAS BURYED HERE NOVEMB. 15. 1635.

She didn't understand a word of it, other than this Parr guy was one hundred and fifty two years old when he was buried here. While she stared at all the abbreviations trying to make some sense of them, a pair of big bulging blue eyes rose up to the surface of the grave and stared back at her.

"You're a witch."

Emma had the presence of mind to place her hands over her mouth and stifle her scream. But still, she tripped over backwards and onto the floor. Grabbing her shoes, she immediately got back onto her feet and looked about to make sure no one saw her fall. She had heard about a few of the sisters at Tipsy Dolls seeing ghosts but she never thought she would. Emma took a few deep breaths to collect herself. Then, leaving her mother's high heels behind, she crept back to where the eyes were. Emma could see a complete head now in the stone. "Who are you and how do you know I'm a witch?" she asked nervously but with a degree of pride.

Now a finger rose up from the underground tomb and went across the ghost's lips. "Shhhh… they'll think thee be mad. Go beyond the door the other witch went in. I shall meet thee there."

On the other side of the door it was dimly lit. There was a stone staircase that twisted up into the Abbey like a corkscrew, but Emma could not see any sign of a ghost. Then slowly, materializing on the third step from the bottom came into view a very old bent-over ghost that propped itself up with a staff.

"It's been a long time since I've seen witches. They don't come here much. To think all this time then two in one day. Oh… yes… you wanted to know who I be. I be the ghost of Thomas Parr. Perchance you've heard of Old Tom Parr?"

"No. I've never seen a ghost before." Emma said half scared and half enthralled with being on conversational terms with a spirit.

"People have forgotten Tom Parr already? Was quite famous in the day. I mean, who lives to be one hundred and fifty two? Kept body and soul together on naught but cheese and bread and cider and ale. Lived through the reigns of Edward IV, Edward the V, Richard III, Henry VII, Henry VIII, Elizabeth, Mary, James, and Charles. Had a child out of wedlock at one hundred and married a second wife at one hundred and twenty two. You'd think people would remember something like that no matter how much times have changed."

"Sorry, I'm not much good with famous people. Maeva… I mean the other witch would tell you that. But I'm trying. Excuse me… but how did you know I'm… I mean Maeva and I are witches?"

"Seen lots of your kind go up in smoke. Take no offense, but we burnt every witch we laid hands on and many folk who were not witches we'd throw into the fires just to be on the safe side. But to answer thee, tis the eyes. They're rolling. Your ghost comes in and out. It takes hold of thee then loses thee. Not so much with the other one. Maeva?"

"Maeva Wolusky. She's our president."

"President? I've heard the American Colonies got one of them. Now witches as well. Somehow seems fitting to me. Your president's eyes don't roll much with her ghost's presence. Absinthe I suspect."

"Green Man's Own. I'm too young for it. But many of my sisters use it."

"I'd keep away from it. Cider and ale and cheese are all a body needs. Take me for instance, there's no older corpse in the Abbey… well there are older spirits but not one of them had a host that lived as long as mine. It took one hundred and fifty two years for him to die. I guess today they'd call me a post-term baby."

Tom Parr laughed at his joke, which Emma suspected that he had made often through the centuries since his death.

"Now you listen to me. Eat cheese. A nice Dorset Blue Vinney would be good victuals for thee. Never get tired of it. What killed my host was a change in diet. He should never have gone to see King Charles. Being a celebrity and all, the king wanted to meet his acquaintance. Had him up to the palace, had Van Dyck and Rubens paint his portrait. Then he fed him some rich food. It killed him. So sort of as a way to make amends, the good king had us buried here. He was such an excellent sovereign. Pity that malcontent upstairs had his head chopped off."

"Oh that's why we're here, to see some Reverend upstairs. Did he have your king killed?"

"Oh no. No. Not the Reverend. No. No. No. The Reverend would never do such a thing. He's the one who puts everything right. No, it was his lackey. That lickspittle, maggot pie, Bradshaw."

"Bradshaw? John Bradshaw?"

"Aye."

"But the security people told us that there was no Reverend Poda… something or another… or a Mr. Bradshaw. Maeva said that they have an office up in the treeformeum. But security said there wasn't."

"What would they know? They're almost all flesh. Just ignorant that's all. There's an office up there. But no one goes up there unless they are invited. Few of us spooks have ever seen it. I never have."

"So it is up there."

"No, it's not."

Emma' s heart jumped into her mouth. It was the second time in a few short minutes that she had been nearly frightened out of her wits.

"I've searched the entire area, just a lot of crates and cigarette butts." Maeva had appeared, rounding the staircase and pausing just a few steps above Tom Parr to answer what she thought was Emma's question.

Emma looked up at her incredulously. "But Tom says there is an office up there."

"Tom who?"

"See? Tis the absinthe. Her brain is all muddled and gripped with it. The witch can neither see nor hear me."

The door they had taken from Poets' Corner unexpectedly opened.

"I did tell you that the triforium was off limits to the general public. I want you two to leave now. I don't expect to see you back again at the Abbey."

Chapter Fifteen

The Summoning

It was but a short drive from Westminster Abbey to Tipsy Dolls in Mayfair, a drive that was punctuated with the squealing of tires from a car that could reach sixty-two miles per hour in three point seven seconds and one hundred and twenty-four miles per hour in ten point six seconds. However, due to snarled traffic, interminable pedestrian crossings, outbursts of rage over being tossed out of the Abbey, it had taken Maeva and Emma a considerable amount of time to traverse less than one-and-a-half miles distance. There had been absolutely no conversation since they had been thrown out of the Abbey. What little communication that took place was through the lurching and abrupt stops of the Mercedes SLR McLaren and the thumping of Maeva's hands on the steering wheel.

Emma decided that all the anger that Maeva was venting with a 5.4 liter super charged V8 engine was being misdirected towards the motoring public and it was best for her, and everybody's safety, if she owned up to causing the mess with the security people at the Abbey.

"I'm soooo sorry Maeva," she said as tears welling up in her eyes, "I should have kept a better lookout."

"No Emma. Don't apologize. You did nothing wrong. I should have guessed that all those cigarette butts on the floor of the triforium belonged to the Chief of Security. I spent far too much time nosing around up there and should have come down and gotten you sooner. It was just a matter of time before I got nabbed. Still, our embarrassment aside, it was a worthwhile trip. At least I know that our peculiar Mr. Wallace Butterfield of Butterfield and Son Architects is as much an architect as a six year old is with a box of Legos. Besides, it's my fault. Believe it. I mean it. It's my fault. I think I'm worldly but I obviously am not. I bought into his cock-and-bull story about this Reverend Poda-Pirudi and the commission to design a tower and his meeting with this Melanesian eccentric up in his posh office in the triforium. Let's face it, Maeva Wolusky is dumb."

A driver, who had been waiting behind the Mercedes at a stoplight, leaned on his horn. "Screw you!" Maeva cursed, as she positioned her middle finger up in front of her rearview mirror for his inspection. She then slowly rolled through the signal. It went abruptly from yellow to red, forcing the impatient fellow behind her to endure another sequence stopped at the light.

"No Maeva... no. You are wrong. He's telling the truth."

"What? Why would you think that?"

"I tried to tell you."

"Told me what?"

"There is a reverend a tri... whatever it's called."

"Why do you think that?"

"Because when you were up there I met a ghost. He told me."

"You met a ghost? Well the place must be full of them but it's rare for one to let you see him. How did you meet this ghost?"

"I was in Poets' Corner where you told me to keep a lookout. He surprised me. Oh was I scared! But he was really kind of nice. He said his name was Tom and he had me meet with him on the other side of the door. You came down when we were talking. But you didn't see that he was there."

"Tom huh? Oh yes... you did mention a Tom. He was a ghost. What did he say to you?"

"He talked about you and me being witches and said he'd met lots of our kind. Also told me what to eat to live as long as he did. Tom lived to be one hundred and fifty-two."

"What did he eat?"

"Mostly cheese."

"I see ... guess longevity isn't everything."

"But Tom also said that there was an office up where you were. However, no one is allowed in unless invited. He also said there is a Reverend and a guy that works for him that nobody likes. Tom seems to like the Reverend though, says he makes things right."

"Makes things right? Emma you are a natural. You are such a gifted girl of fourteen. I bet you'll be our president soon. Look, we're here and it appears a lot of our sisters are here too."

Maeva maneuvered the roadster into a parking space on Salmesbury Avenue near to the musician's entrance of Tipsy Dolls. When they got out Maeva was so excited that she didn't bother with putting the cover over her car. But still found the time to grab hold of one of the cases of Green Man's Own.

"Come Emma. We're going to have a very special meeting and I'm going to announce to our coven what you saw and heard today."

As the two entered the old eatery, Maeva began to sense that something seemed to be out of sorts with the place. It had had some kind of makeover. Things were missing from the hall and there were lots of sounds of commotion coming from just beyond it. Maeva motioned Emma with her head to stop. There, remaining silent, they listened to what was going on in the next room.

—— «» ——

Terrified and shaking, Wallace Butterfield's breathing was becoming restricted from countless wraps of duct tape. The pain of standing so long was causing his leg to convulse, and all of the excitement wasn't easy on his bladder. He hadn't gone to the toilet in hours.

But, Butterfield's ghost was feeling quite differently. He was beside himself with joy. Wallace's torment was always his pleasure. There wasn't any reason for him to create fright and panic within Wallace. There was no need to run up and down his spine. These reformed absinthe drinkers were taking care of all of that for him. He decided to just enjoy the show. However, if his assistance was required— well, he would be more than happy to oblige the ladies.

It seemed like hours, but in time the women of WITCH did return. Now all of them were bare-chested, clothed only in loincloths. That is, except for Hecuba, who was the last to make her entry. She wore a red loincloth and had a mantle of a lioness skin draped over her back, with the skinned face of the lioness secured to the top of her head. Fastened upright upon the lion's head was a large silver lunar disk with an image of a Uraeus, the striking cobra of the Wedjat eye.

"Begin the ceremony!" Hecuba screeched, her vocal chords now very tight from the influence of her ghost melding into all of her organs.

Artemisia ran up before the stone eye with a sermon that Hecuba had compiled for the occasion. It consisted of excerpts from the Pyramid Text and the Egyptian Book of the Dead modified by Artemisia for the occasion.

A gong was rung and the ladies of the coven formed a circle around Hecuba, Artemisia, and Butterfield with his guards, and, of course, Butterfield's ghost.

A drum began to slowly beat as Artemisia commenced with her recitation.

> *"He has taken the hearts of the gods;*
> *He has eaten the Red,*
> *He has swallowed the Green.*
> *Our Lord is nourished on organs,*
> *He is satisfied, living on their hearts*
> *and their magic.*
> *Their magic is in his belly.*
> *He hath swallowed the knowledge of*
> *every god.*
> *The lifetime of our lord is eternity,*
> *His limit is everlasting*
> *He is Mega Therion!*
> *Prince Chioa Khan!*
> *The Great Beast of Revelations!*
> *The Baphomet, 666!*
> *Count Svareff!*

Lord Boleskine!
Aleister Crowley's ghost!"

With this, the ladies in the circle began to move counter-clockwise. Their arms outstretched, they thrust their breasts forward and began to shimmy as they recited,

"Abracadabra! Abracadabra!
Abracadabra!"

Artemisia shrieked with rapture,

"Clouds darken the sky,
The stars rain down,
The constellations stagger,
The bones of the hell-hounds tremble,
The immortals are silent,
When they see our master's ghost,
As a god living on his father's
Feeding on his mothers
Our lord of wisdom.
Who cooks them in his evening kettles
It is he who eats their magic
Devours their souls.
The great ones are for his morning
portion,
The middle-sized ones are for his
evening portion,
The little ones are for his night portion
Old men and their old women are for
his incense-burning.
It is the 'Great-Ones-North-of-the-Sky'
Who set for him the fire to the kettles
containing them,
With the legs of their oldest ones as
fuel."

The gong rang again. "Abracadabra! Abracadabra! Abra-cadabra!" shouted the women from the moving circle.

"We also sing praise to our Lady of Slaughter, our Lady of the Bright Red Linen," Hecuba announced, as she held her arms skyward as an act of invocation.

"Abracadabra! Abracadabra! Abracadabra!" was repeated with even more intensity, and, as it was, a blue swirling pinwheel of light formed within the pupil of the carved stone eye, the Wedjat eye, expanding in size as it spun.

The circle was moving in a frenzy of passion. The shouting was now hysterical. The flames of the torches shot upward, as strange images danced deep within them. Suddenly, there was a flash of blue and the form of a man hovered above them, above the Wedjat eye. He was attired in a long black nightshirt with a matching triangular black turban. Embroidered upon the face of the turban was a silver star radiating light

"Good. Good. I am pleased," he announced as he watched the semi-nude women move past him one by one in their ceremonial circle.

Artemisia stepped closer to the eye and to the ghost of Aleister Crowley. As she did, it became apparent to Butterfield's ghost that she and, in fact, all of the rest of these women could actually see Crowley's spirit. Butterfield's ghost had noticed during the course of his detainment that the WITCHes' eyes were growing larger and larger and more ghostly blue.

Artemisia stepped before Crowley's specter and greeted him with outstretched arms and wiggling breasts.

"Hail Prince Chioa Khan, the Great Beast of Revelations, the Baphomet, our prophet, the ghost of Aleister Crowley!"

"Abracadabra! Abracadabra! Abracadabra!" shouted all the women in the room.

The ghost of Crowley scowled. He turned his head toward Hecuba and said, "No, not this flabby one again. Something younger. Something prettier."

Hecuba grabbed the sermon from Artemisia's hands and abruptly motioned her to take her place within the circle. She then walked over to one of the women there and gestured at her. The ghost of Crowley lowered his head in assent. Hecuba grabbed the girl about her shoulders and pulled her into the middle of the circle. She then thrust the paper into her hands and ordered her to take over the reading.

"From the Egyptian Book of the Dead my lord magus."
"I am the blue egg of the Great Cackler.
I am the egg of the world.
I was asleep inside a mound of dirt,
now I rise from a buried egg.
I live,
I say, I live.
I smell the air.
I sniff the air.
I walk with my toes in the dirt.
I give my family duck meat to eat.
I guard the fledgling in the nest.
What food there is for man in the sky, blue sky.
A swallow darts and circles.
I am the egg. I smell the air."

"Oh that was splendid. Simply splendid!" interrupted Crowley's ghost.

"Now wiggle your tits for me."

When she did so, he intoned, "Good. Good." Then he turned his face to Hecuba.

"Well, okay. What do you want? And what is that?" The ghost of Crowley pointed at Butterfield and his ghost.

"That is why we summoned you my lord," Hecuba rasped, then quickly added, "Oh Great Beast 666."

She then wiggled her tits. Aleister Crowley's ghost nodded approvingly.

"How unusual. Never seen the like of this. So why did you capture it? I assume it's male?"

"Yes my lord magus. He's male. Not much of one, but I agree he is unusual. We've been thinking. If we could figure how he got like that—" Her voice was becoming almost robotic and her face was beginning to twitch. She began to babble incomprehensibly.

Artemisia ran over to her with a secret bottle of Lucifer's Delight, which she had stashed away. Hecuba frowned at her, but still put the bottle to her mouth and took a few pulls. She waited a few minutes for the wormwood to take effect. The room stood quiet. Even the ghost of Aleister Crowley watched attentively.

"Better?" he asked with a bemused smile.

"Better," she said, as she wiped her lips with the back of her hand. "We were hoping that, my lord, that you might help us with him. We want to know how he got that way. We figure that if we could do the same thing to ourselves, we'd be able to function without drinking this stuff all the time." Hecuba held up the bottle of Lucifer's Delight.

"Well, I rather enjoyed it while I was corporeal but I understand your point. But how do you imagine that I'm going to be of any help?"

"Oh Mega Therion, if you could talk to his ghost, perhaps he would reveal how he came to be above this Wallace Butterfield's head?"

"Talk to his ghost? Why you silly cow. He's just a pupa. He hasn't been born yet. You try talking to a fetus and you can summon me again if it talks back. Till then, leave me alone."

"Oh master!" Hecuba was frantic. "For so many centuries our people have been afflicted for—"

"Wait!" The ghost of Crowley held up a hand to silence Hecuba. "Why is it doing that?"

"Doing what my lord?"

"That thing with its eyes?"

Hecuba moved in front of Butterfield and stared into his eyes. She saw nothing. She wanted to turn to the ghost of Crowley and tell him that, but she was too afraid.

"No, no, not the fleshy thing. Look up, or do you have too much wormwood coursing through your brain?"

Hecuba did as she was commanded and saw what she had first missed. Butterfield's ghost was opening and closing his eyes in a deliberate and exaggerated fashion. She kept staring at his eyes. Then she announced, "Damn, his ghost has managed to get control over his eye lids. It's code. Morse code, Lord Magus. I was in communications in the Navy. I spent some time with a signal lamp. He's closing his eyes like they're the sliding shutters on the lamp."

Crowley's ghost laughed with glee. "Oh what a clever young'un! So, what's he saying?"

Butterfield's ghost hadn't been asleep during those endless boring years when Wallace and his dad were monkeying around with radiotelegraphy. He had to listen to countless conversations with the most inane people on the planet by way of a telegraph key. Now it had paid off.

"Dash dot dash... that's K... dot dot... is an I... dot dash dot dot... makes an L... dot dash dot dot... that's another L... dot dot dot dot... for an H... dot dot... I... and dash dash... which makes the letter M. He's spelling "Kill him!" Hecuba shouted.

"Oh, what joy!" Crowley clapped his ghostly hands together repeatedly. "We must oblige him."

"Yes, my lord but how do we find out how he got like this?"

"Sekhmet will rejoice in having a human sacrifice. It's been ages since she has had one. After the festivities, I'll talk directly to this Butterfield's spirit. That's the best way of finding out what has happened here. So, let's get the meat on the barbecue!"

Butterfield had been shaking and groaning throughout the ceremony. The site of the ghostly apparition of Aleister Crowley had almost done him in. If his guards hadn't held him up, he would have swooned. But the talk of sacrificing him to Sekhmet was the last straw. He began to scream through his duct tape gag and thrash about as his bladder finally let go. A puddle of urine formed at his feet. His ghost was humiliated. Once again stuff was coming out of a sack. He couldn't wait till he was rid of Wallace Butterfield.

"How shall we make this offering Count Svareff, Lord Boleskine, Great Prince Chioa Khan?"

"Why at the oldest structure in London, Cleopatra's Needle, of course, and as soon as possible. Tonight at moonrise!"

"It shall be done my lord!" Hecuba shouted.

"No, it shall not! We are not going to start burning men like they used to burn us!" a voice shouted back from the street door.

The entire coven turned and looked towards the musicians' entrance. There was Maeva carrying a twelve-bottle box of Green Man's Own.

"Here sisters, take this. Drink up. Please! You don't know what you are doing."

"They listen to me now Maeva," Hecuba pointed out with a malicious grin.

Maeva lowered the box of liquor to the floor, walked quickly toward Hecuba yelling, "This is my organization. I've subsidized it and I'm the president! You're out. You self-contained bitch! The sisterhood is done with you. Let the evil in your head keep you company."

"Oh the great parachute magnate speaks. Well listen, honey, we've had a revolution around here. It is you who are out! Your boyfriend is ours now."

All the other women in the room mimicked her menacing laugh. Even the ghost of Aleister Crowley joined in.

"Take her sisters!" Hecuba cried, and, as the witches wrapped Maeva up in duct tape, added, "There will be no mercy or pity for your boyfriend, honey. He burns tonight.

Butterfield's guards let him fall to the floor. They ran over to the Wedjat eye and grabbed the torches from the wall. Holding their firebrands high, they joined in the shouting of the coven, "No mercy! No pity! Wallace Butterfield burns tonight!"

Chapter Sixteen

Emma

At the time, Emma didn't know that it would prove to be a blessing that she had left her mother's heels behind when she and Maeva had been escorted from the Abbey. But bare feet gave her traction on the sidewalk and she had needed that. A couple of the coven's sisters had seen her lurking in the hallway when they had grabbed hold of Maeva, and they went directly after her. But though these women had some athletic ability, they couldn't catch up to a determined and very frightened fourteen-year-old girl running for her life.

Emma managed to outpace them as she ran down White Horse Street. As she darted onto Piccadilly, they began to cry after her, calling her sister and encouraging her to come back with them. However, these entreaties didn't slacken Emma's long stride, they increased it. Emma never looked back once. She wouldn't throw away a second of time for that purpose. She instinctually knew that whatever Maeva's fate might be; hers was going to be the same.

After about a mile into the run, she heard what she assumed was the last of the pursuing witches scream, "We know where you live!" Still, Emma kept her pace. She sprinted around Wellington's Arch, onto Knightsbridge and then down the Brompton Road. As she started to weave her way through the shoppers gathered in front of Harrods's Department Store, her lungs gave out. It was a sickening sensation. Emma tried to puke but was too winded to do it. Her legs went wobbly. She had to lean against the building to catch her breath. Now, for the first time, she looked back. Though there was no sign that she was still being dogged by one of her pursuers, it was possible. Perhaps they were coming for her in a car? She didn't know. There would be no point in trying to run anymore if they did. Emma was spent. It was clear that the only safety to be found for her was by following the crowd of shoppers going into the department store.

She didn't mind being pushed and jostled by the throng of people that were here for the sale or who had just come to gawk at luxury items surrounded by a motif of neo-pharaonic opulence. It felt safe to be enveloped by them. They were like fleshy armor, multiple legs and arms swinging and moving and directing her towards the central escalator. Which was just in front of her. Customers were ascending or descending through the seven floors of the department store. Between the escalators was a large golden statue, Tutankhamen like. It was holding massive candles. Emma moved passively onto one of the escalator treads and began to rise upward. Overhead, in the high ceiling was a depiction of the ancient Egyptian gods among stars of the zodiac. The walls supporting this ceiling appeared to be made of sandstone and were inscribed with images from temples and tombs. Emma could see illuminated columns, crafted to look like gigantic stalks of papyrus, grass from the banks of the River Nile. Regarding her from the walls were golden sphinxes, resting in carved niches.

"Mine is a heart of carnelian,
Crimson as murder on a holy day."

The words now echoed through Emma's head.

"Mine is a heart of corneal,
The gnarled roots of a dogwood and
the bursting of flowers.
I am the broken wax seal on my
lover's letters."

She could feel the pull of the coven.

> *"I am the phoenix,*
> *The fiery sun, consuming and*
> *resuming myself.*
> *I will what I will.*
> *Mine is a heart of carnelian,*
> *Blood red as the crest of a phoenix."*

There was another statue of a golden pharaoh just up ahead of her, where the escalator ended. She felt that she was being taken to it. There she would surrender herself. She would find a pay phone, call her sisters and have them come and collect her for whatever purpose they had in store for her.

Then, as she stepped off the escalator into Harrods' Egyptian room, a tall woman in a crisp black skirt stepped in front of her.

"I don't know how you've gotten this far but we do have a dress code." She said as she pointed down to Emma's bare feet.

The floor manager had snapped her out of her trance. Perhaps saved her life? Going down the escalator was a lot different than going up in it. For one thing, she had gotten her breath back and for another it got her thinking about the first building that she had been thrown out of this day. There was something that old Tom Parr had said to her. "He's the one who puts everything right." She now had a plan.

— «» —

Emma hid herself amongst the bushes near the Blue Bridge that spanned the lake in St James' Park. She waited there well into the night, passing the time, watching the London Eye make its rotation above the Royal Horse Guard parade ground. Occasionally, she thought of just phoning home or going to the police. But she remembered the threat about knowing where she lived, and Emma guessed that the witches might all too easily bring the police under their control. So, she decided to remain concealed, determined to give her idea a chance.

Big Ben struck two long before Emma felt that it was safe enough to leave cover. The Abbey was not far away and could be seen from the park. Emma studied it for a while. She was pretty sure that it was empty of all visitors, but she had no idea who else or what else might still be lurking inside.

As she crept towards the building she wondered how on earth she was going to gain access. The only logical choice was to begin with a door.

To Emma's surprise, she didn't have to put much of her weight against the large central door leading into the Abbey to move it open just enough for her to poke her head in. The North Transept was softly lit, having just enough light for her to discern what things were but not enough light to provide any detail. Emma kept her head positioned halfway through the door and watched. She was sure that with the door unlocked, there had to be security about. Guards would have to be everywhere. As her eyes slowly became adapted to the light, she spotted one of them. At first she thought that he was a statue standing in front of the High Altar. He didn't even appear to be moving. She was scared already and this man, behaving more like a mannequin than a human being, was unnerving. But many stranger things had already happened this day and she had managed to pull through them, so Emma decided to give her luck another try. As quietly as she could, she tiptoed into the Abbey and made a wide circle behind him. Safe so far, she pushed her luck a little further and began to slink towards Poets' Corner. It was odd; she could hear the soft chatter of voices all about her. She felt the hair going up on the back of her neck as she realized that the ghosts were talking to one another from their crypts, as she might talk to one of her girlfriends at a sleepover.

"You have returned young witch."

"Ahhhhhhhh…" Emma's scream reverberated throughout the cavernous stone walls of the Abbey.

"Oh… my god you scared me," she stammered as she frantically turned to look at the security guard who was stationed in front of the High Altar.

"Fear him not. His senses are dulled. He and his ilk have no more comprehension than a rag doll, after midnight."

The ghost of Tom Parr clarified. "The Reverend sees to it that we are not disturbed. Odd though, that the door was unlocked. You were fortunate that they had all been busy talking about a football match earlier and failed to secure that door before the Reverend's languorous enchantment came upon them."

"Tom, I'm so happy to see you. I never thought I ever would be glad to see a ghost."

"But of course, the ladies have always liked me."

"Oh I'm sure of that," Emma said, appealing to his vanity, "but I'm actually here to see your Reverend. It's really urgent that I talk to him."

"No one sees him unless invited. I told thee this earlier when thoust were here last."

"Yes, I remember but Maeva... the witch who was with me when thoust told me earlier... is now in big trouble. You also said back then that the Reverend puts everything right. I need to see him! Maybe he can put the entire coven to sleep. I'm so afraid that they might burn her alive. They said that they were going to burn her friend tonight."

"Witches being burned is the natural order of things. I'm pleased that they are now doing everyone the courtesy of burning one another. Why would this matter to the Reverend? Why should he care if your friend goes up in smoke? One fewer witch, I say."

"Well, maybe he wouldn't care but would he care if her friend Butterfield is burned? I know they are definitely going to burn him and he's no witch."

"Butterfield... a Mr. Wallace Butterfield?"

"Yes, Wallace Butterfield. Maeva calls him Wally. You know him?"

"No. But there has been lots of chatter about him coming up from the crypts after midnight. Maybe you do need to see the Reverend. Come with me child. I will take you to his office."

Tom Parr then materialized a wooden staff from thin air. Leaning on it with his left shoulder, he took Emma's left hand in his right. His touch was cold and clammy. She felt as though she had hold of a melting icicle but Emma fought her desire to pull away from his grasp and moved with him as he tugged her towards the small door that led to the stairway.

Neither of them spoke as they ascended the stone turret that would take them to the triforium. Unlike Butterfield, Emma did not screech when she saw the sheeted statues of discarded saints and notables that were backlit by the window at the top of the stairs. Why should she? She was holding hands with the real thing.

Tom Parr's staff thumped along the thick planked unfinished flooring as he guided Emma around battered stone gargoyles and the wooden crates that were labeled Royal Wedding, Coronation, and State Funeral. Eventually, they came upon a rustic medieval door with weathered bronze strap hinges. Standing next to the door was a security guard, like the one by the High Altar. He too appeared to be frozen in time. The ember of the cigarette that was between his lips glowed but did not burn.

"Emma," for the first time Old Tom Parr didn't call her young witch, "I will go no further with thee. The Reverend is beyond that door. I must go." His voice sounded as though he had lost his nerve. The staff fell from his hand, clattering upon the triforium floor, as he faded to a blue shimmer that was absorbed by the darkness.

Most people would have been very relieved to see a ghost go, especially within the dark confines of an ancient abbey, but to Emma it meant that she was alone and truly on her own. Though frightened, she was resolute. She had made it this far, escaping witches, evading security, and enlisting the aid of the spook of a one hundred and fifty-two year old man, why would she shrink away now? Her luck had been holding. Why not test it one more time? This would be it. Beyond the door was the Reverend. Tom Parr said that he was the one who made everything right. All she had to do was knock on the door. Emma was so frightened and it would be so easy to run down the steps and out of the Abbey. But then there was Maeva. Maeva had been so kind to her. Maeva had taught her that she was something special and now she needed her help.

Emma was not going to desert her. Steadying her nerves, she took two deep breaths and then knocked on the door.

She could hear voices and stirring coming from on the other side. Then, with a creak that had been nurtured through the centuries, the door to the office in the triforium opened, but only partially.

An eye stared out through the crack. It was a dark brown eye, surrounded by dark brown skin.

The door slammed shut.

Emma could hear some more conversation, but this time it was heated. Then it stopped, and the door was again opened, this time a little bit wider. It was clear to her that she was being examined, and by a ghost who was dressed very much like Old Tom Parr.

"Go away!" he said as he slammed the door shut.

"But I'm not going to go away!" she shouted loudly enough so that she could be heard in the room on the other side.

There was some more conversation, then the door, now groaning on the hinges, opened all the way out.

"Well, do come in then," said a man dressed like a minister. "My secretary, Mr. Bradshaw has just advised me that you are an associate of that charming woman, Maeva Wolusky. Is that true?"

"Why... yes." Emma was a bit stunned. This wasn't what she was expecting; the office was quite nice, in an old fashioned way. It wasn't at all spooky looking... except for Mr. Bradshaw.

"How nice of you to come pay us a visit. I'm Reverend Poda-Pirudi and you are?"

The Reverend extended his hand. Emma clasped it, expecting it to feel like a melting icicle but it was actually soft and quite warm.

"I'm Emma... Emma Ludshorp."

"I'm so pleased to make your acquaintance Miss Ludshorp. We so rarely get company up here. Gets quite lonely at times. I was just remarking to Mr. Bradshaw the other day that wouldn't it be nice if someone took the bother to climb up all of those steps and negotiate their way through those interminable packing crates to pay a social call on us. And here you are. Oh do come in."

Emma walked into the office and across the ebony and white oak parquet floor to a maroon velvet chair that Mr. Bradshaw had pulled out for her. She hesitantly seated herself in it while the Reverend sat down behind a large elaborately carved wooden desk.

"Dandelion burdock?" he said.

Emma looked confused.

The Reverend thought she hadn't heard him. "Could we offer you a drink of dandelion and burdock? No trouble you know."

"Excuse me? I don't know what that is. Why would I want to drink it?"

"Oh… sorry… sorry. The centuries do fly by. Dandelion and burdock was a very popular drink with the young ladies not too long ago."

John Bradshaw shook his head hoping the Reverend would see him.

"Silly me. It was popular quite some time ago. How the centuries do fly. But it does taste good and is full of all sorts of good things too— dandelion roots, the root of a burr weed, vanilla bean, honey, ground ginger, and black treacle."

"No. But thank you. I'm not allowed to drink absinthe so I'm sure I shouldn't be drinking that.'

"But it is non-alcoholic. But perhaps you would prefer a phosphate soda of some kind? Johnny, what do they call those things now?"

"Soft drinks, Reverend."

"Ah yes. Could we offer you a soft drink?"

The Reverend's hospitality wasn't making Emma feel at ease and she certainly didn't want to socialize. She wanted to get help to Maeva even at the risk of offending the guy who seemed to have all the ghosts in the Abbey at his beck and call.

"I want nothing to drink. Please be quiet, and let me tell you what's wrong. Why I'm here!"

At first the Reverend appeared to be stunned, downright flabbergasted. Then he placed his hands on his chest and began to laugh.

"Oh thank you Miss. Ludshorp. It has been a very long time since anyone has put me in my place. And I'm not at all accustomed to the feeling. I imagine that such a sensation will do me a bit of good. But here I am again distracting you from the purpose of your visit. Do go on Miss Ludshorp, tell me what's troubling you. Perhaps I may be of assistance?"

"That's why I came. I was told by Tom Parr that you make everything right and I really need you to do that now."

"Tom Parr? Who is Tom Parr? Johnny do you know a Tom Parr?"

"The cheese eater Reverend."

"Oh that fellow down in Poets' Corner. Johnny would you write Mr. Parr's name in my appointment book for tomorrow?"

"Of course Reverend."

"Please, continue Miss Ludshorp."

"My friend Maeva. She's our president, the president of WITCH. I'm a member of WITCH."

"I have some knowledge of Miss Wolusky and her little club in Mayfair. And if you don't mind me saying so, your being a witch… well it shows. But do go on."

"Well, there's another witch— Hecuba. She's grabbed a hold of Maeva and I'm sure she plans to do something awful to her."

"A revolution in the clubhouse, how distressing. But why do you think they are going to do anything awful to her… beyond tear up her membership card?"

"Because they've got her friend Wally too. They've got him all wrapped up in tape and some nasty ghost… Albert Crowsfeet… or something like that… told them to burn Wally tonight. If they do that to him, they probably will do something like that or even worse to Maeva. Hecuba doesn't like her much."

"Well I guess she doesn't! But you will be relieved to hear Miss Ludshorp that the situation is well in hand. I have one of my associates down there as we speak. He is a very capable gentleman and I'm sure that if the situation gets out of control with either the fate of Miss Maeva Wolusky or Mr. Wallace Butterfield that I would most certainly receive a phone call apprising me of this information. Wouldn't I Johnny?"

"Why yes Reverend."

"Good. By the way, Johnny, who is presently monitoring the activity at Tipsy Dolls?"

"Well it was supposed to be Mr. Darwin... but he was suffering from some malady. I believe... chronic fatigue syndrome... or perhaps it was a migraine? Anyhow, he told me that he was having Sir Isaac stand his watch for him."

The Reverend appeared to be in some discomfort as he sprung up from his chair.

"Excuse me Miss Ludshorp. I need to have a private discussion with my secretary," he said as he glowered at Bradshaw. Pointing his finger in the direction of a back room he added, "Perhaps it would be best to have our little chat in your office Mr. Bradshaw."

The Reverend and his now dejected looking secretary disappeared into a small room just off of the Reverend's office. When the door to this mini-office closed, the shouting began. Emma could tell that it was the Reverend who was doing all of the shouting.

Within a few minutes, the door to Mr. Bradshaw's office opened again. As it did, the ghost of John Bradshaw flew through the closed door that led out into the triforium like he was some kind of blue comet.

The Reverend Poda-Pirudi now came back into the room and again sat at his desk. He took in a couple of deep breaths, then turned his attention to Emma.

"A minor snag I assure you. We have this well in hand. Are you sure I couldn't interest you in a phosphate soda?"

"Oh no... are Maeva and Wally going to be all right?" Emma asked now with even greater urgency than before.

"Yes. Yes, just a little glitch. We'll see what Johnny has to say when he returns from downstairs. It shouldn't take more than a minute or two."

No sooner had the Reverend spoken than John Bradshaw shot through the closed door that he had exited from.

"Perfect timing Johnny. What news do you bring?"

"There has been some confusion over who was responsible for being at Tipsy Dolls this evening. As you know, Darwin handed the responsibility to Sir Isaac. I've just had word with Sir Isaac and apparently he's under the misapprehension that you preferred having Sir Frederick Herschel take over for him."

The Reverend Poda-Pirudi's eyes bulged. His face puffed. His hands, which had been folded in front of him on his desk, unclasped and formed fists, which he used to bang the top of his desk with. A strange high-pitched whining noise came from him. It almost sounded girlish. But it subsided quickly and as it did, his composure returned to him.

"Forgive me my dear Emma. Just a momentary loss of our bearings. Everything will soon be tippity-top. Johnny would you get my appointment book please?"

John Bradshaw went into his office, returning with the Reverend's appointment book.

"Please remove Tom Parr's name from my appointment book for tomorrow and replace it with the names of Mr. Charles Darwin and Sir Isaac Newton."

"Yes, Reverend. Anything else?"

"There is one thing more. Under Sir Isaac's name place yours as well."

"Oh… of course Reverend," Bradshaw said, visibly shaken.

Now I believe that you and I have a night's work to do. Miss Ludshorp, I'm afraid I'm going to insist that you stay here for a little while."

Emma began to rise from her seat to protest.

"No. No. I know you want to come with us and that is most admirable but I will not hear of it. In this I am firm. However, I will have Mr. Darwin and Sir Isaac come up here and tend to your needs while we are away. I'm sure that by now you are most sick of the company of old ghosts, and who could blame you? But it will not be for long. And they will be on their very best behavior. On this I can assure you."

Chapter Seventeen

The Sacrifice

It was a little after three in the morning when the black cab containing the immobilized body of Wallace Butterfield showed up at the Embankment. Earlier, Hecuba had sent out most of her crew to start dumpster fires around Victoria Station. If their missions were successful, the police would spend the night searching for arsonists on the other side of town. They'd be oblivious to the main event, and Hecuba and her confederates would be well clear of Cleopatra's Needle by the time the Metropolitan Police arrived. It would take them days to identify the charred remains.

As Butterfield was carried from the cab, Artemisia began to mutter some Egyptian mumbo-jumbo over him and to rub some perfumed ointment on his head.

Hecuba had planned this like she had the first operation. It would go down like a commando raid, a surgical strike: in and out. No time for lollygagging or excess of ceremony.

Artemisia had consulted the paper for official moonrise. It would be at 3:17. At that hour, Butterfield would be dead and they would all be on their way home ten minutes after that.

Wallace Butterfield was exhausted from squirming and was now quite easy for the women to carry. Like a mouse gone limp in a cat's jaws, he had surrendered, knowing that he was experiencing his last few minutes on earth. All that was left for him was to suppress his panic and take in as much of life as he could, while he could. He moaned and tears welled up in his eyes as they lugged him past one of the two large bronze sphinxes that guarded the side entrances to Cleopatra's Needle. His life had been uneventful up to now, a bit stale and reclusive; still it was his life and they were going to take what little pleasure he derived from it away.

Butterfield was placed standing up against the granite obelisk that, over three thousand years ago, had been erected in the Egyptian city of Heliopolis, as commanded by the pharaoh Thuthmosis III. Now it jutted out over the Thames. Floodlights illuminated it. The hieroglyphics that had been carved into the stone long ago could still be read even though equatorial heat, sand storms, London pollution, and a Nazi bomb had weathered and scorched them.

Illumination from the dolphin-ornamented lampposts that ran along the Embankment was revealing too much of what was going on. Hecuba ordered that Butterfield be hidden from the light and had him placed under a park bench. Then she and her three companions sat on the bench, using their legs to further obscure him.

They had removed all of their Egyptian trappings back at Tipsy Dolls and had re-dressed and were now looking quite ordinary. Only the time of night could call attention to them. They waited anxiously. It was only a few minutes before moonrise and the promised appearance of Aleister Crowley.

Artemisia passed a brown paper bag that hid a bottle of absinthe to Hecuba and then asked a little sheepishly, "Does our master appear in the form of a lion?"

The question caused Hecuba to remove the bottle from her mouth. She answered Artemisia peevishly. "No, of course not. Why? Do you see the Goddess?"

"No, I don't think so. It's just that those lions are beginning to creep me out."

Artemisia pointed at the large bronze lion heads affixed to the river wall just above the waterline of the River Thames. They had been placed there in 1860. Though not used much anymore, each lion still had a mooring ring in the grasp of its jaw.

"You are getting jumpy! You've got to be calm! I have enough to do here without you causing me additional problems. We've got a lot to get done tonight and I still don't know what to do with Maeva."

"Of course. How foolish of me. It shouldn't be much longer… Maeva? What do you mean?"

"She's not going to let us get away with this without causing some kind of stink. When we are done here, perhaps we should go back to the clubhouse and knock her on the head and then throw her in the Thames? Better yet, maybe untie her and then slit her wrists. We could make it look like she killed Butterfield in some kind of jealous rage and then took her own life. The press would have a field day with a headline that read OCCULT LOVING RICH GIRL MAKES A HUMAN SACRIFICE OF HER BOYFRIEND THEN KILLS HERSELF. It might throw the cops off our scent long enough for us to scatter. But still, I'll have to think of something nice to do with Zoraida as well. That may take a little more thought."

"No, we can't do that! We can't kill Maeva or Zoraida."

"Of course we can. Once Crowley and the Goddess rid us of our affliction they'll be no stopping us. The cops will be no match for us. We'll outwit them at every turn. You'll see."

"I don't think we should do that. Burning Butterfield is bad enough. No, let's talk about this later. We will all calmly discuss what's to be done with them. Put it to a vote. I'm sure everyone will see reason."

"Yes, of course," Hecuba said feigning a reassuring tone. Then she added, "We are a sisterhood after all."

"That's right," Artemisia muttered. She was no longer looking at Hecuba but instead was staring distractedly up at the big Art Deco clock on the top of the Shell-Mex building. It was showing a quarter after three. She then turned around to face the river.

"Look!" She motioned frantically to her right. "Over by the London Eye."

A peculiar looking moon was peeking through the spokes of the Ferris wheel. As it rose upward, the lights of the London Eye changed from a fiery red to the strange opalescence of this full moon. Both circles, the moon and the London Eye, were reflected in the flood tide of the Thames. The river was rapidly rising, causing a choppy backwash, which was distorting and elongating the images upon the water.

"Where is he?" gasped Artemisia. "You know what they say about the Thames?"

"No, what now?" Hecuba said derisively.

"When the Thames lions drink, London will flood."

"Stop obsessing on those lions!" Hecuba snarled. "Crowley said he will be here at moonrise and I'm sure he'll be here any second now. If he's not here already."

The mirror images of the Ferris wheel and the moon rocked and twisted on the surface of the river. The images suddenly narrowed, merged, and reached across the Thames in the form of a beam of blue. Light struck the obelisk on the opposite shore like a laser beam. Then it diminished as the ghost of Aleister Crowley appeared triumphantly at the base of Cleopatra's needle.

"Where's our birthday boy?" He mirthfully intoned.

The four women jumped in unison off the park bench and went running to him.

"Master! Master! Prince Chioa Khan! Oh Mega Therion! Great Beast of Revelations! The Baphomet! 666! Abracadabra! Abracadabra! Abracadabra!" they shouted.

"Yes— yes— yes. Enough groveling. What have you done with our infant?"

"He's under the bench, master," volunteered Hecuba.

She and the others ran back to the park bench. Artemisia and the guards grabbed Butterfield by his taped-up legs and pulled him out. They carried him toward the base of the obelisk, while Hecuba fished out a jerry can full of petrol from a nearby clump of bushes.

Lifted to his feet by his female guards, Butterfield was groaning and emitting a pitiful whine through his duct tape and panty gag. His body was shaking convulsively and he was now messing himself from several orifices.

But his ghost paid no attention to this. He no longer cared. Wallace Butterfield was nothing more than a conveyance and would soon be but a memory. His immolation would have no more sentimentality attached to it than a clunker of a car being towed off to the salvage yard.

The guards now propped him up against the base of the obelisk and Hecuba pored petrol all over him. Butterfield tried to scream but the sound would not come out.

"There, now!" Aleister Crowley's ghost admonished. "This is a great honor. Human sacrifices release great magic! Try and control yourself. The amount of energy you are about to release is dependent on how willing you are to be slaughtered. I know. I know. In the olden days you would have garlands of fragrant flowers draped around your neck and tiny bells about your ankles. And there would be sweet music to send you off; flutes, tambourines, drums, lutes, and lyres all would be playing in your honor. But poor fellow, this is the twenty-first century— and you appear none too willing. So, suck it up. Duct tape and petrol will have to do."

"Master?" Artemisia inquired.

Crowley's ghost looked down upon the chubby one with a contemptuous smile. "Yes?" It obviously pained him to even recognize her.

"Master, will the Goddess receive this sacrifice considering his state?"

"Why, of course. It's been a long time since Sekhmet has received a burnt offering and this is a very good place to slaughter Mr.— Cowfield?"

"Butterfield, master."

"Yes, well, of no consequence— he'll burn well whatever he's called."

Hecuba decided to throw her lot in with Artemisia and question Crowley's ghost. "Why is this a good place? Because it's Egyptian? It doesn't appear to me that sacrificing at an obelisk put up for Thutmose has anything to do with our Goddess."

Crowley's ghost drew himself up large and towered over the women. "It doesn't occur to you that Thutmose was a devoted servant of hers? He lined the boulevard to her temple at Karnak with hundreds of statues of her, made from the finest and blackest basalt. Her altar was always kept clean. The city was commanded to bring Sekhmet daily offerings of bread, fruits, wine, and beer. He himself placed precious vessels of gold and silver upon her temple floor and filled them with precious stones. It was upon his command that a throne of electrum was made for her and that the blood of sacrifices of old were renewed. And yet you dare to question the sanctity of this place?"

Hecuba and Artemisia went to their knees. "No master. No. Forgive us," they pleaded.

Hecuba felt compelled to explain. "It's just that we wanted to make sure our Goddess would be pleased with this site and of our offering. We do so wish that she will be merciful and consider our predicament."

Crowley's ghost then calmed and shrunk back into the stature of a man.

"As I said, I shall speak to her on your behalf and I will also speak to the ghost hatchling to find out how it came to be unstuck. We will sort out that muddle in your minds. Soon you will be able to live normally— that is, up until you decay. Which I'm sure won't be for some time." He smiled benevolently. "Now get up off the ground and go light a torch."

Obediently, Artemisia jumped to her feet and went off to the bushes where the petrol had been hidden and pulled out an unlit torch. As she did, she could see that the level of the Thames was rising. She ran back to Hecuba, handed her the torch and attempted to tell her what she had just seen.

"The river is going up—"

"Stop it!" Hecuba hissed. "No more of your river nonsense. Let's just get this over with and get out of here. Whether the Goddess is pleased or not, the police won't be, and I don't want to spend the time I have until I decay in a prison cell."

Hecuba then took out a butane candle lighter and pressed the trigger. A little flame formed at its end. She touched the flame to her torch. A bright crimson blaze whirled upward from its end. She held it high and, letting go of all of her concerns about being discovered, shouted,

"Mine is a heart of carnelian,
Crimson as murder on a holy day.
Mine is a heart of corneal,

> *The gnarled roots of a dogwood and*
> *the bursting of flowers.*
> *I am the broken wax seal on my*
> *lover's letters.*
> *I am the phoenix,*
> *The fiery sun,*
> *Consuming and resuming myself.*
> *I will what I will.*
> *Mine is a heart of carnelian,*
> *Blood red as the crest of a phoenix."*

Aleister Crowley's ghost merrily watched. Rocking back and forth on his heels, he hugged himself. Then, raising his arms to the night sky, he pronounced: "Oh Mistress Sekhmet, take this mortal offering as an act of obedience to your will. Feed upon his singeing hair, his boiling blood, and his spitting fat! Let him cook well within your sacred fire. We show him no pity! But we beg of you pity. If this sacrifice pleases you, pity these wretched WITCHes. Grant them peace from the torments within their minds."

Crowley's ghost nodded to Hecuba. She was standing at the base of the obelisks with her firebrand held high above the heads of the squealing Butterfield and his ecstatic ghost.

But nothing happened.

So, Crowley's ghost nodded again.

Still nothing happened.

"Set the victim ablaze!" he commanded while furiously motioning with his hands for Hecuba to get on with it.

But Hecuba wasn't paying any attention to him. Her eyes seemed fixed on something behind him.

Perplexed, Aleister Crowley's ghost swung round and faced the Thames to see what could possibly be holding up the sacrifice.

"Oh crap!" he said.

A duck-shaped pedal boat approached along the river. A large red bowtie around the duck's neck formed the prow of the boat, making the craft appear to be utterly ridiculous, but yet it still had an ominous air.

John Bradshaw was seated in the boat and working hard at the pedal boat mechanism, cycling madly to keep the big yellow plastic duck from drifting backwards with the tide.

Reverend Poda-Pirudi was standing up in the prow of the boat with a bronze lantern hanging down by his side. He was staring intently at Hecuba, but said nothing.

She was dumbfounded. She lowered her torch so that it now pointed toward the ground. Growing confident by the Reverend's silence, she raised the torch again over her head. Standing on her tiptoes, she held the lit end of the firebrand as high up as she could get it, singeing the tape on Butterfields head. Reverend Poda-Pirudi just stared at her, as though he was anticipating something.

But Aleister Crowley's ghost was too distraught over the present turn of events to allow the ceremony to continue. Turning toward Hecuba, he waved his arms about and shouted. "No! No!"

Hecuba paused briefly, but then shouted back at him in defiance. "We can't live this way any longer. Butterfield will feed the Goddess!"

Then she brought down the torch to do a proper job of igniting Wallace's head. As she did so, Reverend Poda-Pirudi raised his lantern. Across the Thames the thirteen-ton white stoneware statue, the South Bank Lion, rose up on its hind haunches and roared.

With this, the mooring lions, on either bank of the Thames, spit out their mooring rings and began a dreadful bellow.

But Reverend Poda-Pirudi's bellow was even louder. "Drop that torch or I'll cut your legs into strips and use your skin for flypaper ribbons at the Mucking Marshes Landfill!"

With this threat, Aleister Crowley's ghost fell to his knees in front of Hecuba. He was sniveling and covered with a ghostly sweat. Clasping his hands beseechingly he pleaded, "Please. Please. Dearest Hecuba, don't do it! Please!"

Hecuba made a motion as though she was going to ignite Butterfield, but faltered. The torch dropped from her hand to the pavement.

"Oh thank you." Crowley's ghost whimpered. "Oh thank you sweet Hecuba."

When the torch fell, the Thames began to recede. The South Bank Lion went back to all fours and the mooring rings rose up from the river and returned to the jaws of the Thames Lions.

"You are all in very serious trouble," said the Reverend. He brought a nickel-plated bobby's whistle up to his mouth with his free hand.

Then, he blew on it several times.

In response to the shrill calls of the whistle, ghostly specters dressed in Victorian police uniforms suddenly appeared all about the obelisk.

"Good lads!" shouted Reverend Poda-Pirudi. "Good lads! Ladies, I give you straight from London's Brompton Cemetery, Police Division L of the Woolwich Dockyards and their inspector, the renowned Charles Frederick Field."

The specter of Inspector Field flashed into form just in front of Hecuba. He was a clean-shaven ghost, fortyish, that is, if he had been alive. There was a dimple in his chin and a bowler hat on his head. And he seemed to be quite enjoying himself.

"You're all under arrest!" he proclaimed.

"Indeed you are!" affirmed Reverend Poda-Pirudi.

With this, the Reverend Poda-Pirudi placed his police whistle in his pocket. He opened the door to the lantern and allowed the light within to escape. All went bright white. Then the dazzling light vanished, and in the moonlight that remained, the scene was very different. The duck boat was gone, so were the WITCHes, the bobbies, Aleister Crowley's ghost, and Wallace Butterfield.

Now, the scene at Cleopatra's Needle appeared just as it had at three o'clock, just before Hecuba and her WITCHes had arrived. Even the big illuminated clock atop the Shell-Mex building confirmed that it was three o'clock.

Chapter Eighteen

The Trial

Inside the flash of light, it was bright and unpigmented; as though color could not exist within such intense brilliance. There was no definition here, nor substance. There was only the sense of being part of a radiant void.

Though it took Wallace Butterfield some time to arrive, time had no meaning during his journey. It was an unnecessary construct, arbitrary and of no purpose. All was present, a present without a beginning or an end.

But clarity began to creep in. It started as the color white, and dissolved into subtle variations of the same shade. White contours formed upon a white background, sparingly providing definition, like subtle shadows on the petals of a white rose. Time started to beat again. Shapes sharpened. Gothic design emerged. The interior of a great building embossed itself upon the empty air. Color seeped in, smells rose up, disjointed sounds and muffled speech could be heard in the distance.

Butterfield felt as though he was coming out of anesthesia. He had no knowledge of the things about him. Nothing made sense. He didn't know who he was or, even, that he was.

Gradually, sounds began to take on coherent form. Wallace began to understand their meaning.

A voice boomed, "The prisoner known by the Wicca name of Morgana approach the bench!"

There was a pause followed by, "How do you plead?"

Sobbing followed— widespread sobbing. Butterfield realized that many people were crying.

"Well! Your plea?"

"Guilty, my lord."

"I hereby find the prisoner Morgana guilty of attempted murder as charged. Go stand with the others and await my sentencing!"

"The prisoner known by the Wicca name of Artemisia, approach the bench!"

Butterfield knew this name. In fact, he could now see her. She was standing before a long table. There was a man in a red robe seated at the table. He had on a long curled white wig, quite a contrast to his very black skin.

"How do you plead?" The question was asked again. "How do you plead?"

But Artemisia stood before the man seated at the table trembling, unable to speak. Another woman ran up to her and whispered in her ear. Wallace knew this woman too. She was Hecuba.

Now, things were beginning to make sense to Wallace Butterfield's brain. One particular after another was becoming clear to him. This was the Abbey. He could see its grandeur all about him. The long table was in front of the ornately carved gold High Altar. A golden cross and two large gold candlesticks stood directly behind where the judge was seated. He realized that the judge was Reverend Poda-Pirudi. But the fact that Reverend Poda-Pirudi was officiating at a trial wasn't half as strange to Butterfield as the recent memories that were now rushing in on him. He shook in horror at the thought of the evil blue man, the obelisk, the torches, and the fact that the women were going to burn him alive and that he had spent hours and hours wrapped up in duct tape. Wallace glanced at his arms and realized that he was no longer so constrained. And to his relief he seemed to be no worse for wear. Someone had even taken the time to clean and press his father's suit.

His hands were gripping the wooden armrests of a fancy chair. He must have been in that chair for some time, because he felt awfully uncomfortable. His arms had that painful tingling sensation, as though they were no longer part of him. Butterfield attempted to move them and get his circulation going but they wouldn't budge. He tried again, but something held them fast. He began to squirm about in his seat. Then what was holding him in place became clear to him. Several pairs of hands gripped him. Hands were pressing down on both his wrists. Hands were on his shoulders— and these hands were a luminescent blue.

In a panic, he looked to his left. A lanky spirit with long hair had hold of him. Wallace turned in horror towards the Reverend to ask for help, but there were other creatures like this one seated just to the left of the Reverend's table and the Reverend appeared to be quite comfortable having them there.

Yet again, during the course of this very long day, Wallace Butterfield felt compelled to scream.

"Ahhhhhhh!!!! Ahhhhhhhhhh!!!!!" The "creatures" were all dead queens and kings whose pictures he had been required to memorize in school.

Butterfield looked again at the ghost who was holding his left side down. There was another face that he had to memorize in school. It was Sir Isaac Newton's. Butterfield tried to pull himself free from the grip of Newton's ghost by lunging to the right. As he did so, he came face to face with the specter that was holding him down on his other side.

"Mr. ... Berwyn?"

The ghost of Charles Darwin smiled at Wallace and gave him a friendly nod.

"Wally! So glad that you're with us!" Reverend Poda-Pirudi announced from the table where he had been officiating. "Got a lot on our agenda today. Lots of justice to be meted out. But I'm sure that Newton and Darwin will look after you," he said as he stared disdainfully at the two of them.

Butterfield was stunned. He opened his mouth to say something, but Reverend Poda-Pirudi waved him off.

"No time. No time. Would love to chat— perhaps later." Then he frowned and glared at Artemisia. "Has the prisoner considered making her plea? Or should I add the additional charge of interfering with the course of justice? There is such a charge, isn't there Bradshaw?"

Dressed in a black robe with a barrister's wig atop his blue head, John Bradshaw stood in front of the table and just to the right of the Reverend.

"Well, the charge I think you are referring to is actually called 'perverting the course of justice.' It is meant for perjury or jury tampering, fabricating evidence— that sort of thing."

It was apparent by his demeanor that Reverend Poda-Pirudi did not approve of this answer. The ghost of John Bradshaw stopped the legal discourse and promptly executed a legal about-face.

"But, after all, this is the highest court in the land. All precedence would naturally devolve from here. So, if it pleases the Old Soul— I mean if it pleases the Reverend Poda-Pirudi— such a charge is hereby entered into common law."

"Why Johnny, your understanding of legal matters never ceases to amaze me. And you're right, it does please me."

He turned again to Artemisia. "Well, you've just heard from our legal scholar. He's been practicing law for over three hundred years. Do you wish me to add this additional charge?"

The Reverend then turned his attention back to Bradshaw. "Johnny, I assume that making up penalties is also within my purview?"

"Why of course, Reverend."

"Good. Good. Artemisia, I'm now thinking of a particularly nasty penalty for interfering with the course of justice. Again, how do you plead?"

Artemisia desperately wanted to speak. She was opening and closing her mouth like a fish gasping for air, but all she could manage to do was sweat. Hecuba again whispered into her ear and sounds started forming out of Artemisia's mouth. "Gu…il…ty. Gui…lty. Guilty!"

"Ah yes. I thought you were guilty all along. Please step over there with the others and await your sentencing."

As he said this, Hecuba tried to slink back to where she had been standing. The Reverend had had no need to hear any evidence yet because everyone was pleading guilty. It would just be a matter of minutes before he got to her, but she apparently wanted to prolong her arraignment for as long as possible.

"No. No. Stay right where you are. Hecuba isn't it?"

"Yes sir."

"It's not sir, it's Reverend, but that's okay. No need for formality here, just a plea."

"Guilty, Reverend," Hecuba said with a little girl's voice.

"Of course you are. Never doubted it. Now get along over there with the others."

Hecuba moved off and disappeared within the ranks of her all-guilty and now-defunct organization, which was bunched up in a semicircle one step below the High Altar.

The dead monarchs were seated just above them. There were twelve of them. Butterfield had counted. He was hoping very much that what he was experiencing was a complete mental collapse. No doubt brought about by too much anxiety concerning coming up with some decent idea for a tower for this place. The notion that he was going through a massive nervous breakdown was somehow very soothing to him. It certainly helped explain why he was watching ghastly bluish forms of some of Britain's most famous monarchs constantly change their ancient and bizarre costumes. Black satins turned into clothes of gold, which in turn became red brocades, which then became the deepest green velvets. Butterfield laughed audibly as he watched ruff collars come and go, as did farthingales covered with pearls and doublets studded with precious gems. Within a wink of an eye coronation robes of sable or ermine dissolved into the air, only to reappear a moment later in a newer, but still outdated, fashion.

It was apparent to him that this was all part of some sort of delusional fit. The dead faces of Charles II, Elizabeth I, Edward the Confessor, Edward I, Edward III, Richard II, Henry III, Henry V, Henry VII, Mary Queen of Scots, Queen Anne, and James I were staring at him. All, no doubt, symptoms of his craziness, maybe brought on by drinking too much of that absinthe stuff with Maeva. He chuckled again, thinking that this was all due to La Bleue Clandestin, and that he must have killed off a sizeable number of his brain cells with it.

"Wally, please, you are interfering with this trial. Your laughter is distracting the jury," Reverend Poda-Pirudi admonished.

Butterfield nodded his compliance with a bold grin on his face. However, Butterfield's ghost wasn't taking things so lightly. For the first time in the ghost's and Butterfield's relationship, it was his ghost, and not Butterfield who was in absolute terror.

Wallace was stuck in his high-back chair, held there by Darwin and Newton. He couldn't turn left. He couldn't turn right. He couldn't see what was behind him. But Butterfield's ghost could. Since their arrival at the Abbey, he had grown a little taller and needed merely to twist his head around to see well over the back of the chair.

In complete disbelief, Butterfield's ghost stared at the pews behind him. Except for the members of the court, everyone who had ever been buried at the abbey was seated there. Sir Lawrence Olivier's ghost was seated in the front row. Next to him was the Unknown Warrior's ghost. Next to him was the ghost of Father Benedictus. And so it went, one illustrious ghost after another: Ben Jonson's, David Livingstone's, Neville Chamberlain's, William Pitt the Younger's, Geoffrey Chaucer's, George Frideric Handel's, and so on, over three thousand of them... except for a one living person. Seated in the front row, next to the ghost of Tom Parr, was a teenage girl.

It was a congregation of the dead, and they were moving through the costumes of their once-living hosts in full luciferase bioluminescence, winking off and on like giant florescent fireflies. But there was more to this situation than the dead being glow-in-the-dark, quick-change artists. They were angry, very angry, with Butterfield's ghost.

"Will the prisoner who calls himself, Mega Therion, Count Svareff, Lord Boleskine, Great Prince Chioa Khan, the Great Beast of Revelations, the Baphomet, 666, and I suppose I've missed a few titles, approach the bench?"

The ghost of Aleister Crowley scurried forward. He stood before Reverend Poda-Pirudi furtively clutching his hands while bobbing up and down, as though he was just waiting for the opportunity to get down on his knees.

"I take it you are Mega Therion, Count Svareff, Lord Boleskine, Great Prince Chioa Khan, the Great Beast of Revelations, the Baphomet, 666?"

"Oh no my lord! Those are just some foolish pet names the girls gave me. I'm sure that someone as important as yourself wouldn't know my name."

"You're the ghost of Aleister Crowley," the Reverend Poda-Pirudi butted in as a point of fact.

"Oh, so you do know my name. You do me such an honor. How can I be of service to you Old Soul, Great Phantasm, Spirit of Spirits, Shepherd of Shadows, the Shining One, the Bright One?"

"Well, first of all by keeping quiet long enough so I may ask you a few questions."

Crowley's ghost pursed his lips and made a zip motion across the front of his mouth with a ghostly hand and nodded his compliance.

"Good. How do you plead? Guilty or not guilty?"

"Of what, my lord?"

"Of the attempted murder of Wallace Butterfield over there. Have you been listening to these proceedings?"

"Oh yes. Yes. Yes. But I thought that I was here to bear witness against that vile cult of deranged women." He nodded toward where Hecuba and her associates were standing. "I never dreamed it possible that I would be charged. I'm just another victim, like Mr. Butterfield over there. Those WITCHes summoned me against my will. They intimidated me so with their black magic that, against my better judgment, I divulged the sacred rights of Sekhmet to them. My participation was involuntary and more of an historical discourse. A lecture. I never thought that they would attempt to put any of what I told them into practice."

"I see. So you are entering a plea of not guilty?" The Reverend gave Crowley's ghost a deep penetrating stare. He continued, "Of course the court is far more lenient when it receives an admission of guilt, but if you insist upon your innocence— the punishments that I can devise— I'm very creative, you know?"

"Oh yes! Of course! Master! Forgive me!" Crowley's ghost was on his knees before the bench frantically bowing up and down. "Guilty my lord! Guilty!"

"Guilty are we?"

"Yes. Yes. Most guilty. Repugnantly guilty. Reprehensibly guilty."

"Very good. I shall find you to be simply guilty. Now step over there with— I believe you called the ladies a 'vile cult of deranged women'— go stand over there with them."

As the ghost of Aleister Crowley crossed the sacrarium, Hecuba came forward to meet him.

"The Great Beast of Revelations, my ass! You're nothing more than an old tosser!"

This caused Crowley's ghost's bluishness to pinken. He glided around Hecuba and hid himself at the back of the WITCHes, just as the Reverend brought his gavel down.

"Quiet! I will not have any more disruption in my court. Bradshaw, how many more prisoners to go?"

"Well, Reverend, I'm afraid just one more. So far the fugitive, Maeva has eluded our sweep of the city. So, we only have one left that is available for today's trial."

"Fugitive? Maeva? Johnny, I don't recall Ms. Wolusky having taken an active role in the attempted immolation of our dear Mr.Butterfield? I fear, Johnny, that you are once again being overzealous in the apprehension of your duties. You are no longer serving that tyrant, the alleged Lord Protector, Oliver Cromwell! Excuse me, excuse me— sorry. I do warm to that subject. As you know, you serve me, the gentle and eminently fair Reverend Poda-Pirudi. So, you may call of your dogs. No need to have her here."

"Yes, Reverend. Of course. I'll attend to that immediately." Johnathan Bradshaw then motioned a constable from Division L to approach him, and then whispered something in his ear.

"Good. Now that that's settled, who remains to receive their just punishment to what ever maximum severity the law will allow?"

"Why that would be a Mr.Wallace Butterfield."

"Oh yes…I see him on my list here. Wallace Butterfield, approach the bench!"

"Me?" Butterfield said incredulously.

"Why, yes, Wally. You."

"But I've done nothing. They tried to torch me!"

"I'm more than happy to hear the facts but you must approach the bench. A plea must be entered. Now come here. Up. Up."

Butterfield didn't want to move. He tightened his grip upon the arms of his chair, but the ghosts of Sir Isaac Newton and Charles Darwin broke his hold effortlessly. Hauling him to his feet, they dragged him unceremoniously across the Cosmati Pavement and up to the High Altar.

Reverend Poda-Pirudi looked down upon Wallace from his judicial perch.

"Well, how do you plead?"

"Plead? Plead to what?"

"Wally, do keep quiet. This is serious business. How do you plead?"

"What am I supposed to have done?" Butterfield was losing his conviction that this was all just a stress-induced figment of his imagination.

"If you must know, the charge is attempted murder."

"Murder of whom?"

"Why of you my dear boy."

"There must be some mistake. They— those women and that blue thing tried to murder me. I certainly wasn't trying to commit suicide by having them dose me with petrol."

"Wallace, this really doesn't require your testimony. Please be silent. This is serious business. Johnny, what is he doing?"

"Apparently blinking my lord."

The Reverend Poda-Pirudi stared into Wallace Butterfield's eyes. "Odd. But of course, he hasn't been born yet. Can't talk, can he? Just blinking hey? That's not much of a response. Not good enough you know? You see, I don't speak blink. Bradshaw, what does it mean when the prisoner is silent?"

"He stands mute, Reverend"

"I can see that."

"No my lord, if a prisoner refuses to enter a plea it is automatically assumed that he is pleading not guilty."

"Wonderful! So we are going to actually hear some evidence. I'm so excited. You may return the prisoner to his chair."

Reverend Poda-Pirudi motioned to Newton and Darwin's ghosts, who dutifully dragged the unruly Butterfield back across the marble floor. As they did so, Wallace Butterfield caught sight of the assembly of ghosts that were seated just behind him. Abruptly, he stopped protesting his innocence and began to scream again. As Newton and Darwin forced him back into his chair, they each placed a hand over his mouth.

"Oh this is so delicious. We are going to have a trial. Johnny, will you please present the case?"

"Why yes Reverend. What we have here is a conspiracy between the organization known as Women In Therapeutic Chemical Healing, the ghost of one Aleister Crowley, and the unborn ghost of the victim, Wallace Butterfield. The object of this conspiracy was to burn alive the aforementioned Butterfield at the site of Cleopatra's Needle. The motivation being the release of Mr. Butterfield's spirit, so that it could be interrogated by the now self-confessed malefactor Aleister Crowley incorporeal. Oh yes, there was some hocus pocus concerning the sacrifice of Mr. Butterfield to some ancient mythological deity. The prosecution is now willing to present a witness to this conspiracy. Miss Emma Ludshorp, a member of this coven and a polite and upright teenage girl."

"Those are outstanding credentials for a witness Johnny, do continue."

John Bradshaw bowed as a gesture to Emma who smiled back nervously.

"To conclude, your lordship, Miss Emma Ludshorp was in a hallway, at the abandoned restaurant, Tipsy Dolls, in Mayfair and overheard all of these foul plans. With your lordship's forbearance, the prosecution will now call Miss Emma Ludshorp forward to take the stand and give evidence as to the entire nefarious conspiracy, whereby

Mr. Butterfield's unborn ghost first suggested the murder of his host to the assemble miscreants gathered there. As you know, since you were involved in their arrest by our local constabulary, they all came very close to murdering Mr. Butterfield. I would also put forward that these deeds go beyond attempted murder, and that an additional charge of treason should also be entertained by your lordship."

"Treason, Johnny?"

"Yes Reverend. Petty treason. As delineated in Parliament's Treason Act of 1351: No one shall attempt to murder or actually murder his or her superior. It is primarily meant to curb wives' acting unkindly towards their husbands, but I think it would be good common law to extend it to ghosts against hosts."

"Really? I was unaware of this. I haven't been paying much attention to the newer laws— still boning up on Hammurabi's Code, don't you know. Well, if you say so Johnny. I'm willing to add this extra charge. But I don't see any need to call the inestimable Miss Ludshorp to the witness stand. For one we don't have one, a witness stand, that is. I suppose we could use the pulpit over there, but I really see no need. I'm sure that the jury doesn't need to be inconvenienced by too much testimony. As I recall, when you were the presiding judge during King Charles's trial, you missed the first three days of testimony. You didn't need to be filled in on all that extraneous evidence did you?"

"Ah, no my lord."

"Well, why should this court?"

"No reason, my lord."

"Thought not. I guess the only thing we should consider is that Mr. Butterfield's ghost gets some good legal counsel. Have we someone from our public defender service available?"

"Why, yes, my lord. The spirit of Mr. Charles John Huffam Dickens is willing to take his case on."

"Oh, this is very satisfactory. What sort of legal training does he have?"

"It is my understanding that, back in the day, Dickens and Inspector Charles Frederick Field chummed around a lot. In fact, Mr. Dickens wrote several articles about him and even used him as a model for the character of Inspector Bucket in his novel— I've forgotten which one your lordship."

"It was 'Bleak House,' Johnny."

"Right, 'Bleak House.'"

"So he knows our chief investigator. Acquaintance with someone in law enforcement is as good as any apprenticeship one can get at the Inns of Court. He'll do fine. Are you done presenting your case?"

"I am, my lord."

"Well then, Mr. Dickens' ghost front and center."

An elegant specter, well-tailored in a lint-free black frockcoat that refused to cycle into the numerous pieces of apparel that he had worn during his host's life, stepped forward. He did not glide, but walked up to Butterfield's chair, punctuating each one of his steps with an ivory-topped bog oak cane. There was a sense of purpose communicated in his gait, a deep profundity to his every step.

The ghost of Charles Dickens was apparently still embarrassed by his thinning hair and wore a comb over, with the remaining hair on either side of his head brushed forward, to form a coiffeur resembling wavy blue wings. The mustache of his youth was gone. Dickens' ghost chose to present himself in his later days, sporting a long wiry goatee.

As he approached Butterfield, the ghosts of Sir Isaac and Charles Darwin both let go of their grip on Wallace's mouth.

"This is unfair! This is madness! Let go of me! Get me out of here!"

Dickens' ghost shot an angry look at both Newton and Darwin. They immediately recovered Butterfield's mouth.

Wallace choked and sputtered under their ghostly stifling as Dickens proceeded to lecture him.

"You have been advised that this matter does not need your participation. I am here to represent my client, who so happens to be your spirit. I will not allow you, through these perturbations, to hamper the defendant's case. It is impossible for me to have you removed from this court, but I shall do everything in my power to keep these disruptions of yours contained. Be silent, sir."

If Butterfield's ghost could have shaken Dickens' hand he would have, if for nothing else than for telling Butterfield to shut up.

Charles Dickens' ghost turned and faced the bench. "My lord, the defense would like to call its first witness."

Reverend Poda-Pirudi, who was engaged lighting up one of his cigars, paused for a moment and then nodded his ascent.

"The defense calls the ghost of Inspector Charles Frederick Field to the witness stand."

Strobe-like flashes of blue preceded the materialization of the celebrated Victorian detective. He stood before the bench and looked about quizzically.

"Oh, I'm sorry," Reverend Poda-Pirudi apologized. "It was silly of me. I didn't anticipate that we were going to have a need for a witness stand and failed to provide one," the Reverend said as he glanced at Charles Dickens' ghost. "Inspector, do you mind standing while you give your testimony? I'm sure you won't be needed too long."

"Oh no, me lord. Being dead I don't have any pressing plans."

The Reverend chuckled. "Good. Good. But I promise we won't detain you long. Will we, Mr. Dickens?"

"Oh no, your lordship, perish the thought. I'll be very brief. Let me start. Inspector Field, you were present with the other members of the constabulary's Division L of the Woolwich Dockyard at Cleopatra's Needle when this crime allegedly took place?"

"Why, of course, Charlie. Why do you think I'm here?"

"Well, could you tell us if, during this time, you made any observations that would lead you to believe that my client was an active participant in this crime?"

"That would have been hard to. He was all buggered up in tape."

"So, there was no evidence at the time to show any complicity?"

"Complicity? "

"I mean, is there any reason for you to have formulated an opinion that the defendant is guilty of the crimes that he's been charged with?"

"Why no, none; that is, beyond the fact that he is guilty."

The Reverend cleared his throat and again glanced hard and long at Dickens.

Dickens understood well enough the implied threat behind the throat clearing. "My lord." He hastened. "I think we have had all of the testimony that we need upon this matter and the defense now rests."

"Very good, Mr. Dickens. Inspector Field you are excused and again my apologies for the inconvenience. It is time for the jury to consider a verdict."

He turned to the assemblage of monarchs whom he had appointed as jurors. "Do we need any time to consider the facts?"

The ghost of Queen Elizabeth I stood. "My lord, Reverend, I believe we are all sufficiently acquainted with the qualities of this case and can speak honestly to the charge. The defendant is most guilty."

"Aye!" thundered the other jurors.

"Then guilty he is," declared Reverend Poda-Pirudi.

With this pronouncement, Butterfield began to wriggle out of the grip of Newton and Darwin, but was once again subdued.

"Apparently," the Reverend announced, "I've got a lot of sentencing to do. Let's start with those fortunates who pleaded guilty. All of the members of WITCH who are in our custody, approach the bench."

Under the guidance of the boys from Division L, the coven was herded in front of the Reverend.

The Reverend summoned up his deepest and most magisterial voice. "For the living to go about tampering with the affairs of the dead is a very serious matter. The two species are distinct and must remain so. To have it otherwise would disrupt the patterns of nature and disturb the forces of being. My word, next you'd want to marry. Won't do, you know. However, that being said, I do feel that there is some mitigation caused by your peculiar state. You are not quite normal— sort of an unpleasant admixture of the living and the dead. So to this end, I've decided to be lenient with you— that is, all of you but for Hecuba."

Hecuba groaned.

"For all of you, except Hecuba, I sentence you to five years as laborers in the village of Val-de-Travers in Switzerland. You may know that that was where absinthe was first distilled. Several sympathetic wormwood growers have consented to take you in. My advice to you is that you seize upon this opportunity to reform yourselves from those nasty occult habits that you've taken on. Work hard and stay drunk."

There were several exclamations of joy and thanks, as the constables of Division L led out the crowd of women to an awaiting double decker bus.

"Ah yes... Hecuba get over here."

Hecuba ran to the bench and stood before the Reverend visibly shaken.

"You madam are evil. Evil, pure and simple. But still I feel that to be too hard on you would be like beating a blind man because he can't see. Perhaps it's a sign of the times, but I've again chosen to be merciful. Hecuba, you are sentenced to transportation to our prison colony in the Commonwealth of Massachusetts. There you shall remain for the rest of your life within the confines of the Township of Salem. I think I shall place you there around 1692. Perhaps Sir Isaac might give you some advice on your travel plans. It's his century, you know."

Hecuba shrieked, "That's a death sentence! Reverend, please, not during the Salem witch hysteria. Have mercy!"

"Oh well, okay. I always like to see those that I convict leave happy. How about we say contemporary Salem, Massachusetts? That way you'll become a tourist attraction and a boon to the local economy. I'd suggest you make a go of it reading palms, selling travel bags, mugs, T-shirts, and herbal teas, that sort of thing. But listen, if you ever attempt to leave the town you will find yourself back in 1692. Do we have an understanding?"

"Oh yes, Reverend. Never will you have a problem with Hecuba again."

"Of that I'm sure. One of the constables will see you to Heathrow Airport. I've got you all booked, economy class, of course. Now off with you."

Hecuba was led away from the bench.

"Oh we have just a few more to go. Mr. Crowley's ghost would you mind approaching the bench?"

The blue specter of the Aleister Crowley crawled across the Cosmati Pavement on his hands and knees. Once he was in front of the table on the high altar, Crowley's ghost placed his head upon the stone floor. Sobbing, he beseeched the Reverend for forgiveness.

"Oh master, this poor erring spirit begs you for mercy. I did not know that you had any interest in this matter. If I had, I would have stayed far, far away from those accursed WITCHes. Oh, please let me redeem myself in your eyes. I promise you that I shall devote the eternity of my existence to your instruction and command."

"Indeed you will," interrupted the Reverend. "Mr. Crowley, you don't mind that I'm not using your many titles, do you?"

"Oh no. Oh no, Great Phantasm, Spirit of Spirits, Shepherd of Shadows."

"Honestly, Reverend will do. But let's move along, shall we? Mr. Crowley, have you ever stayed at the Hotel Cecil?"

"Why, why, yes Reverend. Capital place you know. One of the best grand hotels I ever stayed in. Over eight hundred rooms, you know. I used to live there. Of course, it's all gone now."

"I can imagine it. Highly ornate, very posh, no doubt catered to every one of your needs. And I'm sure somebody like you had varied and highly unique needs."

"Yes. Quite. Wonderful place. Why do you ask?"

"Mr. Crowley, where are you from?"

"Well, I was born in the Royal Leamington Spa in Warwickshire."

"No. No. That's not what I meant. I want to know where you were buried."

"Oh, I was cremated and my ashes were scattered under a tree in Hampton, New Jersey."

"Excellent! Well here's your sentence. You will return to that tree. There you shall secrete your soul in the root of your choice and remain there for the eternity of your existence. If you move even a centimeter from it, you'll find that the time spent within that root was like your stay at the Cecil, that is, when you compare it with what I will have in store for you. Do you understand me?"

Crowley's ghost nodded his head up and down in terror.

"Good. You now have less than a half a second to get there."

Poof! Aleister Crowley's ghost disappeared in a cloud of blue smoke.

"Does anyone find that the air is appreciably better around here?" The entire congregation of ghosts shouted their agreement. "Good. That's taken care of. Moving on, bring the ghost of Mr. Wallace Butterfield to me."

The ghosts of Sir Isaac and Charles Darwin once again snatched Wallace from his seat and dragged him before the Reverend.

"Why is he still blinking at me? I've told you that this court does not recognize blink. You had your chance to confess to your crime a while back. It is too late now."

The Reverend reached down and lifted up the black cap of sentencing the condemned. As he placed it upon his head, Butterfield began to protest.

"This isn't fair! How can you punish my ghost and not harm me?"

Placing a finger over his lips, the Reverend shushed him and proceeded with the sentencing.

"Unborn ghost of Wallace Butterfield, you have been found guilty of attempted murder and treason against your host, a creature that has nurtured and sheltered you during your development. During my 27,711 years of existence I have never seen a case wherein a spirit has attempted to destroy the womb from which it will spring. There can be but one sentence for such a heinous deed and that is death. It is a sentence I do not impose lightly. I have never required that a ghost give up its existence before, but I do so require it now. Ghost of Wallace Butterfield you are to be immediately executed, here and on that spot."

The Reverend pointed to the central roundel of the Cosmati Pavement, which was just in front of the ornately carved chair that Wallace had been seated in during the trial. To Butterfield's horror, a ghostly headsman was now standing there with an axe in his hands and wooden block at his feet.

"Well now, it's the ghost of Jack Ketch, isn't it?" exclaimed Reverend Poda-Pirudi. "I haven't seen you in a dog's age. What have you been up to?"

"Oh not much my lord, Reverend, just the Mrs. and me, if you pardon the pun, just hanging about Saint James's Burying Ground. That's in Clerkenwell, you know?"

The Reverend smiled broadly; he loved listening to the puns of the ghost of Jack Ketch.

"No, I didn't know. Well, how wonderful for the two of you. You had such a busy life with all of those executions, Lord Russell, the Duke of Monmouth and all those others. Quite a strain I imagine, hanging people up by their necks, then chopping off heads and limbs, all that disemboweling, and, I imagine, frying up the livers of screaming victims— I mean prisoners, It must have gotten on your nerves a bit?"

"Yes Reverend it did. I know most people hold it against me and my host, old Jack Ketch, that it took us several attempts to lop off the head of Lord Russell. We did send out a printed apology about botching the job. Still people felt poorly about the whole thing. It didn't help any that we had a couple of bad swings trying to take off the Duke of Monmouth's head. We used a butcher's knife to finish that job. And the Duke being so kind as to provide a handsome tip for a good beheading beforehand. He said to us, 'Here are six guineas for you. Do not hack me as you did my Lord Russell. I have heard that you struck him three or four times. My servant will give you some more gold if you do the work well.' And it takes me host more than five chops and a slice with a knife to do him in. Embarrassing it was."

"I dare say. Your job was over after that as I recall."

"Aye! Off to prison it was and they gave our job to the assistant executioner. But he was caught embezzling, so they needed him to be hanged up at Tyburn. So, all was forgiven then. And me and me host got the chance— again, pardon the pun, Reverend— to teach that miserable upstart the ropes."

The Reverend snickered. "Oh quite. Well I can see how all of that could lead to a lot of stress. I'm so glad that you are taking it easy these days. But I've called you out of retirement— well, pardon my pun, Mr. Ketch— to get Butterfield here to give up the ghost. I must warn you that Wally is a particularly good friend of mine. I want a clean chop right through the vertebrae. Well, two or three at the most."

"Oh, I wished you hadn't said that, Reverend. I'll do my best… just feeling a bit out of practice. It's been over three hundred years since the last beheading."

"Of course. Can't expect too much under these circumstances. Do your best that's all."

Between screams, Wallace Butterfield had picked up most of this conversation. Oddly enough, his ghost was screaming in concert with him. Nobody buried in the Abbey had ever heard an unborn ghost make any sound before.

"Mercy, Reverend. Please have mercy, Reverend," Butterfield sobbed as the ghosts of Sir Isaac and Charles Darwin dragged him to the block and positioned his head on the chopping block.

"Come, come, Wally you are sounding like Aleister Crowley's ghost. Buck up and this will all be over soon enough. Mr. Ketch would you position yourself and take a couple of practice strokes."

"Right you are, Reverend. Now Mr. Butterfield, if all goes well I'll have your head off on the count of three."

"One!" The axe came down gently but was a bit off course and just kissed the side of Wallace's neck.

"Two!" The axe came down squarely and lightly tapped the nape of Butterfield's neck.

"Oh, I think I got the swing of things. Sorry, me and me puns. Here we go— THREE!"

The cacophony created by the screaming of both Butterfield and his ghost was deafening. And then there was an abrupt popping noise, like a champagne cork taking flight. Butterfield's ghost shot out of Wallace's body and headed upward toward the vaulted ceiling of the Abbey.

"Get him!" cried the Reverend as he pointed out the flight of Butterfield's ghost.

The entire congregation lifted off their seats and into the air. The assembly of over three thousand spirits began the chase. Through the South Transept, Poet's Corner, and Henry VII's Chapel they pursued him, while he screamed the entire time.

As Butterfield's ghost rounded a corner and fled back into the South Transept, John Bradshaw's ghost handed Reverend Poda-Pirudi a purple egg-shaped bottle embossed with the words, "W. O. Smith Chemist, Titchfield."

"Why thank you Johnny… oh I remember this one… a poison bottle from an old bottle dump in Devon. Right?"

"Why yes, Reverend. Right as always."

"Of course, it's coming to me— Mary Ann Cotton's arsenic bottle! She poisoned all four of her husbands with this and cleaned up on the insurance money. That is, till they hanged her. Is the ghost of Mary Ann Cotton about? No, she wouldn't be. Now what did I do with her? Oh well, I'll figure that out later."

Reverend Poda-Pirudi uncorked the bottle. Holding it above his head with his left hand, he placed two fingers in his mouth and whistled.

It was as if thousands of border collies had responded to his command and began to herd what was the equivalent of one sheep toward its enclosure. Butterfield's ghost couldn't move, but forward. In a panic, his ghost flew straight down and into the Reverend's purple poison bottle, which the Reverend secured with a cork.

"Well done! Thank you all!" the Reverend exclaimed. "Now how's poor Wally doing?"

The ghost of the sainted king, Edward the Confessor, had evidently been tending to Wallace during all of this commotion and had managed to get him back into the chair that he had been sitting in during the course of the trial.

"I beg pardon. It is an ill-fitting throne but still it has served this country well for almost eight hundred years." King Edward's ghost said as he knelt before Wallace Butterfield. And with this, the entire congregation also went to their knees.

Half dazed, Wallace Butterfield looked about Westminster Abbey. The interior had become resplendent with strange and beautiful flags, pennants and bunting. A hymn started in the back pews and was carried forward. Everyone began singing, "Oh Protect and Guide Us Old Soul."

Reverend Poda-Pirudi walked up to Butterfield, mopping some sweat from his forehead with a handkerchief. He plopped himself onto the Cosmati Pavement, taking a seat on the floor right next to where Butterfield was sitting.

"Wally, I know this has been an awful ordeal for you, but it had to be done this way. I tell you that I've never appreciated a midwife's skills as much as I do now."

A long line now formed before King Edward's coronation chair. One by one, dead monarchs, dignitaries, and notables approached the throne and made their bow or courtesy to Butterfield. And he was no longer afraid of them. Somehow, this all seemed to be natural and not in the least frighteningly supernatural.

Three thousand three hundred and twenty-nine disembodied spirits presented themselves to him. Butterfield didn't know how he knew what the exact number was, but somehow he did.

"Your flock," the Reverend explained, as though he had picked up on Wallace's thought. You'll always know their number. Here and everywhere else in the world. But we shall talk about that later. However, I would like to formally present to you Sir Isaac Newton and Mr. Charles Darwin. I know that you've recently had their acquaintance, and can imagine that they left you with rather a negative impression of their characters." The Reverend scowled at them and added, "That can happen."

Charles Darwin moved respectfully forward and started to address Butterfield. "I hope that you understand…", but then was cut off in midsentence by an emphatic Sir Isaac Newton.

"We wanted thee to know that we meant no offense in our maltreatment of thy person. And, as I've oft heard expressed in these newer times, 'We were only following orders.'"

"That will be quite enough Sir Isaac," The Reverend pointed at him, indicating that he was too close to the coronation chair. "Only if the two of you did follow orders. You know, I was considering rewarding you, for the thorough way you carried out your orders, with a two-month stay haunting the Swine Manure Nutrient Recovery Plant in Bugscuffle, Tennesse. Pretty hot there this time of year. But upon further reflection I decided not to mar this joyous occasion by disciplining you. Therefore, I will grant you clemency. Now, I'd suggest that the two of you be off to your crypts."

Newton and Darwin were not going to tempt the Reverend a second time, though they both wanted to hang about and enjoy the festivities with the rest of the spirits, they decided that it was better to immediately comply with the Reverend's wishes and disappear into the safety of their crypts.

At the end of the line of disembodied spirits who had come to pay their respects to Butterfield came an elderly ghost with a staff in one hand. In the other he held the hand of someone who wasn't dead at all but very much alive.

"Wally, this is Old Tom Parr and the young lady is very special to me… to the two of us I think. If it hadn't been for her I'm not sure what would have happened. Things could have gotten quite muddled I suspect. Don't know. Anyhow, it is my privilege to introduce to you Miss Emma Ludshorp."

"Oh… the witness," Butterfield muttered a bit incoherently.

"Please to meet you sir… Old Soul… I mean," Emma said as she curtseyed.

He gave her a weak smile as his attention drifted down to her feet.

"Nice shoes."

"Aren't they? They are actually slippers. Ruby slippers."

"Yes," the Reverend interjected. "I thought, considering all she's done and the fact that I couldn't let her walk about upon these cold stone floors barefoot, that she deserved a pair. After all Miss Ludshorp has done far more service for the community than merely dropping a house upon a solitary witch. I hope you enjoy them Emma."

"Oh I will Reverend", she exclaimed with delight as she clicked her heels and vanished before Old Tom Parr could follow after her.

"Well that's the end of the line Wally. More than enough ceremony for one day eh?"

"No. No. Wait… Reverend. You promised," Bradshaw's ghost exclaimed as he rushed over to the north transept door and opened it.

A tall woman, with an impressive braid of silver hair, tentatively edged her way through the proffered opening.

John Bradshaw's ghost grabbed her hands and pulled her through.

The woman was anxious, confused, and understandably reluctant to enter a dimly lit specter-filled church. She dug in her heels, literally, but eventually succumbed to the ghost's fawning protestations and insistence that she allow him to convey her to where Butterfield and the Reverend were holding court.

"Here she is Reverend," the ghost of Bradshaw said with great pride, "Ms. Zoraida Fernsby!"

"Oh yes Ms. Fernsby. Pleasure to meet you. I almost feel as though I know you. Johnny has been positively gushing to me about your artwork for years. What a stroke of luck that the ill-advised actions of WITCH have provided him with the perfect social setting to make your acquaintance."

"Reverend, may I remind you that she had nothing to do with those ill-advised actions."

"Yes. Yes. Of course Johnny. Calm yourself. I'm quite aware of Ms. Fernsby's heroic stand against the misguided Hecuba."

"Ms. Fernsby," the Reverend continued dotingly, "I'm so pleased that you could join us today. As I was saying, Johnny is a great fan of your paintings. Garbage isn't it?"

Zoraida was beginning to sort out some of the events going on around her. Being a WITCH, she knew a lot about ghosts. Their presence in the Abbey didn't surprise her much. But the Reverend was something else. He was obviously pretty powerful. All the ghosts were bowing and scraping around him. The ghosts were also being very deferential to the wrung-out young man seated near him on a throne. Zoraida speculated that he was that Wallace Butterfield person that Maeva had been talking to her so much about on the telephone. His being exalted and seemingly worshiped somehow put her at ease, made her feel that she couldn't be in any danger if they were going to treat a mortal like that. So, Zoraida relaxed and warmed to the Reverend's welcoming attention.

"Yes. I do paint garbage."

"Well, that makes sense. I mean, that's why Johnny here is so smitten with your work. He spends most of his free time at the Mucking Marshes Landfill. I believe he's caught a glimpse or two of you out there with your paintbrush and easel. Strange thing that— he detests being encased in garbage, but over the centuries he's developed a certain aesthetic appreciation for refuse. I've heard him wax poetic about one of your landscapes… I think it depicted a steaming transfer station at sundown?"

"Oh I did paint that. I do think I did a good job of capturing the moment."

"As did our Mr. Bradshaw. Bet you didn't know he was spying on you? Mind you he's no perv— just a regicide."

"No I didn't know that he was about but I'm normally pretty toasted on absinthe when I do my best work."

"Of course, not that I'm trying to play matchmaker here, but I promised Johnny a vacation after this whole Butterfield thing had come to an end. He had this idea that you might like to take a couple of art lessons from some Polish chap."

Bradshaw's ghost chimed in, "Reverend, that would be Zdzislaw Beksinski."

"Yes, of course, the ghost of Mr. Zdzislaw Beksinski. And I do believe he's willing to take you on as a pupil Ms. Fernsby. However, there is a wrinkle. He is a bit of a shy fellow— reclusive. But aren't all ghosts. I'm afraid the only way you can study with him is by going to see him. As I recall he resides in Poland."

"The Sanok Cemetery in Podkapacle is his place of residence," the Ghost of John Bradshaw added.

"Thank you Johnny… I guess the question is Ms. Fernsby, are you willing to take the trip on us— with Mr. Bradshaw here— to Poland? If you find the idea of traveling alone with him to be inappropriate, I could arrange for a chaperon. The ghost of Amelia Bloomer perhaps? I assure you that she's more than a match for Johnny."

"Oh, I'm sure that won't be necessary. Mr. Bradshaw seems to be quite the gentleman."

"Well Ms. Fernsby don't let his clothing fool you. A laced collar alone is no sign of character. But I take your response as a yes. Delightful! Johnny will conduct you to your plane. Remember, all expenses are on us and you'll find a gift of a complete trousseau in your new Louis Vuitton luggage."

Zoraida smiled appreciatively as the ghost of John Bradshaw rushed up to the Reverend and for the first time in their acquaintance grasped his hand.

"Oh… steady on Johnny. It's just a holiday. The Marshes still are waiting for you. But enjoy yourself for the time being. Who knows, perhaps you'll learn to paint happy little trees, happy little clouds, happy little mausoleums— that sort of thing?"

As Zoraida Fernsby and the ghost of John Bradshaw disappeared out the north transept door, the Reverend turned his attention back to Butterfield. "You know, I think it's time for us to take a vacation too and I know just the place. Stand up me boy, I'll have us there in just a matter of seconds."

The Reverend and King Edward's ghost helped Wallace to his feet. Then the Reverend held up his lantern. As he did so, the Cosmati Pavement began to glow and move as though it was a carousel.

"It's liminal space. Think of it as sort of twilight between what is and what isn't. This is a threshold into it and out of it. It's kind of a place where the boundaries of math and science— reality itself— dissolve and reconstitute into a myriad of different forms."

Reverend Poda-Pirudi began to circle Butterfield, still holding up his lantern, the pavement moved more and more rapidly beneath their feet.

"I had this one built years ago. I've made many others since then and placed them all about the world. But, I must tell you this one is pretty powerful. Well, we should be off."

He opened the door to his lantern. Again, a bright light shot forth.

Chapter Nineteen

The Holiday

It was so odd. He was a good kilometer up in the air and was falling through a fluffy cloud, but wasn't scared. Wallace Butterfield was not tense or apprehensive. As Butterfield exited the cloud, he saw a large archipelago below. Around it, the sea turned from a deep sapphire blue to a bright green. Squealing with delight, he clasped his knees to his chest and spun wildly. Wallace crashed into the sea, sending up a huge geyser of water in his wake. Dropping like an anchor, Butterfield continued to descend till he hit bottom. As he did so, hundreds of blue ribbon eels with brilliant yellow dorsal fins popped their heads out their holes and stared at Butterfield in amazement. He was grabbing at his throat, tearing at his collar as saltwater came rushing into his lungs. Wallace Butterfield had heard how people who were drowning didn't experience pain. Certainly, this appeared to be the case. Strangely, it was somehow exhilarating. He had heard about that too.

The ribbon eels' heads swiveled from side to side as they tracked Butterfield's movements. He contorted and convulsed and paddled in circles about the sea floor. But he was not dying. The ribbon eels knew that. And after a while, so did Wallace.

At some point it began to dawn on him that, though he was breathing in water, he was not choking and certainly wasn't in the throes of death. He really hadn't panicked. It was more like aquatic theater. Butterfield had felt an obligation to be in terror for his life, since he was at the bottom of the ocean. But upon reflection, he realized that being at the bottom of the ocean and breathing in water was just one of these new states that he had been experiencing— like falling out of the sky. Things like this had been happening to him whenever the Reverend opened his lantern door. Butterfield began to relax, and as he did so he discovered that breathing in water now seemed as natural to him as laughter was to a baby. And indeed Butterfield was laughing,— hysterically.

Being here was a delight. Exotic fish were everywhere; schools of silver trevally and blue and yellow fusilier rushed by him, giant manta rays lumbered about, parrotfish, lionfish, damselfish, regal angelfish, surgeon fishes were everywhere amongst the eccentrically twisted corals and sea fans. All were pulsating with a richness of color that he had never beheld in anything. Thousands of shades of reds, oranges, yellows, greens, blues, and violets shimmered all about him, but they seemed drab compared to the new colors he was seeing. The colors embraced the far ends of the electromagnetic spectrum. He saw infrareds, ultra violet, polarized light, even left and right circular and elliptical polarized light. Along with his vision, his sense of smell was heightened. Butterfield could detect the individual components that made up the salt water he was swimming in. He knew the identities of the fresh water streams and tributaries that had intermingled with it. And, as he breathed water in and out of his lungs, he could tell which currents had conveyed the ocean here. He could name them too, as well as the deep-sea vent that had added a hint of sulfur to the mix. His hearing was intensified too. Wallace Butterfield could hear anything he chose to, from the seismic movement of the Solomon Sea plate deep below him to the sound waves that were being pushed ahead of the local sharks that were cruising along the chasm.

Sharks were plentiful. Black-tipped sharks and grey whales were patrolling the corals looking for their dinner. They were intrigued with Butterfield and made runs at him, veering off to go around him at the last minute. He could feel their fins brush by him. To Butterfield's surprise it was a pleasant sensation, very friendly, very comforting.

There were other creatures here as well, but not of the present time. Long-dead fishes and saltwater crocodiles and prehistoric animals like mosasaurs, a behemoth cross between a fish and a crocodile. They were stacked up on the bottom of the canyon, snoozing, like the ghosts in their crypts on the floor of the Abbey.

"Wally."

Butterfield heard his name being called.

"Wally would you mind coming up here?"

It was the Reverend. Butterfield could see his reflection dancing and shimmering across the surface of the water.

Pushing his feet off the bottom, Wallace Butterfield began to swim upward with the dexterity and power of a gigantic frog.

As his head popped out of the water, the Reverend exclaimed, "There you are my boy. Having a good swim, are we?"

"Why, yes, I think so. To tell you the truth, I'm feeling ecstatic, not at all like myself."

"Well, of course, you're not. I remember feeling the same way when it all happened to me."

"When what happened?"

"When I became the Old Soul, as you've become— though you aren't very old yet— but that will come with time."

The Reverend was sitting on a small sandy beach. Most of the shore had been taken over by mangrove roots. The interior consisted mostly of coconut palms, and kerosene, queen ebony, and rosewood trees. It was a little island surrounded by much bigger ones, all mountainous. Butterfield could see the volcanic cone of a large summit off in the distance. The Reverend's island was just a bump in a string of islands that formed the outer part of the huge lagoon.

"It's the Marovo Lagoon."

"Yes it is. I don't know why I know this, but I do."

"Oh you would. You'll find that you will know more and more things as the days go on, some incredible things. But let's have lunch shall we? I've had a picnic basket packed for us. And to tell you the truth, I'm famished."

Butterfield noticed the large wicker basket next to the Reverend, who was fondly patting it with his right hand. He had also changed for this outing. He still had on his black shirt with its clerical collar, but, from the waist down, he was dressed in local traditional garb: a warrior's tapa skirt made from pounded tree bark and painted with a pattern of intricate geometric designs in brown and black on a background of light grey.

"Well, we have a small feast here. There's coconut milk, crab, banana, pineapple, and papaya. Oh look, Johnny has packed some char-broiled tuna steaks and this." Reverend Poda-Pirudi held up a six-pack of ale. "It's Nuzu Nuzu Ale. I love the stuff. Made locally you know. It's the best ale brewed on the Solomon Islands. Well, actually it could be the only ale brewed here, but it's good stuff."

He uncapped a bottle and handed it to Butterfield, along with a plate of food. The two of them began to eat in silence. In a short time the picnic basket was nearly empty. Taking his eyes off their feast for a moment, Wallace noticed that the Reverend was leaning against something that appeared to be very old and manmade.

"I don't know what that is, but I know it is very important." Butterfield gestured to a large stone box.

"Oh good. You're picking this up very quickly. I am pleased. It is indeed very important. It's as important as the Abbey. It's been here much longer than the Abbey has been around too. I used to come here when I was about your age. I was quite the lad back then. These islands hadn't been inhabited with people that long, but, still, there were clans across the length of them." The Reverend then pointed his thumb against his own chest and said with mock swagger, "I was a great warrior."

"You? I wouldn't have pictured you as a warrior."

The Reverend laughed. "Of course not. But time can change a man and I've had lots of time. I hate to say this, but back in the old days I was a fierce headhunter, the scourge of these neighboring islands. I had a great war canoe with tens of warriors. We'd paddle out to other islands and take heads and prisoners. I used to come to this place to stack up the heads of my victims near this stone box you've noticed."

Butterfield's face twisted with disgust. "Why would you do that? Taking heads?"

"Well, I was driven by— let us call it an ill-fitting spirit. I had bad dreams all the time. Like you— but I hadn't manage that first-rate technique of yours of pushing it up out of my head. It totally controlled me. Awake or asleep, it was always whispering in my ear to go out and kill. So, taking heads became a passion with me. Maybe like playing with a telegraph key was to you? Or maybe not."

"I'm not following you. I pushed my spirit up out of my head?"

"Yes indeed. Quite a feat that."

"Anyhow, once you've got an impressive collection of heads, what do you do with them? I decided the best thing to do was to put them on display next to this sacred stone box—"

"How did I push my soul out of my head?" Butterfield insisted, feeling a bit put out.

"Sorry. I'm leaving out some details, aren't I? When you were awake, you wouldn't let it take hold of you. But at night, when your defenses were down, it would force its way into your brain. Then, you would simply toss it out. What an amazing display of willpower and such a simple solution to a complex problem. I wished I had figured that one out. As I was going to say, this box contains the skulls of some of my people's greatest chiefs and warriors. Many of them were from other lands that my people inhabited before they came to these islands. They were carried across the land for thousands of miles and transported across the sea for thousands of miles too. My folks believe that this is a very sacred spot. In our legends this is where our souls are collected when we die. From here, at sunset, they are transported across the ocean in a great stone war canoe—"

"Wait a minute," Butterfield interrupted, "is this another place of twilight— you called it— a threshold between what is and what isn't?"

"Precious boy! You are quite right. It is more liminal space. And it's a natural phenomenon that really doesn't require an answer for how it works; that is, till some meddler tries to supply one."

He sighed and added, "No need for cause-and-effect here. Reasoning is no more than the coarse convention of human ape's minds. It is clumsy and idiosyncratic and has more to do with language and style than true understanding. I swear that a woolly bear asleep in its cocoon discerns more about the universe than men can grasp with all their facts strung together in tidy succession."

The Reverend giggled self-effacingly. "I do warm to that subject. But let's not get ahead of ourselves. But Wally, look about. Can you detect anything?"

Butterfield ran his eyes up and down the entirety of the little island. Up in the sky were frigate birds and red-footed boobies. But there were many more spirits of frigate birds and boobies roosting in the ghosts of expired trees. Finally, his eyes came back to the stone box the Reverend was sitting next to. At first it looked just like any other primitive container. But then he noted a faint pattern radiating out of it like fractured light through cut glass. Shapes in the light began to move together. As they merged, translucent images of long dead people in ancient dress suddenly stood before him.

"Great job! I see them too. You've just called them up through time. But that's enough. Let them rest."

Wally did and the ghosts vanished into the heavy tropical air.

"Reverend, what's this all about? I should be shrieking in fear. I can't explain why I'm not. I can't explain any of this, but, strangely, I'm comfortable with everything that has happened. I've been kidnapped, almost burned alive, almost had my head cut off, seen more ghosts than could fill a cemetery. I see, smell, and hear things no one else can. I've been lied to, especially by you. Yet strangely, I'm not perturbed by all of this. In fact I feel rather good."

"First of all Wally, do call me Jae. I've asked you to before."

"Yes, sorry, Jae, but please tell me what's going on?"

"Kiso pa Jae is actually the first name. My full name is Kiso pa Jae Poda-Pirudi. It means shark of Jae and the rest roughly translates into a wild spirit that haunts the reefs and wilderness. But to answer your question, and you may welcome this idea, you are not an architect any more. That is, you won't have to design another le Mareschal's Supermarket in order to make a living. You see, you are rapidly changing, the same way I did. That's why I brought you here. This is where it happened to me."

Butterfield shook his head in utter confusion.

"Give me time Wally. There's a lot to tell. To start with, I've been keeping an eye on you since you were a boy. You are unique. But let me start by filling in some more of my own history. My people moved into these islands a few thousand years after they inhabited Papua New Guinea. I was born in this lagoon shortly after that. As I mentioned, I was a warrior— of some distinction. Back then, it was very much as it is today when it comes to fending for yourself. Of course no one had to go out and get a degree in architecture, but we worked hard tending our gardens and fishing to feed our families. So it was with me. This passage into the lagoon was where I'd frequently come for fish.

It was here, while I was spear fishing underwater that everything in my life changed. I had many silver trevally on my stringer. There were lots of them about, more than I could possibly eat. Still, I felt driven to keep killing them. I wasn't paying attention to much around me, except for that school of trevally. Then, as I stabbed yet another fish, I realized that a large school of scalloped hammerheads had moved into the passage. The sharks were being drawn to the fish blood oozing from my stringer and had been circling above me for some time. Suddenly, one spun down and came straight for me and my stringer. This frightened me out of my wits. I fended him off with the point of my spear, while trying to surface at the same time. This meant that I had to come up for air through the other sharks circling above me. I remember how my lungs were aching, I had already held my breath far too long, but there was no safe place to surface. Then two more came down and joined the other one. It was so terrifying that I panicked and sucked in a mouthful of saltwater.

"I should have died right then, but then I heard this loud popping sound. As soon as this happened, the sharks stopped coming in at me. To my amazement, I found that I was breathing in water, not air, and not dying because of it. And just like you, my senses changed. Oh, by the way, did you see any mantis shrimp when you were down on the bottom of the passage?"

"Mantis shrimp? I don't think so. Actually I don't think I've ever heard of a mantis shrimp. Guess I don't know the names of everything yet."

"Oh, no worries. They look like little lobsters but are spotted and have nasty little pincers. You see, the mantis shrimp have sixteen different types of light sensitive cones in their eyes. Butterflies have five. Humans have three, and dogs, just two, but they make up for the color deficiency in their eyes with their superior brains. Nothing in the world can see the variety of light and color as well as a mantis shrimp; that is, except for you and me of course."

"Dogs have superior brains?"

"Why of course. Nice stable brains. They domesticated man didn't they?"

"No. No. It has to have been the other way around."

"So dogs would have you think. That's how clever they are. Dogs knew that men were out of control and something had to be done. So they befriended them. Dogs taught man how to hunt successfully by working together cooperatively in stalking and circling their prey. They also did some manipulation of the human gene pool. If a hunter was cruel to his dogs, his dog would run off. The man couldn't hunt well and he would starve to death. The most vicious and least accommodating people perished. Believe it or not, that helped cut down on some of the worst aspects of human behavior. You should have seen people before dogs. What a mess. They civilized man. As I said, dogs like to tinker with genetics. They took man on as sort of a pet project. Oh, sorry about that pun. Where is that Jack Ketch? Sorry. As I was saying, dogs very well may have saved man so they could use him as some kind of genetic beauticians."

"Beauticians?"

"Yes. I strongly suspect that men shape and color dogs to dog's specifications. But that's only my theory. Anyhow, not only do you and I have eyes better than a mantis shrimp, we have noses and ears that are far better than a dog's. That's pretty good. If I dropped a cup of sugar into the Thames you'd be able to smell it. But even better, like a mole, you'll smell it in stereo. But I'm getting way off course here. The popping sound was my ghost leaving me."

"You mean like with mine? They just can run off like that?"

"Oh no, only in extraordinary cases like with you and me. And they didn't run off, we threw them out. But I'll get to that. When I came out of the water after that shark attack, it took me thousands of years to figure out what happened. I was seemingly indestructible with incredible powers. You know, I did whatever I wanted and, even though my ghost had left me, was still in the habit of taking heads and women. But this frightened my clan. Eventually, they tried to kill me. When that didn't work, they fled to the mountains. Several hundred years had to pass before some people were brave enough to drift back into the area. And guess what, I was still hanging about this reef. And I was as confused as ever. The only difference was that I was determined to keep on their good side. I really did need the company.

"So, I took it upon myself to guard this passage against any other headhunters who might like to come through here on a raid and take some of my friend's heads. I also made sure that the local sharks got the message not to bite any of the local fishermen. It's strange that the people of this lagoon figured out long before I did that the ghost that had inhabited me was that of a hammerhead. How they did that, I'll never know, but they began to call me Kiso pa Jae Poda-Pirudi, the shark spirit, the spirit that haunts the reef. This relationship worked out for some time, but then the Brotherhood located me."

Wallace interrupted him again. "The Melanesian Brotherhood? And what do you mean that your ghost was a hammerhead?"

"Oh yes, I did mention the Melanesian Brotherhood to you didn't I. Well, you can forget about that and the bit about me attending the University of the South Pacific and Saint Stephen's House in Oxford. I'm afraid that it didn't happen. It's a different brotherhood that you and I belong to. And we don't get terribly worked up over an occasional lie. But more about the Brotherhood in a minute, I'm very much hoping that Bradshaw remembered— ah, he did!"

Reverend Poda-Pirudi reached into the picnic basket and pulled out two lanterns. Then he placed them on the beach next to Butterfield. He rummaged around some more and then pulled out a box of cigars. Smiling with delight, he opened the lid.

"The Brotherhood has promised to always have a supply of these for me no matter what the anti-tobacconist mob has to say." He sighed, and then offered Butterfield a Ignatsio Gaudelupe maduro torpedo No.2 cigar. Butterfield shook his head at the offer.

"Pity. You know they won't kill you?" He chuckled at his joke as he lit up.

"Let's see where was I? Got it. I was telling you about me not knowing about the shark soul. You see, eventually a group of odd-looking chaps with lanterns appeared right here on this beach. They and their clothing were quite uncouth. My, my, did they give me a start. So much so, that I ran off into the bush. However, they managed to first track me down and then calm me down."

"I must say Wally that you are doing a much better job of keeping your nerve about this than I did."

Butterfield looked doubtful.

"No. No. It's true. Anyhow, they proclaimed me as one of them. You see, for some inexplicable reason, on every inhabited planet there is this genetic anomaly. It only happens every so many of tens of thousands of years. Quite peculiar, but a host is born with the wrong soul. In my case my soul was that of a hammerhead. Over time the host rejects it. Expels it the way that we did.

"But the queer thing is that after that, the host doesn't die. I mean dry up like some empty skate egg casing and wash up on this beach. From what they've told me, the body somehow learns to cope with having a foreign soul in it by generating its own soul. Once this happens the host becomes as immortal as any ghost and much more powerful. The Brotherhood said that it is nature's way of taking care of things. Well, actually, it is you and I that are in charge of taking care of things. Oh, by the way, thank you, Wally, for showing up. I was getting quite tired of taking care of things. My boy, I guess you have gathered by now that you are my replacement? The new Old Soul in charge of everything?"

Butterfield had been receiving one successive verbal shock after another during the course of their picnic, but this was too much.

"No I'm not! No way! I'm not going to move into the Abbey and babysit all of those dead spooks! I don't know what has happened to me but I'm going to find a nice island of my own and hide until I've got this all sorted out. For all I know, I could be strapped into a bed in some insane asylum right now being pumped full of Thorazine. It's not going to happen!"

The Reverend listened appreciatively, and when he figured Butterfield had calmed down sufficiently he continued.

"I'm so sorry, but I regret to tell you that it already has happened. Cheer up Wally, you've got control of space and time, and, as far as I know, you can never die."

"Well, why am I so lucky?" Butterfield asked sarcastically.

"Oh, you aren't. You never can die, though I can't imagine what would have become of you if I let Hecuba put a torch to you... talking ash I imagine. Anyhow, the dead are the lucky ones. As I said, you can never die but also you can never sleep and never dream. I'm afraid you will look back at your insomnia as the blissful sleep of your youth. And you are in charge of more than the ghosts in the Abbey. You've got the whole shebang, everything from the tiniest mites in people's noses to great whales, fathoms below the surface of the oceans. All have souls and all souls need a shepherd and that shepherd would be you, Wallace Butterfield. Actually I should say Reverend Wallace Butterfield. I know the task sounds daunting. The people alone are a staggering responsibility. There are close to nine billion human hosts inhabiting the earth right now. Six thousand eight hundred and eleven have been born since we started our little chat and two thousand and ten have just expired. Which means that there are two thousand and ten new ghosts. Keeping spirits in the background isn't always easy either. Ghosts can be such egotists. And of course you are going to have to keep on top of punishing the wicked. What a chore that is."

The Reverend stopped, took a long drag from his cigar, and then continued.

"To tell you the truth, I thought I was going to lose it last century. Over 160 million people died in the wars. And then there was the genocide: Mao Zedong with 78,000,000 people. Joseph Stalin, 20,000,000. Adolph Hitler with 12,000,000. King Leopold the II of Belgium, 8,000,000. Hideki Tojo, 5,000,000. Pol Pot had 1,700,000. Kim Il-sung, 1,600,000.

"It was like they were competing in an International Olympic event for psychotic dictators. Souls were coming at me fast and furious. You know, if scientists were ever able to extend life forever, I believe that mankind would reject the idea as being too limiting. Human beings are really having a lot of fun knocking one another off! Truly, there was a time, back in the twentieth century that I was convinced that the whole world was going to go up in a series of mushroom clouds. I hate to say it, but, if that had happened, I wouldn't have to concern myself with any more murdering hosts. There would be this nice static population of spirits to manage. If I could have whipped them into shape, maybe I could have retired. But it didn't happen."

Groaning, the Reverend reached into his shirt pocket and pulled out a handkerchief. Mopping the sweat off his brow, he continued.

"You must see by now Wally that man's great leaps of mental logic are merely the manifestations of the hormonal secretions of an overly developed gland. I mean the brain."

Butterfields face went blank.

"Frontal lobes expanded too fast while filling up with too much dopamine. It gave man the smarts and the drive to develop a wonderful technical advantage over everything, but not the maturity to use this advantage wisely. Oh, how preachy I'm sounding. But then again, I think a preacher is allowed to preach. Anyhow, I'm sure it will be a while before you can retire. Wally, you are just going to have to hang on until the Cosmati Pavement back at the Abbey falls in sync with time, and the world really does come to an end. I could have done a better job when I made it. It's a bit out of time you know.

"But Wally, by no means do I want to give you the impression that it is all bad. The skin on this planet is literally coated with seemingly limitless life forms. Each has its own identity, its own soul that glimmers with originality. It's a kaleidoscope of shapes and colors, twisting together and disentangling— an array of ever-changing patterns— a cosmic skyrocket exploding in a flash of organic geometry. It's as though creation's numeric tumblers fall into place. As they align, the fresh mathematical relationship creates a new kind of state. But then the tumblers shift again, realign, and there is a new form of reality and the most elemental properties of matter shift into position. Precious things come and go in a succession of cognitive awareness. All states seem to be possible within this kaleidoscope, both living and dead. Wally, it's wonderful!

"Oh, I'm sorry. It almost slipped my mind." Reverend Poda-Pirudi rose to his feet and reached into his shirt pocket and pulled out the purple poison bottle embossed with W. O. Smith Chemist, Titchfield.

"Speaking of souls, it's time to release this one." The Reverend tossed the bottle into Jae Passage.

Butterfield jumped to his feet. "Hey that's my soul!"

"No, Wally, it was never your soul. Don't worry, the cork will eventually rot away and then your ex-ghost will get loose and swim amongst the plankton till it eventually grows inside a host and becomes the creature it was meant to be."

This idea intrigued Butterfield. "Was it meant to be in a hammerhead like yours?"

"Ah no. Not quite."

"What then?"

"I'm afraid that your soul was meant for a mud crab. They're very cannibalistic. Love to eat one another, especially when molting. Explains a lot doesn't it?"

Butterfield was a bit crestfallen. He had hoped that he had been sharing quarters with a giant manta ray or a killer whale, not such a puny creature as a mud crab. He had had the soul of an intertidal muck dweller.

"Sorry, but you are rid of him now, and I have to be off."

"Off where?" Wallace was on the verge of panic.

"Some place out on the edge of the universe called the Eridanus Supervoid. Ever hear of it?"

Butterfield shook his head.

"Well, it must be my version of the mantis shrimp because I've never heard of it either. But the Brotherhood has. It's the coldest spot in the universe. Over a billion light years in diameter and contains nothing. Someone in the Brotherhood has gotten this bright idea that God might be out there and I'm supposed to go find him. But don't concern yourself Wally. You'll do just fine and I'll be back. Oh yes, almost forgot. I have a gift for you."

Reverend Poda-Pirudi reached down and picked up the two lanterns and handed one to Wallace.

"It's just like mine. Play around with it. You will soon find that you can do incredible things with it. But, as I said, I really must be off."

Butterfield seized hold of one of Reverend Poda-Pirudi's shoulders with his free hand. "Can't you stay for a while? Give me some pointers? I'm just not capable of doing this. You've got the wrong architect!"

"It's a piece of cake Wally. See that lantern in your hand, it is quite a gizmo. It contains an ember from the Big Bang that is held in stasis by the offsetting polarity of a minute array of black holes. As I told you, it's quite a handy gadget. If I had the wrong architect, he wouldn't be able to hold the thing up. It weighs much more than everything on this planet. You are ready. You just don't know it yet."

As Butterfield looked in amazement at his arm holding up the lantern, the Reverend added. "You see, we of the Brotherhood just don't know where God is. He may be hiding, or in reclusion somewhere, or he may not even exist at all. But if he doesn't exist, something is going to have to be done about that. Someone or something is going to have to step up to the plate and evolve into him. But don't you worry Wally; I think we'll find him. And when we do, he'll have a lot of explaining to do. Oh by the way, could I ask you for a small favor?"

"Yes, yes, of course, Reverend— I mean Jae."

The Reverend laughed. "Yes Jae. That's right it's Jae. I'm glad to see after all I've put you through that we are on a first-name basis. But what I would like to ask you is, would you mind awfully, I mean in a few centuries or so, having Johnny Bradshaw's remains removed from the Mucking Marshes Landfill? You could have them interred at Trelawney Parish, in Jamaica. That's where his folks are buried."

Now it was Butterfield's turn to laugh. "It will be my pleasure. But there is something you can do for me as well."

"What's that Wally?"

"When you find God, say hello to him for me."

"I'll do that Wally. I'll do that." With that, Reverend Poda-Pirudi held up his lantern and with a brilliant flash of piercing white light was gone.

Butterfield glumly pondered the empty space that had just contained the Reverend and wondered what would be in store for the two of them. But no sooner had he considered this then there was another flash of light and the Reverend reappeared.

Wallace Butterfield was completely baffled.

"Oh I hope I didn't startle you Wally. I have one more thing to do."

The Reverend pointed to a spot on the beach just in front of Butterfield's toes. A case of Green Man's Own suddenly materialized there. Before Wallace could ask what it was for, the Reverend pointed up, and again disappeared in a tremendous flash.

Butterfield looked up to where Reverend Poda-Pirudi had indicated. At first he saw only a speck just below the clouds. This speck was making its way leisurely toward the island. Then the wind blew the object directly over him.

At this point he could discern that he had been staring at a parachute. The parachute drifted downward, till it was just over his head. Then he realized that the chute's canopy was covered in polka-dots., and dangling from the harness, was Maeva!

Historical Notes

Where Westminster Abbey stands today there was once an island called Thorney Island. Two branching rivulets of the Tyburn River created this island. The Tyburn River still flows underneath the city of Westminster and still empties into the Thames. There is a belief that Thorney Island was the original site for the Roman Temple of Apollo outside of the ancient city of Londinium. The Roman town of Londinium was sacked by Boudicca, Queen of the Celtic Iceni, around 61 A.D. after she was stripped naked and whipped and her daughters raped by the Romans. She raised armies from some of the tribes of Briton and then defeated a Roman legion, IX Hispana before she and her army were destroyed by the army of the Roman governor of Britannia. There has been some speculation that Thorney Island was also a sacred site to the Celtic peoples before the Roman occupation.

It is believed that the first church to be erected on this site was built at the command of King Sebert, king of the East Saxons, in the 7th century.

Later on, in the 10th century, another Saxon king, King Edgar, granted the lands surrounding this church to the Benedictine order of monks. Then, between 1042 and 1052, Edward the Confessor constructed the Abbey that occupies the site today.

Alexander Wood in his "Ecclesiastical Antiquities of London and its Suburbs," 1774, recounted a popular tale concerning the consecration of the church built by King Sebert, "The night before the dedication, it is related that St. Peter, in an unknown garb, showed himself to a fisher on the Surrey side, and bade him carry him over, with promise of reward. The fisher complied, and saw his fare enter the new-built Church of Sebert, that suddenly seemed on fire, with a glow that enkindled the firmament."

In the 13th century, King Henry III had a master stone-mason, called Odoricus, come from Rome to install the Cosmati Pavement, which forms the front of the High Altar at Westminster Abbey. Odoricus used polished semi-precious stones from far-off Egypt and the mines of ancient Sparta to form spectacular geometric flooring that bore a brass-lettered inscription that forecasted the end of the world. Which, if all goes as predicted, will be in another 19,000 years.

There are over 3,000 people who have been interred within the Abbey, which includes many of Britain's most celebrated monarchs, nobles, scientists, composers, soldiers, authors and poets, and politicians. However, with such a potential for generating ghost stories the Abbey has had few. Father Benedictus is one. He is allegedly seen on occasion talking to visitors or floating about. I should emphasize that he never stole the reliquary arm of Saint Cyriacus. John Bradshaw, the First President of the Council of State and presiding judge during the trial of King Charles, is the other. There have been reports of his ghostly appearance in his old office in , along with sightings of him walking about the Abbey on the anniversary date of the execution of the king.

There is a legend that when the Thames lions drop their rings that London will flood.

Baron Thomas Babington Macaulay wrote of the execution of the Duke of Monmouth in his History of England. He credits the duke with the quote that the headsman Jack Ketch recites in this book, "Here are six guineas for you. Do not hack me as you did my Lord Russell. I have heard that you struck him three or four times. My servant will give you some more gold if you do the work well."

Charles Fredrick Field was a famous Victorian detective in Scotland Yard. Charles Dickens was a good friend of his and he did like to chum about with him on his investigations. Dickens did model his character Inspector Bucket after him in his novel "Bleak House."

In the WITCHes' ceremonies there are excerpts from the 3,000-year-old Egyptian funerary text, *Book of the Dead*.

The passages involving *Giving Birth To Osiris* and *The Heart of Carnelian* are from AWAKENING OSIRIS © 1988 Normandi Ellis, with permission from Red Wheel/ Weiser, LLC Newburyport, MA and San Francisco, CA.

The excerpt concerning eating magic and devouring the gods, is known as the Cannibal Hymn, it is from the Ancient Egyptian Pyramid Text (2,400–2,500 B.C.), which I adapted from James Henry Breasted's 1906 translation. The Pyramid Text is considered to be the world's oldest collection of written spells. They were transcribed from hieroglyphics that were carved into the pyramids of Saqqara.

Tom Parr was a Shropshire farmer who was alleged to have been one hundred and fifty-two years old at the time of his death. Among Parr's many claims was that he fathered an illegitimate child at age one hundred. Due to the popular belief that he was so ancient, the Earl of Arundel had Parr conveyed out of the countryside of Shropshire and brought to London. In London, Parr was presented to King Charles I. During this time he became quite a celebrity and both Sir Anthony van Dyck and Sir Peter Paul Rubens painted his portrait. Unfortunately for Parr, the limelight didn't agree with him and he died shortly after his arrival. William Harvey, the famous physician who mapped the human circulatory system and described its workings, was called upon to perform an autopsy. One of the conclusions of this autopsy was that the change of diet from simple food to rich cuisine had contributed to Parr's demise. Notes from the autopsy also described his internal organs as being those of a considerably younger man. Based on Doctor Harvey's findings and apparent confusion over the actual year of Parr's birth, it is now believed that Parr may have been in his seventies when he succumbed to illness. Nevertheless, King Charles was impressed enough by Parr's credentials to have him buried among the notables of Westminster Abbey.

In the Marovo Lagoon, of the Island of New Georgia, Solomon Islands, the people tell tales of poda, spirits of their ancient ancestors, who inhabit various natural aspects of the region, stones, forests, and reefs, awaiting their eventual trip to the afterworld. This is supposed to happen when they are picked up by other poda in great stone war canoes. Poda pirudi are particularly powerful and untamed spirits that haunt the woodlands or reefs. Kiso pa Jae is the protective shark spirit of Jae Passage in the Marovo Lagoon. It is the custom of the people of this area to honor sharks and never do them any harm. It is believed that the sharks are aware of this and reciprocate by not attacking local divers and fishermen.

Carl Linnaeus, the famous seventeenth century zoologist, first used the word larva to describe immature insects. However, there is an older meaning for the word larva, a Latin meaning. To the Romans larva meant ghost.

If you enjoyed this read

Please leave a review on Amazon, Facebook, Good Reads or Instagram.

It takes less than five minutes and it really does make a difference.

If you're not sure how to leave a review on Amazon:

1. *Go to amazon.com.*

2. *Type in The Haunting of Westminster Abbey by Mark Patton and when you see it, click on it.*

3. *Scroll down to Customer Reviews. Nearby you'll see a box labeled Write a Review. Click it.*

4. *Now, if you've never written a review before on Amazon, they might ask you to create a name for yourself.*

5. *Reviews can be as simple as, "Loved the book! Can't wait for the Next!" (Please don't give the story away.)*

And that's it!

Brian Hades, publisher

ABOUT THE AUTHOR

At nineteen Mark Patton shipped aboard the Research Vessel Chain as a helmsman for the Woods Hole Oceanographic Institution. By his mid-twenties he was flying out of Otis Air Force Base for the National Marine Fisheries Service on weekly North Atlantic Fisheries patrols. After graduating from Northeastern University, he became a roughneck for Delta Drilling in the Texas oil patch. He left Texas to become a police officer and later a head of Natural Resources on Cape Cod. Now retired, he devotes his time between the mountains of northern New Hampshire and his home on Cape Cod, where with his cellist wife, he composes music and pursues his longtime passion for writing.

Need something new to read?

If you liked The Haunting of Westminster Abbey, you should also
consider these other EDGE-Lite titles...

TransMIGRATIONS

by Eddie Louise

Mad Science? Obsession? Folly?

Telesensation agent Justin Bremer studies time — specifically the effects of journeying through it. His assignment is to observe the timeline of a young Victorian scientist, Dr. Petronella Sage and her archeologist companion, Professor Erasmus Savant, who have, themselves, been bouncing back and forth through time, experiencing different people's lives first hand. Novelized from the popular Tales of Sage and Savant podcast.

TransMIGRATIONS is the first installment of a must-read new Steampunk adventure series!

About Eddie Louise

Eddie Louise has always been a yarn-spinner, dream-weaver, and a teller of tales. She lives in sunny Southern California where she makes a living as a ghostwriter and writes in a variety of genres including science fiction, young adult fiction, English-as-aSecond-Language textbooks, and the monthly speculative fiction audio-drama "The Tales of Sage and Savant."

Endless Hunger

by Kevin Weir

Corporate Espionage, Cults, and Faeries.

It's 2133, and Earth has rebuilt after a global catastrophe.

Megacities, wireless tech, and augmented humans are all commonplace. What isn't common, is Kraft. Kraft sees monsters. This tends to get him in trouble, especially when the rest of the world doesn't believe they exist. For Kraft, even an easy job like cleaning a corporation's computer system involves a dark cult, a battle with faeries, and a computer virus that reaches into the real world.

About Kevin Weir

Kevin Weir is an AMPIA Award winning writer of science fiction, fantasy, and comedy. A multidisciplinary storyteller, he has written short films, webseries, stageplays, as well as short stories. These short stories have appeared in places such as *Red Sun Magazine*, *Enigma Front*, and *In Places Between*. He lives in Alberta where he hosts *The Third Space Podcast* and lives with two dogs that he does not own, but are always around.

Pick Your Teeth with my Bones

by Carrie Newberry

She Has a Tail. Normal Is Relative.

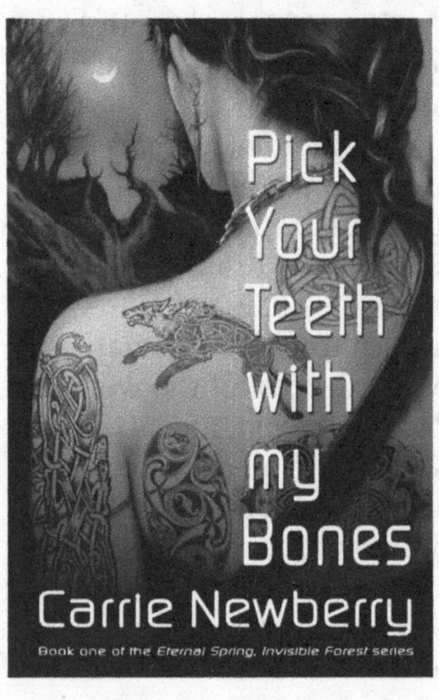

Kellan is a shape-shifter and a member of a secret society, the Sankhain, who protect a fountain of youth hidden in an invisible forest outside Madison, Wisconsin. When a stranger asks Kellan for her help with some documents, documents which shouldn't exist, about the Sankhain, Kellan uses her unique sense of smell to follow the trail, which leads to the very heart of the Sankhain. What Kellan uncovers will shake her world to its core.

About Carrie Newberry

Carrie Newberry is a writer of urban fantasy, horror, and a little bit of everything else. She is a faculty member at All-Writers' Workplace and Workshop and studied Creative Writing at UWMadison. Carrie currently lives in Madison with two rescued mutts and an enormous collection of books.

"Pick Your Teeth With My Bones is an action-packed, emotionpacked rock-your-world tale." — Kathie Giorgio, author

For more EDGE titles and information about upcoming speculative fiction please visit us at:

www.edgewebsite.com

Don't forget to sign-up for our Special Offers